As Long As You're Next to Me

ELIZA STEMMONS

As Long As You're Next to Me
Copyright @ Eliza Stemmons, 2022
All rights reserved.

First paperback edition January 2022

Book design by Eliza Stemmons
Interior formatting by Jennie Lyne Hoitt @ bookcoverit.com
Cover photography by Naomi Linnell

ISBN 978-1-7379066-0-5 (paperback)
ISBN 978-1-7379066-1-2 (ebook)

Copyright inspires creativity, encourages the sharing of voices, and creates a vibrant civilization. Thank you for purchasing an authorized edition of this book and for complying with copyright laws by not reproducing, scanning, or distributing any part of it in any form, electronic or mechanical, without written permission from the author, except in the case of brief quotation embodied in critical articles and reviews.

This is a work of fiction. The names, characters, places, and incidents are products of the writer's imagination or are used fictitiously and should not be construed as real. Any similarities to persons, living or dead, actual events, locale or organizations is entirely coincidental.

*To Marylin Jane Oakey Neubert,
who inspired me to write this book by sharing her stories with me.
And to Harvey "Buddy" Lamon Neubert.
I can't wait to meet you.*

PROLOGUE

May 8th, 1945

Dorothy

I flipped through my sketchbook, trying to find inspiration among its pages. The cheerful voices of The Andrews Sisters came from the record player in the corner, singing about a bugle boy from Chicago. The sunlight shone through the window and lit up the front room where I sat on the couch.

I turned to a random page of my sketchbook, hoping to find something I could redraw or improve. The page I opened showed a boy standing in front of a door, his arm raised to knock. My heart skipped a beat. The only way I could improve that drawing was to go back and change the event that had inspired it. I turned the page to hide it, embarrassed that the drawing and the memory still had me blushing like a schoolgirl.

The new sketch I opened to was of my little brother, Bobby. Much better.

I lifted up my pencil and started reworking the smile lines around his eyes and the freckles on his face. Now that summer was approaching, he would have more of those than ever. He was also older now than he had been when I drew the portrait originally.

I was about to start on the other details of Bobby's face when I heard the front door swing open and then thud against the wall. I looked up to see my friend Peggy in the doorway, her usually perfect hair looking disheveled. The screen door bounced against the outside wall, scratching the brick.

"Dottie, it's over!"

I stared at her, trying to piece together what she was saying. I took in her excited expression, and my heart was filled with an unexpected hope. I pushed it away, not wanting to give place to it quite yet. I was too afraid to let myself believe it really could be over.

"What?" I had to be sure of what she meant before I could bring myself to believe it.

"Dot, turn on the radio." Peggy's eyes began to fill with tears, but she was still smiling.

I scrambled over to the radio on the other side of the room and felt a chill run up my arms. Could it be true?

I took the needle off the Andrews Sisters record and switched over to the radio setting.

A voice crackled into existence as I turned the knob, tuning in to the news station.

President Truman's words were filled with a solemn hope: "The Allied armies, through sacrifice and devotion and with God's help, have wrung from Germany a final and unconditional surrender. The western world has been freed of the evil forces which for five years and longer have imprisoned the bodies and broken the lives of millions upon millions of free-born men."

I felt cold tears run down my face and I let out a relieved laugh. I brought my hands up to my face, wiping away some of the tears before realizing it was pointless. I couldn't stop crying, hardly believing the fact that it really could be over. Europe was freed, and we were one step closer to the true end of the war. As I knelt on the floor in front of our radio, Peggy moved to sit right beside me.

"It's finally over," I said, still in awe.

Peggy just nodded and wrapped an arm around my shoulders. There were tears on her face too.

We listened to the rest of the broadcast, laughing and crying together all afternoon.

CHAPTER 1

March 12, 1945

Henry

I couldn't remember the last two months. The soldier next to me in the medic tent had told me I had been unconscious for most of it. I didn't want to believe it at first. I wanted to be dead. That was the only way I could imagine the pain stopping. The pain was my new constant, the identifying factor of my new existence. Even through my sleep, I felt the fire burning in my right arm, and when I finally woke up it was all I could do to focus on anything else.

The longer I stayed conscious, the more I remembered from that night. The scene played before my eyes again and again, sounds of soldiers whispering in the darkness, met with the whistle of a tank shell flying through the air toward us. I couldn't remember the explosion. I think I lost consciousness for a second after the impact. The rest of the memories came in blurs of color and flashes of heat my skin still remembered. I hated remembering.

Mentally, I was confused and exhausted. Physically, I was dying. The French doctor had told me many times in his broken English that I was losing weight too quickly. The American doctor told me the same, though in slightly more colorful terms. If I didn't try to eat and attempt to keep whatever food I was able to swallow inside of me, I wouldn't beat the infection. I would die here, in a small army camp in France.

Sitting up brought waves of pain throughout the right side of my body. Every time I got up to eat, I wanted to vomit from the sensation. So instead, I resigned myself to simply opening my mouth while lying flat on the bed and letting the nurses spoon broth down my throat. It was almost humiliating, but I didn't care what anyone thought of me anymore. I was lucky to be alive, so I didn't want to complain about my pain.

The nurses in the hospital tent had explained to me that, even though the Allies had won the Battle of the Bulge, we had suffered many casualties. I was almost one of them.

During the months of fighting in France, General Harris had been impressed with my observation and leadership skills and had assigned me to a small group of soldiers to spy on the enemy camp. My good friends, Charlie Jones and Tom Davies, were both in the group. We had been assigned to the same company right after our training. We spent months together in Europe training, fighting in battles, and becoming close friends.

I had been glad that both of them were with me on the reconnaissance team—until our mission had been compromised and my two friends were killed.

I was the only one on the entire team who had survived the tank shell explosion.

When I was hit with the shrapnel that had killed the other soldiers around me, I almost gave up. It took work to make myself stand up and get out of those woods. Back when I was drafted, I knew that it was likely I wouldn't make it home in one piece. After surviving D-Day, I thought the worst part of the war had passed and I would be okay. Then we moved into Belgium and the fighting kept getting worse and worse.

Then the night of the recon mission came.

The details of that horrific night were slowly coming back to me, and it was torture just thinking about the expressions on the faces of the soldiers who knew they were going to die and who told me to escape while I could still walk. Their eyes haunted me when I was awake and filled my dreams when I was asleep. I escaped the forest, but I couldn't seem to escape their accusing eyes.

April 15, 1945

I was slowly recovering. I could now sit up without fainting, eat without vomiting, and walk without falling. Although those were all good signs for the doctors, they were not exactly welcome to me. Improvement meant I would be released soon, probably to fight again.

That was not something I was looking forward to. Any mention of picking up a weapon filled me with dread. I knew what they did. I didn't want to use a gun against anyone, ever again.

On the morning of April 15th, I received a bundle of letters. News from home was the only thing that could lift my spirits in those days. The envelope usually included a letter from each of my parents, one from my little sister Jessica, and a letter from my friend Jimmy, who had been too sickly to be drafted like I had been when the USA entered the war. As expected, this envelope included a letter from each of them and I read every word, trying to keep my tears from falling. Dad told me that once I returned home, which he hoped would be soon, I could get my old job at the oil refinery back. Mom's letter consisted of the usual 'I miss you's and 'I love you's. Jessica told me all about her classes at school and about the latest news from around town. Jimmy told me about his school as well.

What the envelope didn't include was a letter from Dot. My monthly envelopes never did. I was beginning to think she had forgotten about me.

When I left, she promised she would write to me, but she obviously didn't care about her best friend enough to send any letters. If we were even "best friends" anymore. I wasn't sure *what* we were now.

I hadn't written to her either, so I couldn't complain about not receiving any letters from her. I would just have to wait to talk to her in person. I needed to explain some things to her. If what the other soldiers said was true, the war would be over soon and I would see her again.

I prayed that was the case and the war would end. I couldn't fight again. Even if I was somewhat physically able, I didn't feel like I could make myself pick up a gun after everything I'd seen.

April 31, 1945

The nurses told me that Hitler was dead. I didn't fully believe them until one of my captains came in and confirmed the news. I hoped that meant the war would be over soon. Maybe I *wouldn't* have to fight again. I could go home. I could see my family! I would be safe from constant reminders that I got out alive when no one else did.

It didn't help that the other soldiers and the nurses kept bringing it up. They would walk past my bed and whisper to each other how lucky I was and how grateful I should be that I escaped. They acted like I wasn't there or that I couldn't hear them. Thanks to my limited understanding of French from the years spent serving with French soldiers, I could even understand the whispers from the French nurses. They spoke about me like my being alive was a miracle. As if they really knew what happened.

I didn't want to be reminded of that night. I wanted to forget that I was the only one who got out. The thought of being grateful to be alive made me feel selfish, like I was forgetting all of the other soldiers who didn't survive. Being grateful meant forgetting that Jones and Davies were dead.

I could only hope the war would really be over soon. If it was, I would be on my way home where no one would know the real circumstances of my injury. I could keep most of the details to myself, and no one would be the wiser. No one would tell me that I was lucky I wasn't one of the five that died that night. No one would even know about the recon mission. I could start over and forget about the war and about that night.

The only thing that would remind me would be my injured arm, but even that would heal. It was already much better and I was getting stronger. I was gaining more weight and I no longer got dizzy after sitting up. I could now make my way across the room a few times before needing to rest. I couldn't carry anything with my right arm or even hold things in my hand yet, but the doctors told me that my strength would eventually get back to normal, though my range of motion would always be limited. I was sure I would be feeling better by the time I finally got home.

That thought brought a rush of relief to my heart. I held on to that hope, even though it was small. It was the only thing I had.

May 8, 1945

It was official. The war in Europe was over. We listened to parts of the broadcast from the States, but the radio signal was so weak that we weren't able to listen in for long. Those of us stuck in the hospital tent listened to the French radio broadcast all day. The other soldiers in the camp had gone into town to celebrate with the locals. We had our own celebration in the hospital tent, though many of us lacked the energy to stand up for long periods of time. The nurses did their best to help us feel at home, dancing with the soldiers who could and talking to the ones who couldn't. It was the happiest day I had had since I got shipped out, but my heart wasn't really in it. I could only think of home and how close I was to returning.

I couldn't think about much else that day. Everyone around me was talking about home and about seeing their families again. Many of the other soldiers were going to the Pacific to fight the Japanese, but I was one of those who wouldn't be going due to my injuries. Most of us in the hospital tent would be going home for good. One of the generals told me I would be shipped off as soon as they organized my passage.

I sat on my bed and took a deep breath. I managed a slight smile, looking at all of the others in the tent. It didn't seem real, but I was finally going home.

CHAPTER 2

May 12, 1945

Dorothy

The news was coming in so fast it all felt like a dream. First, Hitler was found dead, then the war in Europe ended, and now most of the soldiers stationed in Europe were coming home. My brother John, or Buddy as we affectionately called him, was one of them. He had been gone since the US entered the war almost four years ago.

My younger brother, Bobby, and I cried when we heard they were sending the soldiers home. I think Mom cried too, and maybe even Pop, who usually didn't cry in front of us. I knew it affected him and Mom most. My parents dreaded the day when they might have to change the blue star banner in our window for a gold one, showing that we had a family member lost in the war. Luckily, that hadn't happened, and Buddy was officially coming home.

We didn't know how long it would take for Buddy to get home to Ashwood. The letter from his general told us he still had responsibilities to finish up in England before he could come home to us. After almost four years of not seeing him, I was looking forward to just being around him again. He was one of my best friends. I had missed his teasing and his quick thinking. I missed talking to him and getting advice. He was always so level-headed. I knew Bobby missed having him here too. Bobby was only twelve when Buddy left, and he had grown up a lot since then. I could tell he wanted his older brother back just as much as I did. A huge part of our family had been missing for too long and we were about to get it back.

ELIZA STEMMONS

A few days after we got the letter from the army about the soldiers being sent home, I went to Daisy's Diner in the center of Ashwood with Peggy King, Jimmy Sanders, and Marylin Price. They had been my friends for years, and even now we made the effort to get together often. We had been going to Daisy's regularly since our freshman year of high school. It still felt strange for all of us to be at Daisy's without Henry. It had always been the five of us, but Henry had been in the war for over two years. I blushed when I thought of him. I wondered if he was coming home as well.

I got to the diner right at 5:30 and sat down at our usual table. My friends weren't there yet, so I walked to the counter to talk to Daisy. She had practically watched us all grow up. I remember coming to the diner when I was little and listening to my parents talk to Daisy and her husband, Richard. Now, Richard wasn't around as often as he used to be. He had served for a year or two in Europe, but had returned home after suffering an injury to his back. He was doing much better now, but he still had problems moving around. He had to sit in a wheelchair and spent most of his time at home because of it.

"Hi honey, how are you?" Daisy asked when she noticed me.

"I'm great, thank you!" I responded, sitting on one of the red bar stools. "How are you, Ms. Daisy?"

"I'm just wonderful! But I'm certainly ready for the war to be over."

"Me too."

"Is Buddy coming home with the others?"

I nodded emphatically.

Daisy squinted her eyes in a smile. "I'm glad. You poor kids, having your lives turned upside down in your prime." She shook her head. "I don't know how I would have dealt with all of my friends and marriage prospects going off to war like that. In the Great War, no one I knew closely got drafted, so I avoided most of the heartache. So many young boys have gotten drafted and dragged into this war. It's just terrible." At that, Daisy started mumbling under her breath about the government making soldiers out of children. She was always lighthearted until she started talking about politics. At that point, she would mumble to herself like she was now and get distracted from any conversation she had been a part of.

Luckily, Peggy and Marylin came in right then. I heard them both giggling before I saw them. They ran straight to me and practically knocked me down with the force of their hugs.

"Dottie," Peggy said. "We heard Buddy's coming home! Aren't you excited?"

I beamed. "Of course I am! It's been so long! Almost four years, can you believe it?" I shook my head, still not believing it was true.

Jimmy walked in then and we all greeted him as we sat down at our table. He looked happier than he had in awhile.

"I'm just glad it's almost over," Marylin said. "I'm tired of hearing bad news about the war."

Jimmy's smile disappeared when he heard our topic of conversation. He always looked frustrated when we talked about the war and the men fighting in it. All he had talked about when we were little was being a soldier like his father. Mr. Sanders fought in the Great War as a sergeant, and Jimmy wanted to be just like him. His father always told us stories about his experiences in the war. He always made it seem like he had been a hero in some adventure story. I imagine war wasn't that exciting all the time. Mr. Sanders had probably exaggerated some of the details to keep us interested.

Jimmy had wanted to sign up for the war as soon as he was old enough, but he was diagnosed with asthma during high school, which kept him from passing the physical. He had reluctantly stayed here in the states, going to school and waiting for the war to end, just like the rest of us. It was good to have him around though, with Henry gone.

I would have asked my friends if they had any news from Henry, but I was sure Peggy would start teasing me and I didn't want that. Especially not now when he might be coming home. The less drama surrounding our situation, the better.

I didn't have to mention Henry though, since the group shifted their conversation to the people in our graduating class who were possibly going to be coming home. They brought up Henry quickly, and I felt my face get hot. I worried that my friends might notice, but I don't think any of them did.

"I heard from Jessica that since he got injured so badly, he's coming home soon," Marylin said.

My heart stopped. I hadn't heard he had been injured.

"What happened to him?" I asked, my voice shaky. I couldn't hold myself back.

"You mean you didn't hear?" Jimmy looked surprised.

"I thought you two wrote to each other every week." Marylin knit her eyebrows together. "This happened months ago."

I looked away from her. I didn't want her to see the tears forming in my eyes. "I...I haven't had the chance lately." I lied. "I've been so busy with my bakery plans."

Peggy looked at me with sympathy. "Hon, he almost died back in January. We all thought you knew."

The blood drained from my face. I pushed my cola away from me. My stomach churned and I prayed I wouldn't get sick.

"He's been in a hospital somewhere all this time. His family hasn't heard much else, other than that he's slowly recovering."

I hardly heard her. I continued to stare straight at a scratch on the table. For some reason staring into space always made me feel more grounded, like I wasn't about to either float away or fall to the floor.

"Dottie, are you okay?" I heard Marylin call.

I shook my head, breaking my stupor.

"Sorry," I said in a quiet voice. "I just hadn't heard anything. I feel bad that I didn't know."

Peggy put her hand on my arm and whispered just to me, "It'll be okay. He'll be home soon."

Later that night, I settled down in my bed with my sketchbook open. I wanted to start a new drawing, but I had no inspiration. Even with the war in Europe over and with Buddy and Henry coming home, I didn't feel it. I was too distracted by the mental image of Henry lying in a hospital bed.

I was interrupted by a knock at my window. I hid my sketchbook and pencil underneath my pillow and walked over to open the latch. Peggy always used my window at night, so I wasn't worried it was someone else.

I opened the curtains to see her looking at me.

"Hey." She was wearing a jacket over her pajamas. It was beginning to get warmer, but a breeze still lingered from Pennsylvania's chilly spring nights.

"Hey," I replied, helping her get a leg over the windowsill and climb into my room.

She shut the window and pulled the curtain back over it while I turned and plopped myself on my bed again. I almost grabbed my pillow to hug it, but I remembered I had hidden my sketchbook under it. I didn't want Peggy to ask about the book. She was my friend and I loved her, but she wouldn't be able to keep a secret, especially one that seemed trivial to her. She wouldn't understand that I wanted my drawings to stay private. They were a part of me.

"You told me that you wrote to him." Peggy sat next to me on the bed.

I shook my head. There was no excuse for what I had done.

"I lied. I haven't written to him at all."

"Not even in the beginning? Dottie, it's been two years." Peggy looked both shocked and sad.

"I know." I closed my eyes, trying to shut out the guilt I felt.

"You two were so close. What happened?"

I opened my mouth, but no words came out.

Once she saw that I wasn't able to say anything, Peggy continued: "I thought you knew about his injury and just didn't want to talk about it. We all did. Marylin, Jimmy, and I decided it would be better if you brought it up first. We didn't want to upset you by mentioning it." Peggy knitted her eyebrows. "Apparently Henry's been pretty sick ever since it happened."

I wanted to cry, I really did, but I just inhaled a shaky gasp of air and sighed loudly. I didn't know how to react.

Peggy scooted closer on the bed and wrapped her arm around my shoulders. "Why haven't you written to him?"

I laid my head on her shoulder. "Something changed between us. Growing up, it was always so easy to be around him. He was my best friend and I loved him. But then I realized he wasn't the little boy who used to tease me on the playground anymore. He was a young man and I was a young woman. I started to suspect that he felt something for me. I didn't know what to do."

"Oh Dottie, all of us could see that. There was always something between you two. It just took you both a while to see it. But I still don't understand why you haven't written to him at all!"

"He *was* my best friend, but I think he wanted to be something more. I was confused and scared. Then the war started and he got drafted. I didn't want to lose him, so I pushed him away."

Peggy looked at me with her eyebrows raised. She smirked and looked like she was holding in a laugh.

"I know, I know," I continued. "I'm an idiot. But Peggy, I thought we were just friends and I wanted to stay that way. I was so scared." I shook my head back and forth. I was still so confused, even after all this time.

I paused, trying not to cry at the image that resurfaced in my memory. Henry stood at my doorstep. I held his hand to keep him from tripping. He looked at me intently with his dark green eyes. He smiled, and my heart melted.

"The day before Henry left, he came over to say goodbye." A rebellious tear fell down my cheek. "He was going to kiss me."

Peggy gasped, both her smile and her eyes wide.

"But I didn't let him. I turned away."

Her face fell, reminding me of how Henry looked at me that day. He had looked devastated. I felt awful. I still did.

"But didn't you like him?" Peggy asked.

"I wasn't sure if I did. I was confused. If I did like him, I didn't realize it until after I watched him walk away. I was embarrassed. I never wrote to him because I didn't want to make things worse. I hurt him and he hurt me too by putting me in that situation. I wasn't expecting him to tell me he was in love with me the day before he left for war."

"But how do you feel about him now, putting all this aside?"

I shook my head and shrugged. "I don't know. It's been so long since I've seen him, and I don't know if he'll even want to see me again after all of this. He hasn't written to me either. I thought he would, but then he didn't. I waited for a letter for months, and then I just gave up. If he didn't want to write to me, I didn't feel like I was in a place where I should write to him. And now here we are, years later. He's coming home soon and I have no idea what we'll say to each other."

"Well, once he comes home, we'll have to see. Things might be just like they used to be! But if it doesn't work out between you two, I still have a cousin that you could go out with!"

I pushed her shoulder with mine and laughed. "The thirty-year-old?"

"But that's only a ten-year difference, right?"

I shook my head, sticking out my tongue in disgust.

Peggy left shortly after that, leaving me with a lighter heart. I hoped it was possible to fix the relationship between Henry and me. I would try my hardest to get my best friend back.

CHAPTER 3

May 25, 1945

Henry

There was a huge weight off my shoulders. I never had to fight again. I almost couldn't believe it. I could go home and forget this ever happened. Or, at least I would try.

The army shipped me out of France about two weeks after the surrender was finalized. They told me I would have to wait in England until further plans were made to get us home. There were many of us who were too injured to go fight in the Pacific and the army was doing their best to get us home to the states as soon as possible so we could have better care and rest.

Luckily, my fever and infection had both disappeared long before plans were made for our return, or else I would've had a miserable trip ahead of me. I was left only with a dull ache in my shoulder and a decreased ability to move my arm. That, I could live with.

We were all bunked together in a school in London that had been turned into a barracks, waiting for more news to arrive of our departure. The injured soldiers were on the second floor of the school. The other floors were taken up by soldiers that had been stationed all across England and France who were also waiting to return home. Sometimes I would see soldiers that I knew from training, and we would catch up a bit. There usually wasn't much to catch up on. We had all been fighting. We knew what the war was like and we didn't need to tell each other. It was just good to see familiar faces.

I spent most of my days in London sitting on my bed, writing letters to my family and friends. Another soldier brought me a desk from one of the unused classrooms. My hand was getting stronger now that I was using it more, but it still hurt too much to write. I realized early on that I would have to learn to write with my left hand, at least until I could hold a pen with my right without dropping it. I began practicing with my left hand by writing the alphabet. Doing it made me smile. I remembered my mom teaching a much younger me to form the lines of each letter and to say their names out loud as I did. I laughed as I wrote out a clumsy 'D E A R M O M' and named each letter aloud like I did back then.

"What're you doing?" a confused voice asked, almost laughing. I looked up quickly. I hadn't heard anyone enter the room. The sound of the shell exploding so close on the night of the recon mission must have rattled my brain a bit and affected my hearing. It used to be top-notch.

An American soldier I vaguely recognized was walking into the room. As I was trying to recall his name, he held out his hand. "Sergeant Hansen," he said, then shrugged and said "Frank."

I tried lifting my right arm to shake his hand, but a sudden pain ran from my tricep to my upper back and forced my arm down again.

"Ah, you're injured. Sorry." Hansen lowered his right arm and offered his left. We shook hands. "Is that why your handwritin's so messy?" I noticed he was looking down at my shaky script.

I breathed out a laugh. "Yeah. I've been practicing all day, and it still looks like chicken scratches."

"Ah, you'll get it. I've seen a few injured boys learn to do it. One a' them had their arm blown clean off, and he had to learn how to do it all with jus' one arm."

My eyes went wide with shock, but he kept going.

"Hey, what's your name?"

"Corporal Henry Oakey."

"You were on the mainland." He said it as a statement, not a question. I nodded.

"Golly." He shook his head. "I sure am glad I was stationed here in Britain. A lot less fightin' goin' on up here."

I simply nodded.

"You don't say much, do you?"

I smiled and shook my head.

Frank laughed. "I'm from Florida. Where're you from?"

"Pennsylvania," I said quietly. As I did, a longing for my hometown, Ashwood, and my family filled me to the brim. I couldn't wait to get home.

"Hey, I know a guy who's from Pennsylvania. He's here actually. Downstairs, I think. D'you wanna meet him?" He slurred his words together, like he was already thinking three words ahead as he spoke the first.

"Um, sure." Frank was friendly, and I decided to let him introduce me to his Pennsylvanian friend, even though the 'normal me' would have been fine just sitting on my bed alone for the rest of the day.

Frank ran off, muttering something like "Now, where is that man?"

I finally had the chance to breathe after he had left. I felt exhausted, even after the short conversation. I got back to work on my writing practice, trying to make every 'A' and 'B' look identical to the last. Working with my left hand would take just that: work. I was more than willing to put forth the effort. I simply needed to be able to write. It kept me sane. I was always more comfortable writing out my feelings than trying to explain them to people. I didn't want to give that up.

After a few more minutes of writing out the alphabet, I switched to writing short words. As I began, Frank ran back into the room with someone following not far behind him.

I looked up to greet them, mustering a smile. Frank moved out of the way, revealing the soldier standing behind him. Memories of summers playing games outside of the Banks' house came flooding back to me.

"Buddy!" I cried, standing up as quickly as I was able to give him a hug.

"Gosh, Frank," he said, embracing me and patting my back hard. I tried not to wince. I was just glad to see my friend. "Why didn't you tell me it was Henry Oakey I was coming to see?"

"How was I s'posed to know you knew each other?" Frank laughed, looking at the two of us. "I'll be over there while you two catch up." He walked to the other side of the room and sat down in front of a window. He pulled a knife out of his pocket along with a small block of wood and began whittling.

Buddy's pat on the back had sent a string of pain down to my fingers and up into my head. I sat down after he let me go and struggled to catch my breath. Stars once again swam in front of my eyes.

"Henry, are you all right?" Bud sat down next to me, thankfully on my left side.

"Yeah," I managed to get out. "I'm fine."

"No, you're not. I know you better than that, Henry. You're hurt."

I nodded once, wincing. "I'm fine, though. It's nothing. I just gotta catch my breath."

"Does your family know?"

"I think my captain sent them a letter a while ago."

"You *think*?"

I looked up at him. He was giving me a 'big brother' look. It was a look he had given me often. He had always been the big brother figure for our friends because he was Dot's older brother. I ignored the familiar ache in my heart when I thought of her. Why hadn't she written to me? Was she okay?

"I'm writing to them right now, so don't worry," I said, smiling. I held up my left hand. "It's just taking a while. How is your family?" Dot probably wrote to him often. They were siblings, after all.

"Ah, they're all right." Bud smiled. "Pop is still working at the refinery, and Mom got a job at the school. Bobby is in high school now and says he hates it, but I know he's exaggerating. He always does. And Dot, well, she's still baking and going dancing and spending time with her friends. But I assume she's told you all of that herself."

I lowered my eyes. I knew from his scoff that Bud had caught on immediately.

"She hasn't written to you?"

I shook my head.

"Not even once?"

"No."

"And what about you, my friend, have you written to her?" He raised an eyebrow.

"No. I tried and just couldn't. I couldn't get the words I wanted to on the page." I looked at Bud's face again, and he was staring at me thoughtfully.

"I don't believe it! I thought you two would have written as often as you could! You were practically inseparable back home." He paused and shook his head again. "Henry, I think you should write a letter to Dot along with the ones you're writing to your family. She's one of your best friends, after all! Haven't you written to Jimmy?"

I nodded.

"See? It should be as easy to write to her as it is to write to him, shouldn't it?"

"It's not easy to write a letter to anyone with my right arm like it is, but maybe I'll try."

"That's the spirit," Bud said, bringing me out of my painful memories of Dot. "Now, let's go see what's for supper. Come on, Frank!"

Frank hurried over to us again, and the three of us went downstairs to eat.

I would try to write to Dot. I had tried a thousand times it seemed, but I never sent a single letter. Most of them ended up in the trash or in the fire. The rest I still had in a bag I kept in my trunk. I didn't know if I would ever send them to her. Many of the letters I had kept were simply cold updates of my health and the few details I could bear to share about the war. They were nothing compared to what I wanted to write to her. The letters I actually put my heart into were the ones I had burned. How could I send them to her when she didn't even want me?

I put Dorothy Banks out of my mind and tried to enjoy myself the best I could for the rest of the night.

CHAPTER 4

May 26, 1945

Dorothy

It was a Saturday morning and I was walking around our neighborhood, delivering the fresh bread I had made earlier that day. Soon I would have a bakery of my own. Then I wouldn't need to personally deliver my goods, but for now, I enjoyed the solitude of the mid-morning walk I took three times a week.

I pulled my bread loaves in a red wagon behind me, protecting them from the sun and the breeze with a towel. I learned to make bread from my Grandma Jane when I was little and began selling it to help pay for the family expenses during the Depression. We made it through those years alive and well thanks to that extra money. We were poor, but we were happy. Things had gotten a lot better since then. The oil refinery at the edge of Ashwood had kept Pop employed since he started working there before the Depression. Mom began working at the elementary school when the war started. Together, they earned enough to keep our little family on its feet. Their combined income allowed me to finally save up for my bakery. I had been dreaming about owning a bakery for years. The one in town was owned by Mr. and Mrs. Devon, an older couple on the verge of retiring, and they offered to sell me the building once they did. I saved almost every penny I could for that bakery.

I dropped my last two loaves of bread off to the Johnsons, who were always kind enough to order every week, despite their own financial struggle. I continued walking, immersed in my own thoughts, not paying attention to where I was until I looked up and saw that I had subconsciously walked to the Oakey's house. *Henry's* house.

ELIZA STEMMONS

I didn't know what led me to walk there. Maybe it was the thought that he would probably be returning soon. Maybe it was my guilt about our past. Whatever it was, I was here, and I might as well stop by to say hello to his sister, Jessica. We were friends despite the age gap between us.

I knocked on their door before I could let my nervousness stop me.

It was Mrs. Oakey who answered, not Jessica. Her already cheery face broke into a huge grin when she saw me through the tattered screen door.

"Dorothy! What a joy to see you!"

"Hello, Mrs. Oakey." I smiled as well.

"Oh dear, call me Anna. You are a woman yourself now!"

She invited me inside, and I entered hesitantly. I sat on their floral couch in the front living room. It felt strange to be in the Oakey's house again. I had spent so many days of my childhood here. It had been a second home to me. I hadn't come back except to deliver bread since Henry left.

"Now, how have you been faring, dear?" Anna sat down in the arm chair across from me.

"I've been doing well," I said. "I've been building up my bakery business. I've just come from delivering bread, actually. I plan on buying the bakery in town when the Devons are ready to retire."

"How wonderful. I remember when you and Henry would sell bread together when you were younger. He always came home from those walks so happy." She had a sad look in her eyes now.

I paused before speaking to build up enough courage. "I heard he was injured a few months ago. I didn't know." I shook my head, not quite knowing how to express my sadness. "I feel awful."

"Yes, he was injured badly in a reconnaissance mission in January. His general sent us a letter a few weeks ago. He said Henry was lucky to be alive." It seemed like this was all a memorized piece of information. Her voice was monotone, and her eyes were empty.

"But will he be coming home soon?" I had to know. Would Henry be here in just a few short days, like Buddy?

"I assume so." She breathed out, and some of the joy from before came back into her eyes. "I *hope* so."

"I do as well. It will be nice to see him again." I did miss him. I had realized it more in the last few weeks since my conversation with Peggy. I missed my friend.

"You two were always so close. It will be good for both of you to be together again, I think." She smiled at me, the sadness disappearing almost as easily as it had appeared.

I nodded. It *would* be good to be together again.

After a few more minutes of catching up, I left the Oakey's house with the promise that I would be back the following week with a plate full of my famous chocolate chip cookies and two loaves of bread.

Later that day, my family and I went to the movies. We saw *The Clock*, starring Judy Garland and Robert Walker. I watched the entire film, but I couldn't focus on the plot.

All I could think about was Henry and how he had almost died, and I hadn't even known. What kind of a friend was I? How had I let a bit of awkwardness ruin our relationship? I decided that once Henry came home, I would treat him exactly like I had before he went to the war, before that almost-kiss ruined everything. I just wanted to be friends with him, and so that's exactly what we would be.

Coming out of the theater, Bobby nudged me in the arm and said, quite sarcastically, "You were sure paying attention, Dottie! Why'd you even come if you weren't gonna watch?"

"I was watching," I said, smiling. "Just not as well as you were. Judy Garland was in love with Robert Walker's character, but he had to go back to the war." I stuck my nose up proudly and quickened my pace to catch up to my parents who were already making their way toward our Ford Deluxe. I linked my arm in my father's.

"Hey Pop!" I said.

"How'd you enjoy the movie, Dottie?" he said. He was a lot taller than I was, and I had to look up in order to answer him.

"It was all right, I guess."

"She wasn't even watching it." Bobby was now right behind us.

"Was too," I whined back in the same tone.

He rolled his eyes and opened our car door. "No, you were too busy daydreaming about your boyfriend." Bobby and I were used to teasing each other like this.

"Of course." I folded my arms. "Too bad I don't know him. Would you mind introducing us?" I smiled sweetly at him.

Bobby glared at me from the seat next to mine.

Pop let out a chuckle from the driver's seat. Mom looked back at us with a warning glance, but I could tell she was smiling beneath it.

"Now, you two stop fighting," she said.

"Yeah." Pop looked at me and Bobby from the rear-view mirror. "No more fighting."

Bobby and I smiled at each other. It was always fun to banter with him, especially since Bud, who loved to tease us, had been gone for so long. Even though we weren't children anymore, it was nice to joke around.

"Mom," Bobby said. "When is Buddy coming home?" He echoed my thoughts exactly.

"Hopefully soon," she practically whispered. "I pray he comes home soon."

"I wish he were already here."

"I know, honey. I do too."

CHAPTER 5

January 10, 1945
The night Henry got injured

Henry

I hid behind some bushes and signaled for Jones to go in front of me. I prayed he would tread lightly. Any sound from any one of us would mean our mission was compromised.

I could barely see in the darkness, but my other senses compensated for my lost vision. I could hear the sound of an owl hooting in a tree high above us. I could feel the decaying leaves, softened by melting snow, beneath my feet. The constant smell of burning from the distant campfires and from the battlefield filled my nostrils and the metallic taste of blood from biting my lip out of worry had become all too familiar.

General Harris had sent me with this group in hopes that my observation skills would be beneficial in scouting out the enemy's camp in Belgium. I just hoped my skills would help me and the others last the night in enemy territory.

As we advanced through the forest, the trees provided us enough protection from the enemy's sight. Each movement I made was instinctive. Every step, every breath calculated. I was relaxed, even in my anxious hope that we would get the information we needed. I knew where we were going and why. 'Everything is fine,' I told myself with each breath. *Everything was fine.*

As soon as I heard shouting in the distance, I knew *nothing* was fine. The angry voices were coming closer. I heard the whir of a tank engine from the other side of the trees. I called out a retreat to the other soldiers, but it was too late.

There was a loud whistling as the tank fired a mortar shell. I turned around to run from it, but the explosion was close enough for me to feel the strong blast of air and the intense heat on my back.

I fell to the ground and everything went black.

The next thing I knew, everything was on fire. The trees behind me were burning. Everything was burning. I was burning. My eyes stung with smoky air, and what little light remained from the moon became smoky and filled with sparks. My right shoulder screamed with pain, and I knew I had been hit. I dragged myself to my feet and tried not to cry out for fear I'd be heard.

Shots erupted in the night and shouts in a foreign language followed. We were compromised, and I knew I had to get out of there or die trying. I could not be captured. I didn't want to think about how many of our soldiers had already died or been caught. I tried to look for the others, but all I could see was smoke.

As I stood up and began stumbling along, I heard screams. Jones was running alongside me. He yelled to me, but I couldn't hear him over the ringing in my ears. He fell behind. I kept running clumsily. A few seconds after I had lost sight of him, I heard two gunshots, then silence. I turned around to see what had happened to Jones and immediately wished I hadn't. That image still haunts me.

I kept running, however clumsy I was. After making it a short distance from where Jones had been shot, I saw Davies in front of me on the ground. He had so many injuries I didn't know if I could help him up, but I tried anyway. We walked together for a couple steps with his arm over my shoulders and me carrying most of his weight, but eventually he called out over the chaos to leave him behind and get to safety.

I'm ashamed that I left him alone, even though he told me to. I ran off, dodging the flaming pieces of wood falling in my path.

Finally, I broke free of the flaming part of the woods and managed to make it another kilometer or so before I collapsed in an exhausted pile on the snowy ground, one hand reaching out toward the American camp and my heart reaching out toward the soldiers and friends I had left behind.

June 5, 1945
The Present

The memories were still as clear as the day it all happened. I wished I could forget, but can you ever really forget guilt and pain like that? I don't think you can. At least not completely. A small part of me didn't want to forget. Remembering the eyes of those I left behind caused me so much pain, but I felt I deserved it. I couldn't forget, because forgetting would mean betraying them even more.

I survived my remaining days as a soldier by talking to Frank and Bud, trying not to miss home too much. I hadn't had time or energy to feel homesick when we were fighting, and when I was recovering from my injuries I wasn't conscious enough to notice. Now, with nothing to do but wait, it was difficult to just sit here and know that I was so far away.

I finished writing letters to each member of my family and to Jimmy before I started writing one to Dot. It took me a few tries, but I was finally satisfied.

> *Dear Dot,*
>
> *My, I've missed you. It feels like forever since I left home. When I finally get back, it'll sure be good for me to see you and your smile again. By the time you read this, I'll probably be a few streets away, just like old times.*
>
> *I can't tell you how much I regret not writing to you. The truth is, I didn't want to bore you with details of my everyday life here in Europe. It's pretty dreary here, and I had nothing of value to share with you other than memories of our past, ones you already know and remember.*
>
> *You'll have to excuse my handwriting. My right arm is still getting better from an injury I got in January, so I have to write with my left hand. I've been practicing. Can you tell?*
>
> *Dottie, I really have missed you. I don't think I can say that enough. You'll probably get tired of hearing it once I'm home. I'll be shouting it in the streets: "Dorothy Banks, I missed you!" The world is so dark here, with the war and the horror of it all. It's so different from home. I have needed you more than you can understand. But*

ELIZA STEMMONS

I imagine your days haven't changed much. I imagine you, Peggy, Marylin, and Jimmy are going to the movies, dancing, and drinking one too many colas at Daisy's, just as if I were with you. I've missed those days so much. I can't wait to spend time with you all again.

Now, on to the point of my letter. I know I was too forward with you the day I said goodbye to you. If you've forgotten what happened, I won't remind you. I'm way too embarrassed. Back then, I was scared I might not ever see you again, and I couldn't bear the thought of never telling you how I felt for all of those years. It took a whole lot of moxie to tell you, but I was young and, frankly, pretty dumb. Dot, I've grown up a lot, and now I realize how you must have felt in that situation. I feel embarrassed to even remember it now. I am sorry I did it. I am sorry for surprising you with such a thing.

I hope you can forgive me, and we can be friends, just like we were before. I don't think I could bear it if we weren't friends anymore. So, let's just move on and pretend that day never happened.

I look forward to seeing you again, my friend, and hope you have at least one loaf of bread and a plate full of your chocolate chip cookies waiting for me when I get there.

Love, Henry

I knew it wasn't perfect, but I hoped it was good enough for what I wanted to say to her. My handwriting was still pretty awful, but it was the best I could do at this point. It would take years of practice before I could either learn to use my left hand well, or train my right arm back into working order. I didn't know which option would be harder.

I folded up the letter, addressed the envelope, and put it in the pile with the rest of my letters. I figured that if I was going to be home soon, I'd just bring the letters along with me and hand deliver them. If not, I would send all of the letters from England and follow them home.

"Is that a letter to Dot I see?" Buddy walked up to my bed and picked up the letter.

"Yes it is," I said proudly. "I finally got up the nerve to put one in an envelope. Aren't you proud of me?"

"You're pathetic." He laughed. "I still can't believe this is the first one you've written to her!"

"It's not the first one I've written, it's just the first that made it to an envelope instead of a fire."

"Ahh, so you've been writing to her this whole time?"

I nodded. "I just never sent any."

"Why not?"

"I guess I wasn't ready. Or brave enough." I shrugged and let out a sigh. "I couldn't get the right words out. I don't know, Bud. It's hard."

"I know how you feel, man. There's this gal who lives close to where I was stationed, and we danced a few times. I bought her dinner, we danced some more, and that's where it ended. I thought she fancied me. Dames can be confusing."

I blushed. "That's not what—"

"I know what you mean, Henry. Even though you won't admit it to me yourself, I know exactly how you feel about my little sister."

I tried to get more words out, but Bud interrupted me.

"I'm fine with it, honestly. You're a good man, and I know you two are close friends. Just don't ruin that friendship, if you know what I mean."

"I might have already done that."

"Then repair it. Dottie forgives easily. She's good like that. So, if you want to apologize for whatever you did, then do it. Hopefully, whatever is in this letter will fix everything."

"I hope so too." I said. Bud was a good guy. I was glad to have him there to talk me through my worries.

"I'll be your wingman," he said. "You have nothing to worry about."

CHAPTER 6

June 13, 1945

Dorothy

He was coming home! My big brother was finally coming home! We got a letter on Friday morning informing us that Buddy would be arriving at the train station on June 14th. Mom opened the letter right away and started tearing up while reading it out loud. Every one of us cried and hugged. We were overjoyed.

On the morning of June 13th I went on my rounds, delivering both bread and cookies. I stopped at the Oakey's house to drop off a couple of loaves of bread that Anna had requested.

She opened the door shortly after I knocked.

"Dorothy!" She hugged me. "He's coming home!"

"Henry?" I asked hopefully. Could he really be coming home? I wanted to see him so badly.

She nodded enthusiastically. "He'll be here tomorrow. I've hardly slept a wink because of the anticipation."

"That's so exciting! Buddy's coming home tomorrow too! I wonder if they're together."

"I think they must be if Henry stopped in England on his way home. Oh, we'll all be together again tomorrow!" Anna clasped her hands together in front of her and beamed.

"I can't wait!" I couldn't help but smile widely, thinking about seeing my best friend again after such a long time. If he was at the station tomorrow when we picked up Bud, it would be the first time we would see each other since he tried to kiss me. I blushed at the thought.

Hopefully he wasn't still upset with me. I couldn't imagine that Henry would be truly angry though. Maybe things would be a little strained between us for a while, but I'm sure we would be able to work things out. I prayed that I hadn't ruined things permanently by rejecting his kiss or by not writing to him. Now that he was coming home tomorrow I would finally see. We would have to talk to each other, have a real conversation! I was overjoyed at the thought of seeing him again, but I still feared that we wouldn't be friends the same way we were before.

"You must bring some of your cookies over for Henry soon." Anna's comment brought me back to reality. Of course I should make cookies for Henry! It would be a perfect way to welcome him home. I could make some for Bud too. I wouldn't mind the extra time spent in the kitchen this afternoon, even after I had spent the morning baking bread. It would give me something to do to get my mind off of my nerves.

"Of course," I said, laughing. "Chocolate chip is still his favorite, right?"

"Yes, as long as Europe's taste in pastries hasn't changed him."

"Perfect. I'll make a whole dozen, just for him."

"That'll be perfect! You can bring them over tomorrow afternoon to surprise him."

I looked down to my lap. I didn't think cookies were a good enough apology for not writing to Henry for so long. I hoped it would at least be a beginning to repairing our relationship.

"Is everything all right, Dot?" Anna sounded concerned.

I quickly smiled and looked up at her. "Of course, Anna. I was just thinking about how great it will be to have Henry and Buddy home again."

"It'll be wonderful to have them back." Anna gave me a smile.

We talked for a little while longer before I had to go deliver more bread.

"I'll see you tomorrow morning," I said as I walked down the Oakey's steps. "Say hello to Jessica for me."

"I will, Dottie. Have a pleasant day!"

I was in a much happier mood than the last time I had left the Oakey's house. I would not only be seeing my brother tomorrow, but Henry as well. I would finally see if our friendship could be repaired, and I couldn't wait.

When I got home, Mom was talking on the telephone in the kitchen. I walked past her and began pulling the ingredients out of the cupboards for my now-memorized chocolate chip cookie recipe. I was planning on making a dozen cookies for Buddy and a dozen for Henry.

As I started measuring out the dry ingredients, Mom hung up the phone.

"Dottie, you'll have to make a lot more cookies," she said with a laugh. "Harold Oakey told your father that Henry's coming home tomorrow as well."

"I know." I grinned. "I was just at the Oakey's house talking to Anna."

"Look at you, all grown up and making house calls."

"Mom, I *am* 21. I'm quite mature." I made a dramatic face, then laughed.

"Of course." She nodded and laughed. "Anyway, I was just on the phone with your father, and he suggested we invite the Oakeys over for a meal to celebrate Buddy's and Henry's safe return home."

"And you need cookies for dessert?" I knew where this was going. I would have to make a great deal more than I was planning on if we were going to have everyone over. If Jimmy was coming, I would have to make a full batch just for him. Who knew a beanpole like him could eat so much?

"Thank you, Dottie!" Mom said, already assuming I agreed, which she was correct in thinking. I hardly ever turned down a baking job, even if it was for my own family. She gave me a kiss on my forehead and left to buy groceries.

I spent the entire afternoon baking cookies and listening to my Andrews Sisters record over and over. They never got old. I had the entire record memorized from listening to it so much. I sang out loud with my less-than-perfect voice, but it didn't matter to me what I sounded like. I was too happy to care. My brother and Henry were both coming home, and I felt wonderful!

The next morning, my parents woke me and Bobby up bright and early so we could be at the train station when Bud arrived.

I did my hair and makeup quickly, and then debated on whether to wear my forest green or rose-colored dress. While I was finally deciding on the green dress, Mom walked into my room unannounced.

"It's just me, it's just me," she said as she entered.

I looked up at her from the green dress I was putting on, and saw that she was holding a gorgeous navy blue, sailor-style dress.

"Oh no dear, you can't wear that one," she said. "Take this one. I bought it in Pittsburgh last week."

"Are you serious?"

"Of course. Your father and I thought it would be nice for you to have something new to wear, and we figured this would be a good time for you to break it in."

"Oh Mom, you're the best!" I hugged her. "It's gorgeous!"

"Well, put it on, and then come downstairs. We're just about ready to leave. Bobby's been waiting outside for half an hour already. I'm sure his new pants are already covered in grass stains. I should probably go check on him."

She shook her head and walked out of my bedroom, closing the door behind her.

The blue dress fit perfectly. It matched the one pair of shoes I owned, and it was comfortable and easy to move in. I loved it immediately.

I decided a dress like this deserved some more attention to my makeup, so I added a darker shade of red lipstick to contrast with the navy blue of the dress. I fluffed my curls once more, and decided I was as ready as I ever would be.

When the four of us were finally in the car, we headed out to the train station in the neighboring town. It was only about thirty minutes away, but Bobby had already managed to poke fun at my lipstick, asking if it was for Buddy or for Henry that I looked so fancy. You would never know that boy was sixteen. He still teased me like he did when he was eleven. I ignored him, even when Mom turned around to look at me and winked, of all things.

Maybe it was for Henry, maybe it wasn't. I didn't rightly know myself, so I wasn't going to explain it to them. I simply kept my silence until we got to the train station in Riverside, the next town over. It was already crowded with people, undoubtedly waiting for other soldiers that were coming home.

I got out of the car and suddenly felt very nervous. I was excited, that was true, but that excitement was mixed with some fear. I could feel my heartbeat in my throat and hoped I wouldn't make a fool out of myself in front of Henry.

Henry. He was coming. He would be here any minute!

Breathe. I told myself. I wasn't going to overreact, because I was here to see my brother. However many times I repeated it, it did not keep my heart from beating out of my chest. I fiddled with the bow on the front of my dress and scanned the platform of the small outdoor station. There were several other families standing around, anxiously awaiting the arrival of their loved ones. The sun shone and it was finally starting to feel like summer.

As I looked around, the Oakeys pulled up in their Dodge. When Jessica stepped out of the car, she ran over to me and gave me a big hug.

"Dottie! Our brothers are coming home, can you believe it?" Her blonde hair was in two braids with bows on the ends, just like I always did for her whenever I'd go to the Oakey's house to study with Henry in high school. Jess always wanted me to do her hair exactly like that. We both enjoyed the feeling of having a sister. Now that she was twelve, Jessica still loved having her hair in braids, something that made me smile with nostalgia.

"I can't believe it, Jessie!" I hugged her back, careful not to crumple either of our dresses.

We walked together onto the platform. Our parents were talking behind us and Bobby looked a little lost, so I called him over. The three of us visited about how excited we were. When we had exhausted that topic, I asked Jess if she was looking forward to junior high. Buddy began to give her advice about the school, and the two were tied up in a conversation in no time, leaving me to scan the platform again.

Soon enough, I heard the train whistle. My heart beat faster with anticipation and impatience. I craned my neck to look over the heads of the people in front of me and saw the train begin to approach. It pulled into the station much more slowly than I would have liked. I wanted to jump with excitement, but I left that to Jessica, whose braids were swinging back and forth from the motion.

The train finally pulled to a stop with a loud screech of the wheels against the tracks. I tapped my feet, waiting for the doors to open and for people to leave the train. Finally, a mass of people filed out of every train car, and it seemed like everyone was being reunited with their families and friends except us. I looked around frantically for Buddy or Henry, but I couldn't see them anywhere.

I walked away from my family, trying to see either of my two soldiers in the crowd. I stood on my tiptoes, hoping to catch a glimpse of them.

Finally, I saw Buddy, standing next to the train with two large black trunks, looking lost but excited. I ran to him, dodging the last few people who were getting off the train. I heard more than one curse word when I accidentally bumped into a few men in suits. I hugged Buddy as soon as I reached him and didn't let go until I heard him laugh.

"Dottie, I hardly recognized you!" Bud grabbed both of my shoulders and pushed me away from him, staring me up and down. "You look so much older! I thought you were a complete stranger who was just excited to hug a man in uniform."

"Oh Buddy, I missed you so much." I took in the sight of him in his uniform, then hugged him again. He hugged me back, resting his chin on the top of my head. He looked so official, so grown up. "You're home."

"I am home." He looked up and sighed. His eyes went wide, and he grinned and shook his head. "There's Mom!" He let go of me and ran to Mom, who had finally picked us out in the crowd. They hugged, then Pop was there and joined in. Bobby followed right after Pop, and pretty soon the five of us were together again, hugging, laughing, and crying.

At last we walked to the other side of the platform where the Oakeys were still standing, now with a tall soldier in army green who was hugging and spinning Jessica around. It was him. Henry. I took a deep breath and told myself to act normal. It was hard to focus on acting normally when my heart was pounding so hard it felt like I would explode.

Henry stopped spinning and put Jessica down, laughing and breathing hard. He tugged on one of her braids and she swatted his hand away in response. Suddenly, he looked up.

His eyes met mine. I had forgotten how green they were. My heart rose to my throat.

I smiled and waved at him tentatively, trying not to show how nervous I was to see him again. But that part was over. We had seen each other. I had to pretend I wasn't in danger of falling over from my knees shaking. He walked up to me and hugged me. That was something I honestly wasn't expecting, given how our goodbye went and the fact that we hadn't corresponded in over two years.

"Dottie," he said, his voice breaking. "I missed you so much."

"I missed you too, Henry." I settled into his hug, wrapping my arms around him. I breathed in, remembering how it felt to hug Henry Oakey.

I truly had missed him terribly.

CHAPTER 7

June 14, 1945

Henry

I was home. It hadn't completely sunk in that I was going home until I felt the plane take off two mornings before. I hardly remembered the feeling of flying, since the only other time I had been on a plane was when I flew to France after I was drafted.

The plane was full of silent soldiers. All of us were on our way to America. Some of us were going there to stay, others were going to be transferred to the Pacific. I was glad to be in the group going home. The soldiers that were going to the Pacific had bleak expressions on their tired faces. We were all hoping the Pacific front would soon see peace as well.

Bud was sitting next to me on the plane, but neither of us talked much. None of the soldiers did. We were all still in shock from the fact that the war in Europe was over after such a long time.

I hadn't seen my family in exactly two years, seven months, and twenty-three days. I hadn't known the exact amount of time until Frank asked me when I left home. He did the calculating and promptly informed me how much time it had been since I left.

I let that number play in my head a few times throughout our flight. Two years, seven months, and twenty-three days. That was much too long. I was relieved to finally be going home.

The extra time I spent in England gave me a few weeks for my arm to heal. Before I left that morning, the doctors had approved me to travel and sent me home with clear instructions on how to take care of my injury. There was a large scar on my shoulder and upper arm from the burns and cuts, but at least the wound was closed and mostly healed. I could finally start exercising my arm and hopefully get it back to its normal mobility. It had been held to my side in a sling for long enough. I would soon be able to carry things, eat without spilling all over myself, and write legibly. Needless to say, it would be wonderful to be able to use my arm again.

After over a day of travel, the plane landed outside of New York City. Once we got off the plane, we all boarded trains to our respective cities in the New England area. Bud and I were among several soldiers on our train to Pittsburgh. Once we arrived there, we said farewell to the soldiers staying in the city and boarded a train bound for Riverside along with a few others.

Once we reached the station, we got off the train and I was caught up in the crowd. I was pushed further onto the platform, and I struggled to stay upright. I was still weak from my months of sickness, and it was hard for me to push through the crowds. There were so many people that I lost track of where Bud was, but I assumed he had found his family. I hoped he would find me later, since he had my trunk. I still wasn't strong enough to carry it, so Bud had offered to take it for me.

As soon as I saw an opening in the crowd of people, I slipped through. I began to look for my family but couldn't see any of them. I turned around in a full circle, scanning the platform for them. Finally, I saw my parents running towards me.

Mom started crying when she hugged me. I could hardly believe I was actually hugging my mom again. I hugged her back and laughed when she said she'd been waiting for me to come home since the day I left.

I was wrapped in Dad's arms next. He didn't say anything, but I could hear him sniffing. He was crying. That was surprising. He hugged me hard, but I could tell he was careful to avoid touching my right shoulder.

After Dad let me go, Jessica ran up and hugged me right away. I laughed and spun her around. She looked so much older, but she still had her hair in two braids. I set her down and tugged on them. She had always loved having her hair like that.

Pretty soon, they were looking at my uniform, Mom saying how handsome I was, Dad commenting on how grown-up I looked, and Jessica asking why my uniform was such an ugly shade of green. We were laughing and wiping away tears, and that's when I saw her.

Dot.

She was standing a few feet away in a navy blue dress, her dark brown hair curled around the nape of her neck. She looked even more beautiful than I remembered. Her lips were dark red with the lipstick I knew she only wore for special occasions, and she was smiling. At me. She was smiling at me!

She held up her hand and waved at me shyly, and the nervousness I had pushed away came back. I tried to ignore my feelings and took a few careful steps toward her. Before I knew it, I wrapped my arms around her. She hugged me tightly. Hugging her felt like being home again.

"Dottie," I said, trying not to cry. "I missed you so much."

"I missed you too, Henry." She hugged me back tightly.

After a few moments, I pulled away from our embrace, looking at her again. I still held her close, but dropped my arms awkwardly when I realized what I had been doing.

"I can't believe I'm home." I shook my head and smiled.

"I can't believe it either. It's been so long."

"I know. How have you been?"

"I've been fine." She smiled softly. "You?"

"I've been better," I said reluctantly, quickly glancing at my arm.

"Oh, you're injured, I almost forgot."

"How did you hear?"

"Your mom told me. I went to your house to ask about you after Peggy mentioned something had happened."

"I didn't ever write to you to tell you." I was reminded of the same guilt that had been with me for the last few weeks.

"I didn't write either. It's not your fault." Dottie smiled again, her bright blue eyes sparkling. "But how are you, really?"

"My arm hurts like the dickens, but other than that I'm fine, I guess."

"I'm glad you're getting better. What happened?"

I didn't want to tell her. I couldn't even think about that night, let alone talk about it with someone else. I hadn't realized people would want to know the full story. The soldiers hadn't asked about it, probably because they understood that it was painful to talk about. Most of them had gone through similar things. People like Dot who hadn't experienced the war weren't going to understand that it was hard to talk about. I would have to make up some story since I couldn't explain to everyone what had really happened. I could just say I got hit by shrapnel. That was part of the truth.

Dot must have noticed the look on my face, because she said, "Oh, I'm sorry. If you don't want to talk about it…"

"It's fine." I gave her a smile. "I'd just rather not talk about it right now." I hoped she would understand. I didn't want her to feel offended in any way.

Dot smiled again. "That's okay." After a pause, she continued. "My parents invited your family over for supper tonight." She pointed over to our families, who were chatting a few yards away. Dot laughed. I had missed hearing her laugh. "It's probably going to be more like dessert. I don't think we're eating anything other than cookies."

"We can have cookies for supper, can't we?" I winked.

"Of course, but it might not be the best idea."

"I, frankly, would enjoy a feast of cookies. Especially if they're your cookies. Are they chocolate chip?"

Dot rolled her eyes. "You haven't changed a bit, Henry."

"Sure I have! Jessica told me I'm taller, my dad said I matured a whole lot, and my mom said I'm more handsome!"

"I'll have to think about all that. You're definitely taller…" she trailed off, then smirked.

I shoved her shoulder like I used to do often.

She tensed up at first, but then laughed. Maybe things could go back to normal. Just maybe.

Buddy walked over with my luggage.

"Are you coming over later?" he asked me.

I nodded and took my trunk from him. I held it with my left arm, which still felt unnatural.

"See you then, pal." Bud patted me on the back lightly, careful to avoid my right shoulder. He turned to Dot, who was watching our exchange. "Dottie, I think we're going home. Mom said something about cleaning the house before tonight."

I suddenly remembered the letter I wrote to Dot. When could I give it to her? I didn't have it available right now. It was somewhere buried in my trunk. Maybe I would try to give it to her later that night?

"I'll see you tonight?" Dot was already walking toward her family's car. She walked backwards, keeping her eyes on mine.

"I'll wear my best suit!" I said, bowing. As soon as I had done it, I felt embarrassed.

"Perfect. I'll await you in my finest dress." She faked a British accent. It was wonderful to have my best friend again.

"Swell. See you soon."

CHAPTER 8

June 14, 1945

Dorothy

Buddy was home; Henry was home. It felt like a large part of life was back to the way it was before the war started. America was still fighting on the Pacific front, but I didn't personally know anyone who was there. The only people I truly cared about were here with me in Ashwood.

As soon as we got home, Mom rushed us out of the car and into the house to prepare for the party that night. Pop went to help Bobby in the yard, so Bud used that as an excuse to help me in the kitchen, even after our parents told him he should go rest or unpack. Mom went to the grocers to buy the ingredients for a salad that she had forgotten the day before. She left, mumbling about how scattered her brain had been, and Bud and I laughed together after she closed the door behind her.

I decided to start by washing the dishes we used for breakfast. Buddy started wiping off the countertops.

"It's kind of weird being home," Bud said, looking around the room. "I can't believe I'm back."

"I can't believe it either! It's been so long."

"It doesn't seem like anything's changed all that much. You and Bobby look older, though."

"We grew up a lot while you were gone."

"I can tell. I missed you all so much."

"We missed you too. Now, I want to hear all about England." How do you even begin to ask about four years of a person's life?

"I told you most of it in my letters," Buddy said, looking at me from the other side of the room, where he was wiping the countertop.

"I know, but I want to hear it from you!"

Bud ignored me and just smiled.

"Please Bud, please!"

"Okay, okay, stop pestering."

"I'm not..."

He laughed.

I splashed him with water from the sink, where I was washing dishes. I had forgotten how easy it was for Buddy to joke and tease.

"Well," he started. "England itself was great. The people were kind to us and always thanked us for our service. The food was passable, I guess. It was just different from home, you know?"

I nodded.

He continued. "And the war was horrible. That's all I can say. Every time there was an air raid drill I felt sick because I knew it was me who had to protect those people. I had to help them, even though I didn't know how." He was scrubbing vigorously at a stain on the countertop that had been there for years. It wasn't going to wipe off any time soon. I knew from experience.

"I hate blackout drills." I really did. The memory of hiding in our small basement with the lights off was so horrible, I didn't even want to remember it.

"It's even worse when you know for a fact it isn't a drill." Buddy said this with a haunted look in his eyes.

I shuddered. "I can't even imagine."

"Don't. It's not something I want to return to."

"Did anything good happen in England? Or was it just war?"

"The other soldiers and I went dancing a lot, just like we all do here." Buddy lifted up his head, and his smile stretched all the way to his eyes.

"Really?" I couldn't picture my brother and a bunch of soldiers showing up to dance here. They would stick out like a sore thumb.

"Really. There were some gorgeous girls there in England. Too bad they live across an ocean."

Buddy had a wistful look in his eyes, so I snapped him out of it with more water from the sink.

"Oh, stop that," I said. "Don't you go off dreaming about some English girl when you just got home!"

"I'm not gonna leave you all, if that's what you're thinking."

I folded my arms and glared at him.

"I promise I won't, Dottie. I'm here to stay. But speaking of dancing and courting and all that, have you found yourself a beau?"

"Of course not." I quickly turned back to the dishes. I did not want to talk about this with my big brother.

"Jimmy hasn't stolen your heart yet?"

I snorted. "Jimmy? Ha! Jimmy's just a friend, and you know that."

"And what about Henry? Is he just a friend?"

I stopped laughing and tried to brush his comment off. "I don't want to talk about this, but yes, Henry is just a friend. End of story."

"I sense there's more to the 'story' than just that."

"If there was more, which there isn't, I wouldn't tell you."

"Come on, Dottie, I'm your brother!"

"Exactly."

"I deserve to know!"

"No you don't." I knew he was joking, but I knew he really did want to know. And I knew that when John Banks Jr. wanted something, he got it.

He gave me a puppy dog grin as if to remind me of that fact.

"Fine," I said. "I don't know what's going on between us, okay? I have no idea how I feel...or how he feels."

"That's all right," he said. "You just saw him for the first time in more than two years. You have time to figure things out."

I nodded.

"Let me just warn you though. We spent a couple weeks together in London, and he's gone through a lot. He might be fragile after what he's been through. Don't push him so far that he breaks."

"What do you mean?"

"War is horrible. It's worse than I ever imagined it being, and I was only in England. Henry fought in tons of huge battles on the mainland. He had to kill people, Dot. He was injured badly and he's still hurting from all of it. That's what war is. It isn't just waving flags for Uncle Sam. It was horrible."

I didn't know what to say. Of course I knew that war included killing, but I guess I hadn't realized Henry had to...I couldn't imagine someone like him having to do that.

"He'll be fine," Buddy continued. "Just give him time."

I nodded. I was still speechless. I finished wiping the last dish dry and put it on a shelf. I moved on to sweeping the floor. Buddy was silent as he finished wiping the counter.

Mom returned with her arms full of grocery bags. She set them down on the clean counter and scolded Buddy for helping.

"I know, Momma, I just wanted to talk to Dot. I figured I might as well help her while we talked."

"You've been hard at work keeping our country safe. You deserve a nice long nap." She shooed him upstairs.

I finished sweeping and then helped her prepare supper.

CHAPTER 9

June 14th, 1945

Henry

I sat on my bed, staring off into the space above my nightstand. My stomach felt sick with nerves. I didn't know why. I had already seen Dot. I had already talked to her. Why did it make me so nervous to go to her house?

Deep down, I knew why. That's where I tried to kiss her. I groaned at the memory. Why in the world had I done that? She had never given me any reason to believe she liked me romantically, so why did I have to go and ruin everything? We were just friends. We were still just friends, and I should be fine with that. It should not be a problem for me to go to her house and spend time with her and her family.

I also knew I had to give her the letter. I found it among my things while unpacking, and now it sat next to me on the bed. Should I give it to her? I couldn't remember exactly what I had written, and I didn't want to ruin the envelope I had sealed it in by opening it to see. Had I written that I still had feelings for her? I couldn't remember, and that fact worried me. Did I really *want* to tell her I had feelings for her or did I want to start over? The one thing I did owe her was a better explanation for not writing to her during the years I was away.

I mulled all of this over until I was even more confused and finally decided to move on without giving her the letter. I wasn't sure if I still had feelings for her, and I had no idea if she had feelings for me. I decided to wait a little while to see how things were between us, and once things felt normal again, I would give her the letter.

The whole time I was thinking about all of this, I was sitting on a bed in a room that didn't feel like mine anymore. It had become a storage room while I was gone, but my parents and Jessica had taken out the extra chairs, canned food, and old books the day they got the news that I would be coming home. Now it was plain and almost empty, with only a bed, a wardrobe, and a nightstand with an old clock on it.

I didn't feel at home here. I had missed so much, and I had changed. I knew I wasn't the same Henry that lived here years before, and I would never go back to being him. It was odd to me that I didn't feel at home here, since I hadn't felt at home in Europe either. The cold nights sleeping outside and days spent patrolling or fighting kept me from settling in. I had looked at coming back to Ashwood as the time when I could finally feel content again, but I didn't. Did I even have a place to call home anymore?

I was taken out of my daydreams by my dad knocking on my open door.

"Hey, son," he said, standing in the doorway. "How are you settling in?"

"Everything is perfect, thank you." I tried to hide the melancholy in my voice, but I was sure Dad could tell something was off.

"If you need anything, just be sure to let me know." He suddenly laughed. "Gosh, I sound like a hotel manager. But honestly, Henry. If there is anything, just tell me, all right?"

I laughed. "You got it, Dad."

"Your mother wants to be at the Banks' house by six o'clock sharp. Her words, not mine, so get ready to go soon."

I nodded. "Thanks, Dad."

He nodded at me once before he left.

I opened my suitcase to find the majority of my clothes wrinkled or stained. The few non-uniform shirts I had were unwashed and ratty, and I would rather throw them away than put them on again. I checked my wardrobe, and the shirts inside smelled like moth balls and were too big when I put them on. I must have lost more weight than I thought during my months of sickness.

I had no idea what to wear. Gosh, that was such a silly problem to have. I sounded like Jessica. In fact, I thought I heard her down the hall yelling for Mom's help. Maybe I would consult my father. He would know. Maybe he would even have something I could borrow.

I left my room and went down the hall to my parents' room.

"Dad?" I knocked on the open door. "I need to take you up on that offer already."

Dad was tying a bow-tie around his neck. He looked up and smiled. "How can I help?"

"I have no idea what to wear tonight. What do people even wear to this type of thing? I haven't been to a party in forever. Plus, all my old clothes are too big."

He chuckled and motioned me inside his room. "Your mother said I needed to wear a tie. I don't know what people wear to these things either. How about this one?" He went over to his closet and moved around the clothes on the rack until he picked out a dark blue button-up shirt. It was the exact same shade as the dress Dot had worn this morning. If that was what she was still wearing, which I was sure was so, we would be matching.

"Um, do you have a different one?"

He went back to searching around in his shirts and pulled out a dark green button-up.

"Perfect," I said. "I'll try it on."

"Great. Do you still have those khaki pants we sent with you?"

I nodded. "They are a little big around the waist, but I'll wear a belt."

"You slimmed down then, did you?"

I patted my lean stomach jokingly. "A few months of being sick in bed will do that to you."

"*And* months of hard work in the army, you can't forget that."

I let all my breath out at once. "What if I want to forget it?" I hadn't meant to be so serious, but the words slipped out.

Dad stopped what he was doing. "You want to forget the service you gave to your country?"

"Dad, there were so many bad things that happened, and it seems like that's all I can remember right now. I can't be sure there was anything I ever enjoyed."

"It was war, son. You're not really supposed to enjoy it. Hard work like that isn't always pleasant, even when you're saving people's lives every day."

That comment stung. "I was talking with John Banks, and he seemed to really enjoy himself. Same with a couple other guys. I just don't get it. Was I supposed to be happy doing what I was doing?"

"Henry, a lot of those boys weren't on the mainland. They were in England, away from most of the fighting. You were right there in France and Belgium. And no one likes to dwell on the negative experiences they have had. I'm sure they only told you about the good times they had and hid the bad things away."

"I guess you're right. I just regret so much of what I had to do. I want to forget it all, pretend it never happened."

He put his hands on my shoulders and stared me square in the eyes. "You can pretend it never happened, but if you do, you risk forgetting who the war made you become. You've only been here a few hours, and I can already tell how much of a man you are compared to the boy that left here years ago. You grew up thanks to what you went through. Even if it wasn't pleasant."

I didn't know how to respond. I had had a lot of time to think during the past few months lying in a hospital bed, and I realized how much I hated the war. How could something so horrible change me for the better? I didn't see how it could. I definitely felt different, but not in a mature, grown-up way. I felt like a child again, out of place and scared.

"Go try that shirt on," Dad said, patting me on the back. "It's almost time to go."

I guess he realized I didn't want to talk about it anymore.

I went back to my room and tried on Dad's shirt. It was just a little baggy, so I tucked it in and put on the khaki pants with a belt to tighten the waist. I combed my hair and was ready to go.

My family was waiting for me in the living room when I walked out.

"Oh Henry, you look so handsome!" Mom said, clasping her hands together. "I can't believe you're really here!"

"Momma, you look beautiful, as always." I walked over to her and gave her a hug. She hugged me back tightly, like she didn't want to let me go. "I'm so happy I'm home."

Jessica interrupted our hug by asking loudly when we were leaving.

Mom and I laughed and stepped out of our hug.

Jessica grabbed my hand and practically dragged me out the front door, and my parents followed us, laughing. Jessica talked my ears off on the way to the Banks' house about this neighbor and that one, commenting on all of the events I had missed while I was gone. People had gotten married, moved away, and gotten new jobs. Jess seemed to know all of the neighborhood gossip, and I gladly listened, laughing at her innocent commentary. I was glad to be distracted from my nerves, but they all came back a few short minutes later when we reached the Banks' house. We walked up to the doorstep and Dad knocked on the door. My heart was pounding, threatening to escape my chest.

Mr. Banks opened it and invited us in, saying that he was "glad to see us again," and that he hoped I "had settled back in nicely." I nodded politely, then took in the scene around me, hoping to find Buddy or Dot so I would have someone to talk to. Jessica ran off somewhere with my friend Marylin's little sister Millie, and my parents were caught up in a conversation with all of the other parents, so I felt out of place within a few short moments. The living room was just as orderly as I remembered it. Dot's mom always liked to keep it that way, even though Bobby often used to throw the decorative pillows on the ground and climb up on the couches. Now he must be fifteen or sixteen, so I figured he had outgrown that pastime. I laughed, and then felt awkward again, since I was standing in a house full of people, laughing to myself.

In the army, I hardly ever felt out of place. I had my rank, and I knew what my job was. I was surrounded by guys my age, so I always had someone to talk to or banter with. That had been one good thing about the war. It was hard to truly make friends, though, since there was always a chance that someone wouldn't come back to camp at the end of the day. I saw that with Jones and Davies. I shuddered, trying to keep my mind off of the war. It was harder than I thought.

I made my way into the dining room, trying to find Buddy, but I ran into Peggy, Marylin, and Jimmy instead. They screamed with delight when they saw me. Peggy started throwing questions at me, showing that her personality hadn't changed one bit. I tried answering her, but she started laughing and then just hugged me, mentioning something about catching up. Marylin was quieter, but she hugged me and said they had all missed me terribly. Then I looked at Jimmy, expecting to hug him as well, but I paused with my arms awkwardly in front of me. I could only stare at him. It was as if I was seeing Davies again in front of me, the soldier I had left behind to die. Jimmy's eyes had the same pale blue color and held the same innocence and hope for the world as Davies' eyes. I could almost hear Davies call out to me to leave him behind. The sounds of the party slipped away, and all I could hear was Davies' voice over and over again. I let my arms fall to my sides. Jimmy looked at me with hurt and confusion in his eyes, then hugged me anyway. I reached up to hug him back and tried to ignore my pounding chest. I stepped back from the hug and tried to smile, but I couldn't get the image of Davies lying on the ground out of my head.

I felt a pit in my stomach at the memory of that night. The room spun. I couldn't concentrate on what the girls were saying to me. I could hardly hear them over the rushing sound in my ears. I smiled at my three friends and said something about needing to find a glass of water, then left to go to the kitchen.

My vision blurred. I felt like I was back in the hospital bed in France, sitting up for the first time after regaining consciousness. I ran into the doorway of the kitchen and the wound in my arm burned. I wanted to cry out in pain, but I bit down on my lip and tried to ignore the sharp sting running down to my fingers.

I stumbled into the empty kitchen, trying to find a glass of water or something to calm my stomach. I didn't know what was happening. Everything was so loud. I felt hot and knew I was sweating. I found a cup and started to fill it with water from a pitcher that was on the counter. My arm shook from the effort. When I lifted the cup to my mouth, I spilled some water from the cup onto my shirt. I ignored it and took a drink. I tried to breathe deeply. I held my head in my hands on the counter and slowly counted to twenty in French, just like the nurses taught me to do when I felt nauseous. I gradually felt the pit in my stomach go away and started to feel better. I took another sip of water.

"Henry?"

I looked up to see Dot standing on the other side of the countertop, staring at me. She looked concerned.

"Are you all right?" she asked.

"Yeah," I said, wiping my hand on my shirt. "Just really thirsty. I came in here to get a drink, but I spilled."

"Oh, okay." She said, not sounding convinced.

"I'm fine, really." I smiled. "You look really nice." She did. She was gorgeous.

Dot blushed, looking down at her dress, the same dark blue one she wore earlier. "Thanks. My mom bought it for me."

"It's beautiful." I looked down and laughed. "This shirt is my father's."

"I wouldn't say it's beautiful, but it does look nice." There was my Dot, always joking around.

I felt a lot more relaxed now, with whatever had happened to me out of sight. I didn't understand. I felt normal, just a little tired. What was happening to me? Was I getting sick?

"Have you seen Jimmy and the girls yet?" Dot asked.

"Yeah, I just saw them in the dining room. I was talking to them before I came in here to get a drink."

"All right. Are you feeling better?"

I nodded.

"Let's go find them, then. We need a photo of us all together again!"

She grabbed my good hand and pulled me into the dining room. Peggy, Marylin, and Jimmy were all there, talking to Bud. I noticed the looks the three of them gave me as I walked in, a mixture of worry and confusion on their faces. I tried to ignore them and act like nothing had happened, giving them all a smile.

Bud took a picture of the five of us at Dot's request. We posed together in a line, just like the pictures we used to take together at holiday parties and at high school events. We were all together again, and it was almost like it used to be when we were kids, but we were all so different now. So much had changed while I was gone, and I felt somehow out of place. Could it ever be the same again?

Throughout the rest of the night, I tried to act natural. I smiled and responded accordingly when people asked me how I was. I hugged people and got patted on the back and generally tried not to lose control of myself again. I was truly happy to be there, but what I had experienced earlier scared me. Would it happen again? I wondered if I was getting sick. I hadn't had any problems with the infection in my arm for months, but what if it came back?

I made it through supper and dessert without getting sick, which I considered a success.

I was glad when the night ended so I could go back home and sleep off whatever was wrong with me. What had happened scared me, but I knew sleeping always helped when someone was sick. I had personal experience with that. I was sure I would feel better in the morning.

CHAPTER 10

June 14th, 1945

Dorothy

I was exhausted. It had been such a long day with all the excitement of having Bud home and the stress of hosting a party, not to mention the personal stress I felt from seeing Henry again. We were all very tired.

Peggy and Marylin both stayed to help clean up after everyone else had left, which my family was very grateful for. Thanks to them, we were done in no time.

It was late by the time we finished, so they stayed the night. We put lots of extra blankets and pillows on the floor of my room, just like we used to do in high school when we had sleepovers.

"How is it to have your brother home, Dot?" Marylin asked as she sat down among the blankets.

"It's wonderful!" I sat down next to her and Peggy after turning the lights off. "I missed him so much. We talked for a long time today catching up, and it was great having the three of us back together again." I had definitely missed having Bud here so we could tease Bobby together.

"The *real* question is," Peggy gave me a wicked grin, "how is it to have Henry home?"

I shot her a glare. "It's the same for me as it is for you, Margaret." I used her full name, which I knew she hated. "We finally have our group back together again. Now poor Jimmy isn't the only guy spending time with all us girls! It's great. It's just fine." I stuck my nose up in the air.

Peggy snorted. "Sure."

"Henry was acting really odd tonight, wasn't he?" Marylin said.

"Yeah, he was kind of rude to Jimmy when he first saw him," Peggy chimed in. "He couldn't stop staring at him. It was like he had seen a ghost. They hugged each other, and then Henry just walked away like he hadn't even been talking to us. It was very strange."

"Was that before I found him?" I asked. He *had* been acting a little odd. One minute he looked like he was going to be sick, then the next he was joking around and acting just fine. "I was looking for him everywhere. I finally found him in the kitchen. He said he just needed some water. He looked really tired. Was he feeling okay when he was talking to you?"

"I don't think so," Peggy said. "He looked like he was going to vomit."

"Yeah, he looked awful," Marylin said. "He looked at Jimmy like he didn't recognize him, then just left. Poor Jimmy didn't know what to say afterwards. It was really odd."

I thought things over for a little while. The other girls were silent. I couldn't imagine Henry would try to ignore them or make them feel uncomfortable. He was probably just feeling a little sick from all of the travel.

"I don't think he meant to offend Jimmy," I reasoned. "Henry's not like that. Maybe he really *was* sick and just trying to hide it to be a good sport."

"He did have a long trip," Marylin said.

"And he could still be feeling unwell from his injury." Peggy fluffed her pillow and then lay down.

I hadn't even thought about his injury. Of course he would be feeling unwell. I didn't know what had happened to his arm exactly, but I was sure it would require lots of energy to heal. That's probably why Henry hadn't been feeling well. That was definitely it.

We were silent again. Peggy yawned.

"Hey Dot, how close are you to buying the bakery?"

I was glad for the change of topic. "I think I'll have enough money by the end of the year."

"That's wonderful!" Marylin said, sitting up a little straighter. I think she was grateful for the change of topic as well. "I'm so happy for you!"

"I'm very excited," I said. "You'll both help me decorate once I buy it, right?"

Both of my friends nodded enthusiastically.

"As long as we get free cookies for life!" Peggy joked.

I tossed a pillow at her. "You'll eat me out of business if I promise you that."

Peggy tossed it back at me, laughing. I tossed it at Marylin, who tossed it back at Peggy. We threw it around a couple more times before dissolving into laughter.

"I miss our high school days," Peggy said, suddenly serious.

I lay down on one side of our makeshift bed. "What do you miss?"

"Just the simplicity of it all. Not school. I could never miss school."

"Hear, hear!" Marylin said, raising her fist in the air.

I rolled my eyes at my two friends.

Peggy's voice was more somber now. "I miss seeing everyone everyday and just being a kid, you know?"

I did. I missed it a lot.

We were silent again as we let that thought sink in. We weren't kids anymore, and life was a lot different than it was just a few years ago. I closed my eyes and said, "Being 'grown-up' is harder than I thought it would be."

Marylin settled down next to me.

"It's definitely more interesting." Marylin sighed.

"That's for sure," Peggy said.

"I can't imagine being bored ever again," I said. "There's too much to do."

Marylin yawned. "It's exhausting."

"I'm exhausted," Peggy whispered.

The three of us laughed quietly.

"Me too," I agreed. My eyelids were getting heavy. "Goodnight," I said, closing my eyes.

"'Night Dot, 'night Peggy."

"G'night."

As I lay there, falling asleep, my thoughts turned to Henry again. I hoped he would be okay. I hoped *we* would be okay.

CHAPTER 11

June 19, 1945

Henry

I stepped into Mr. Green's office in one of the new suits Mom bought for me in Pittsburgh. Before the war, I had interned here at the oil refinery. I started during high school and I had loved it. I helped in the finance department, filing audits and reports and helping the accountants out wherever I could. It would have bored some of my classmates terribly, but I loved working out the problems and seeing the patterns in the numbers. The other men who worked in finance were surprisingly fun to spend time with, and accepted me right away. And now I was back, taking Mr. Green up on his promise to give me a job when I came home.

I felt overwhelmed with the returning memories as I took in his office with its filing cabinets and photos of the Green family.

"Henry Oakey!" Mr. Green stood up from his desk and took my hand in both of his. He shook it a few times, and I tried to hold back a wince as a jolt of pain ran down my arm. Mr. Green didn't notice and motioned for me to sit down. "How have you been adjusting?" Mr. Green continued.

"It's a process," I said. "My family has been a big help. I'm lucky to have them."

"You are very lucky to have supportive people around you during a time like this." Mr. Green paused and looked at one of the pictures of his family. He had two daughters who were both older than me and married. I seemed to remember that he was a recent grandfather when

I left. He sighed and then continued. "Now, I'm sure you remember I told you that you'd have a job waiting for you when you came home from the war."

I nodded.

"Wonderful. I am happy to tell you we have an opening for an accountant position. However, a college degree is required for the job. You would need to be attending a college in order to accept that position. Have you considered applying to the University?"

I had forgotten about all of that while I was gone. When I was in high school, I had wanted to go to college and study to be an accountant, since I loved working with numbers and enjoyed interning at the oil refinery. However important that had been to me in high school, all of that slipped my mind while I was in Europe. "Honestly, I kind of forgot about it."

"How would you feel about applying to the University of Pittsburgh? I have a few associates in their school of business who could put a good word in for you."

I did want to go. I had always wanted to go to college and get a degree. I had heard about the school of business at the University of Pittsburgh from both my teachers and other employees at the refinery. It was prestigious and yet close enough to commute every day if I needed to. The only problem was, I didn't know how I would ever pay for it. I couldn't possibly ask my parents for help with tuition. They had enough economic worries left over from the Depression. I would have to pay my own way, and I was starting from the bottom when it came to my savings. I just didn't have the money.

"I'll have to think about it," I said.

"Perfect," Mr. Green responded, clasping his hands together in front of him. "While you decide, we'll keep you on as an assistant accountant. Now, let's get you back to work!"

He gave me a desk next to the one I used to use as an intern. There would be a new high school student coming in to intern once school started again in the fall, so my old desk stayed empty. A few of the other people in the accounting department were the same as before the war. It was nice to see more familiar faces. I sat next to a guy named Jason, who was about thirty-two. I remembered that he had been drafted toward the beginning of the war, but had stayed in the states to help train new recruits.

Now, Jason trained me for my new assistant job. He helped me figure out the new way of filing that had been introduced a few months back, and he was joking around the whole time. He was a lot like Frank, the soldier I met back in London. Like Frank, Jason also liked to talk way more than I did, so I let him. He told stories about his experience in the training camps, which, from what I remembered from my training, was a lot less exciting than he made it sound. His only duties had been dealing with paperwork and reading reports from Europe detailing how many soldiers they needed and when. He made the year he served sound like the best thing ever. Maybe it had been. He hadn't seen any of the horrors of the war. He had essentially spent his year as a soldier doing exactly what we were doing here at the refinery. Though his service to his country had been much more boring than mine, it sounded kind of nice. I felt a bit jealous of the way he could happily recount the memories he had made. I didn't even want to talk about what the war had been like for me. Jason told me about the various new recruits and their growth as soldiers, funny pranks he had pulled on the other soldiers working at the base, and about some of the girls that came to work there. Jason had met a girl there during his service, and they had recently gotten married. Our experiences definitely had been different. I knew good things had happened to me while I was in Europe. I had pulled pranks with the other soldiers, and we had talked about the gals back home, but the bad memories clouded over the good ones, and now I could hardly believe all those good things had happened. I could only focus on the tragedy of it all.

Jason interrupted my thoughts by asking me something I didn't know how to answer.

"And what about you, Henry?" Jason asked. "Do you have a gal?"

I laughed uncomfortably. "No, not really."

"Ah, come on, not a single dame has caught your eye?"

I shook my head no, but I was pretty sure I was blushing, giving myself away.

"Well, I have a sister that's about your age, if you want to meet her. She lives in Riverside and comes to Ashwood every so often to visit me."

I thanked him and plastered a polite smile on my face, but I silently dreaded the moment when Jason would try to introduce me to his sister. I didn't want to offend him, but I was only interested in Dot. Though I had kept my feelings secret, she was the only one who had interested me since we started high school. When I finally felt ready to tell her how I felt, it was time for me to leave for the war. I had messed everything up between us the day I left. I would do anything to start over with her, but I knew I would have to wait until things were less awkward between us.

After work, I met my dad downstairs in the lobby of our building. He was in charge of getting shipments of oil out to various gas stations, airports, and other factories and businesses. He had helped me get my high school internship at the refinery, since he was a good friend and colleague of Mr. Green's. I asked him how work had gone as we walked out to the car.

"It's much busier now with the war in Europe over," he said. "I'm sure you've noticed we're slowly transitioning to selling like we were before the rationing started?"

I nodded. I had noticed that the filing and calculating we had to do was a lot heavier than I remembered. It made sense that we would gradually stop rationing gasoline, since many of our fighter planes weren't in use anymore. That was surely something hopeful. Everyone was ready for the war to be over and done with.

When Dad and I got home, we found Mom getting supper ready and Jessica listening to a radio program. I suddenly felt nostalgic. Everything was slowly going back to the way it was. I could get used to this again, even though I felt different than before the war. I was still Henry Oakey, wasn't I? I had my family back, I had my old job back, and I would try to get Dot back. I wanted to win back her friendship and then try to win her heart.

I knew that everything was going to be okay.

Fire. Smoke. Then pain.

I screamed and heard the other soldiers call out around me. Their voices blended together, calling out from all directions.

I fled. Jones ran next to me but fell behind, calling out my name as I continued to run. I lost him in the smoke.

Everything was in flames. I spun around in circles, trying to find an opening in the burning woods. I saw Davies fall to the ground in front of me, and I cried out to him. He was badly injured. I lifted him up and tried to walk with him for a few steps, but I fell to my knees in agony as I realized I was too weak to carry him any further.

I looked down at Davies' face to apologize for not being able to save him, but it wasn't Davies I was seeing. It was Jimmy. Instead of telling me to get out of there and save myself, Jimmy started yelling at me for letting him down. He clawed at my shirt and then my face, screaming at me like some monster.

How dare you?
How could you?
You didn't save me.
You left me to die.

I woke up in a cold sweat. My stomach churned, and I ran across the hall to the bathroom. After I vomited the last bit of supper into the toilet, I stood up and looked at myself in the mirror. I was as white as a ghost, and tears I hadn't realized were falling soaked my pajama shirt.

I left them. The Jimmy in my dream was right. I just left those soldiers there in the forest to die. It didn't matter that I survived. What mattered was that I was the *only* one who survived. I wasn't a hero. I was selfish. I could have gotten my friends out of there before the mission was compromised and ruined. I should have tried, been more careful. They could have been alive right now if I had.

I started to cry even harder. Jimmy's words echoed back to me.

How dare you; how could you; you didn't save me; you left me to die.

I don't know when I sank to the floor, but suddenly I was sitting down, crying and feeling sick.

I must have fallen asleep at some point, because I woke up to Jessica banging on the door.

"Henry, are you done yet? I need to shower!"

I stood up and checked my face in the mirror. My eyes were still red and swollen, and my face was blotchy. At least I wasn't so pale anymore.

"Yeah, Jess, I just need to shower really fast."

"Hurry up. I'm going to be late!"

Late. I had work today. I still had no idea what time it was. I showered off quickly and ran past Jessica in a towel. As soon as I got to my room, I looked at the clock on my bedside table: 7:30.

Oh thank goodness. I thought. I wasn't going to be late to work. I could finish getting ready before Dad and I had to leave.

I got dressed and tried to make my hair look presentable before rushing down the hall to the kitchen. My dad was eating breakfast at the kitchen table while reading the newspaper. I remembered seeing him do the same thing so many times before.

"I wasn't sure if you were awake yet," he said without looking up.

"I am now," I sighed, grabbing an apple and putting some bread in the toaster.

"Rough night?"

"Yes, but I'm fine now." At least I thought I was. I still felt sad, but I didn't feel as weak as I had earlier. I had gone into some sort of panic mode. I didn't understand it. Now I just felt exhausted. I didn't really want to talk about what had happened. "I just didn't sleep well."

With that, the conversation ended, which was fine by me.

I poured myself a glass of water and took a sip before I grabbed my toast. I ate it quickly, barely leaving time to breathe between bites. Everything tasted like cardboard.

When I finished, I nodded to my dad that I was ready to go. He stood up and folded the newspaper again so Mom could read it later, and we left the house. During the drive to work, I rested my head on the window and tried to convince myself that it would be a good day. We drove the few minutes in silence. We separated in the hall between our departments, and I went to sit at my desk next to Jason. I forced a smile and said hello. Jason must have taken my smile and greeting to mean that I wanted to talk while we worked. I listened to him all morning, nodding and laughing in all the right places. I wanted to make it seem like nothing was wrong with me, even though my heart was still beating faster than it should and my head and neck hurt from falling asleep on the bathroom floor.

After pretending to feel normal for too long, I was finally able to take my lunch break. I decided to eat in the nearby park so I could get some fresh air. I needed to relax, and the walk to the park would be good for me.

CHAPTER 12

June 20, 1945

Dorothy

I had just finished my deliveries for the day and wanted a break before I went home. Things had been crazy lately, with Buddy home and Bobby out of school. We were all together again, which was wonderful, but things tended to get a little chaotic. I hadn't had time to draw in what seemed like forever.

I rolled my red wagon to the park and sat down on a bench. The sun was hot on my face, and I squinted up at the sky. June was one of my favorite times of the year, and this weather was the reason why. I pulled my sketchbook out of my dress pocket and started flipping the pages to find a blank one. I passed sketches of the stray cat that wandered around outside my house occasionally, the new jukebox at Daisy's, and lots of familiar faces before I reached a blank page.

I looked around the park for inspiration. My eyes settled on a man walking a large dog. I hummed to myself and was lost in outlining and shading for a while before I felt satisfied with the page. I looked up again for something new to draw.

Nothing really caught my eye until I saw Henry walking toward a bench on the other side of the park. He held a brown paper bag. I knew he was working at the refinery again, which was a short walk away from the park. He must have come here for his lunch break.

My first instinct was to run over and sit right next to him, just like I would have when we were younger and things were uncomplicated. The rational and logical side of my brain held me back from doing that. Wouldn't it be better to just stay here and avoid the awkward interaction? I felt horrible for thinking that, so I decided to calmly walk over and say hello to him. Any conversation with Henry would be well worth the awkwardness I might feel.

I watched him as I walked. He sat on the bench and put the paper bag next to him. Instead of eating his lunch, he just sat there, looking straight ahead.

"Hi, Henry," I said as I reached him. I must have surprised him because he flinched.

"Oh, hi, Dottie," he said. He glanced at me quickly before looking straight ahead again. His voice sounded a bit tired or sad or...something. Just not like himself. He wasn't even looking at me. He lowered his head into his hands and rubbed his eyes with his palms.

"Can I sit next to you?"

He nodded without saying anything. What in the world was wrong with him? I frowned as I sat down next to him.

"Are you all right?" I had to ask. He wasn't like this. At least, he never used to be.

"I'm fine," he said shortly. "I just didn't sleep well."

"I'm sorry."

"It's not your fault."

I was surprised. He was acting so odd.

"Henry, did something happen?" I wanted to put my hand on his arm, but I held myself back.

"I'm fine, Dot." He looked up at me for the first time. I noticed his eyes were red, like he had been crying.

"If you don't want to talk about it, then that's fine, but I'm going to keep sitting here talking to you."

He made a soft sound like he was giving me permission. He continued to stare in front of us. I looked at the same point, trying to figure out if there was something he was staring at. I was almost positive he was glaring at a small patch of grass.

I took a deep breath, then started talking. "Your mom told me you went back to work at the oil refinery. I think that's fantastic. You always really liked it there. You are so talented with math. I can hardly manage my own finances, let alone the finances of a whole company!" I paused and looked at him again to see if he would react. He didn't. "Well, I think it's swell that you're home. I missed you a lot, you know. We all did, I mean. Me, and Peggy, and Marylin, and Jimmy." I noticed he flinched again when I said Jimmy's name. Strange. "We all missed having you here. We need to go to Daisy's again. She bought a new jukebox. It's all nice and shiny. Nothing like the old one. It works much better."

Henry's gaze moved from the patch of grass to the sky. I took that as a good sign and kept talking.

"We all need to go dancing again too! Peggy dragged us out some weekends while you were gone, but it wasn't the same without you. Peggy and I both had to search for partners, since Marylin and Jimmy always wanted to dance with each other. They've been out a few times, you know. Marylin and Jimmy, I mean. I think they are just adorable together. I keep telling Jimmy to just go for it and ask her to go steady, but he says he's too chicken."

Henry looked right at me. His eyes bore straight into mine, as if he wanted to say something, but then he turned away again. He obviously didn't want to talk to me.

"I can leave if you want me to," I said, feeling a bit frustrated. "I know I'm probably being annoying."

"No," Henry said, almost too quiet for me to hear.

"What?"

"No, you're not being annoying."

"Then, should I keep talking or should I stop? I'm confused."

"Um, tell me about your baking." His voice was a little bit stronger now, like he was feeling less tired or sick. I wondered if it was the same problem he was having the other night. He took his lunch out, which was further confirmation that he was feeling better.

"All right," I began. "Well, do you remember when we were kids, and I told everyone I wanted to have a bakery?"

Henry nodded. He was actually looking at me now, which was a good sign.

"Well, I'm actually saving up to buy the bakery in town."

"Dottie, that's amazing!" Henry grinned. I had really missed his smile. His teeth were a bright white, and one side of his mouth went up higher than the other one. I had always loved making him happy so I could see it.

I noticed I had been staring at his mouth, and I quickly looked at his eyes again, hoping he hadn't noticed. "I'm really excited. Mrs. Devon says that she and her husband are looking to retire soon, and they want me to buy the bakery from them. I should have enough money in a few months!"

"Wow."

"I know!"

We were both looking at each other and smiling, and it felt right. It felt like we were back in high school, best friends and partners in everything. For a moment, it felt like nothing had changed. But then I noticed Henry's eyes were still red and knew something *had* changed. He wasn't feeling okay, and he wouldn't tell me why. He always used to tell me when something was wrong. He obviously didn't want to today. At least he let me sit here with him and talk his ears off.

"How's work?" I asked him.

"It's fine," he said. "Mr. Green gave me an assistant job, just like he promised, but he says if I want to be an accountant, I need a college degree."

"And have you thought about that? Going to college?"

"A bit. But honestly I'm having a hard enough time getting used to being home again without thinking about college, so I haven't given it much thought."

"Oh." I nodded. Henry had barely been home a week, and now he was expected to plan his whole future without any warning. I could only imagine how confusing it must be.

Henry continued talking. "I know I should. Go to college, I mean. It means I can get higher paying jobs and understand more of what I'm doing and why. But it's a big decision, you know?"

I nodded. I finally let myself put my hand on his upper arm. "You can do it. This has been your dream for as long as I can even remember. You'll work everything out. I know you will."

"Thanks, Dot." I swore I could almost see him blushing. The thought of him blushing at my touch made my own face get hot, and I quickly put my hand back into my lap.

Henry also turned away from me. He looked at his watch and stood up quickly.

"My lunch break ends soon. I'm gonna be late." He looked at me apologetically.

I smiled up at him. "It's all right, go." I nodded in the direction of his work.

"Bye Dot!" he yelled as he ran toward the oil refinery.

"Bye Henry!" I yelled back. I saw a few people in the park turn toward me, and I laughed under my breath. Maybe Henry and I could be friends like we were before. It certainly felt like we could after our talk today.

CHAPTER 13

June 27, 1945

Henry

That conversation with Dot stayed on my mind for the next few days. Not that it was really a conversation. Dot did most of the talking. I knew I had been rude by not responding much, but I hadn't felt like myself that day and had needed a moment to think. When I saw Dot standing next to my bench, it was a huge surprise. It was an even bigger surprise that I let her sit down and talk for so long. I was glad that I had, though. Her smiles and laughter helped me feel better and forget about my worries for a while.

Those worries eventually returned, but I kept going to work every day. I had to. I knew I couldn't put my life on hold just because of some bad dreams and memories. I had to carry on, even if I was becoming more and more tired every day from all the sleepless nights.

I tried not to pay attention to the feeling of guilt that had been with me since I dreamt about Jimmy, but I couldn't. That sick feeling resurfaced at random moments of the day, and I'd feel horrible again. I didn't have any more dreams about the war after the one with Jimmy, but I couldn't shake the feelings of the first. I felt like I was living in one of my dreams, and I struggled through my days feeling exhausted and numb. I still didn't feel like I was really home. Physically I was here in Ashwood, but emotionally I was somewhere else entirely.

I tried to forget about the war, but it felt impossible. Even waking up early in the morning caused me to remember my days as a soldier, when we had to get up before the sun for our training. I often remembered the war when I sat down for supper with my family and saw the meager meals we still had to eat due to rationing. I couldn't live in peace for even a few hours. Something always brought me back to the war, and scenes from my dream mixed in with the memories of fighting battles and the horrors I witnessed. The memories always made me feel sick. It was horrible knowing deep down that it was my fault those soldiers died. I couldn't talk about it with anyone. I didn't want others to know how terrible I felt. I couldn't have people looking at me the way Jimmy had in my dream. *How dare you; how could you; you didn't save me; you left me to die.* His voice played over and over in my mind, and I couldn't concentrate on anything else.

In the brief moments when it felt more possible to forget the memories and the guilt of the war, other worries seemed to fill my head in their place. I knew I would have to decide if I was going to college soon, but I was having trouble adjusting to normal life as it was. For now, my answer to Mr. Green about attending was a firm "I don't know." He told me I could have a month to make a decision, but I would need to apply to the University of Pittsburgh quickly or I wouldn't be able to get in. He had told his colleague in the business school that I would be applying and to hold a place for me, but the opening would only be there for a few more weeks.

Mr. Green called me in on a Wednesday morning to talk about this. I left his office more stressed than when I entered it, but I sat down to work all the same. After a few hours of filling out paperwork, I needed a walk and a drink of water. I had been sitting down for so long that I felt antsy, so I told Jason I would be back in a minute and I left my desk.

I walked down the hallway that connected to the refinery. I stopped to drink some water at the drinking fountain.

That's when I heard the explosion. The sound filled my head, and I was in a forest again. I could almost hear the screams. I instinctively dropped to the ground, knowing I was in danger. I reached for my gun, then felt absolute panic come over me as I realized I didn't have one. What was I going to do? I was alone and without backup or a weapon. Dread filled me to the brim. I looked up and to my right, but only saw the empty hallway. Odd. I could have sworn I heard something from that direction. I turned to my left, and there was nothing there either. I turned back to my right and saw a man about my dad's age walking toward me. He was dressed in a black jumpsuit and was holding a clipboard. A moment of confusion brought me back to reality. I wasn't in Europe. I was home. There wasn't an explosion. That wasn't a soldier. He was a worker. *I* was a worker. What was I doing on the floor?

I noticed him looking at me strangely. I quickly stood up and brushed off my khaki slacks. I could still feel my heart beating heavily. What was wrong with me?

"You all right?" the man asked.

"Yes, um, I thought I heard a crash from over there." I tried to sound normal, but I knew he had seen me crouching near the ground. I could hear my voice shaking, and I was positive this man thought I was crazy.

"Oh, someone dropped a replacement pipe over by the distiller. Everything's fine."

"Oh." I felt embarrassed. Why did I react the way I had? I knew I was at work. Loud sounds were normal at a refinery, especially as close to the distiller room as I was in this hallway. Thinking through everything logically this way, I felt extremely foolish for thinking I was back in Europe.

"You fought in the war?" the man asked me gently.

I nodded, confused as to why he had asked such a question.

"My pop was like you. He fought in the Great War and always jumped at the smallest noises. My mama called them episodes. Said they happened 'cause he almost got blown up a few times and thought it was gonna happen to him again."

My eyes grew wide. Was that why I had immediately reached for my gun and had assumed the sound I heard was an explosion? Was I having an episode? It made sense. I had fought in a war just like this man's father. Maybe I was like him. Maybe this was perfectly normal.

"You'll be fine, boy. Everything is under control."

I nodded, trying to process what he had told me about his father. What if that was what was wrong with me? I started linking together the way I felt at Dot's house that first night I was home, the dream about Jimmy, and what had just happened in the hall. Were they all "episodes"?

"Son?" The man's voice brought me back to the present, and I saw he was watching me with wary eyes. "You're gonna be fine. Let's get you back to your office."

I nodded again, still in a daze, and followed him back down the hall to the offices.

I couldn't shake that weird feeling for the rest of the week. I felt like I was living someone else's life. My head was still in Europe, and it felt odd to be here in Pennsylvania, trying to lead an ordinary life. I knew I was supposed to be here, but it felt strange.

I walked out of work on Friday feeling relieved. I didn't have to go back until Monday. I knew it was bad that work had become so tedious after only two weeks, but it was becoming hard for me to sit still. I was used to being outside all the time, training or fighting or traveling. Being stuck in an air-conditioned building all day was making me strangely restless and even nervous at times.

As my dad and I drove home together, we talked about how work went. I hadn't mentioned what had happened a few days before, and I didn't want to. Luckily, Dad steered the conversation toward college. I had spoken to my parents about the opportunity Mr. Green had offered, and they were both very pleased I would have the chance to go.

"Have you thought any more about what Mr. Green said about college?" Dad asked. He was especially excited for me. He agreed that it was important for me to further my education so that I could keep my assistant job and eventually advance in the company.

"A little bit." I honestly had, but I was still stumped. I wanted to go, but it was a big commitment, and it scared me. I didn't know if I could handle going to college while working at the same time. Mr. Green had explained that if I did decide to go to the University of Pittsburgh, I could continue working at the oil refinery part time. He also explained I would receive a full grant from the government, thanks to a bill they passed allowing any veteran to attend college for free. I no longer had worries about paying for school. My only worries now were ones I couldn't put into words Mr. Green or even my parents would understand. I knew it would be hard to balance school and work, and I was scared of creating even more chaos in my mind. With my life like it was now, I was already having problems sleeping, and I always felt on edge.

"And what do you think?" Dad looked at me from the driver's seat. We were driving past the park, and I remembered my conversation with Dot. She believed that I could do it, but she didn't know half of what was going on inside my head. No one did.

"I don't know," I said numbly.

"Don't you only have a few more days to decide?"

"I have until the end of July."

"Keep thinking about it. You know that your mother and I will support you in whatever you decide to do."

"Thanks Dad."

"But make sure it's the right choice." He looked at me, raising one of his eyebrows.

"Dad..."

"I'm just kidding you." He laughed heartily.

I laughed too. It felt good to laugh. I needed to do that more often.

When we got home I went to my room to change into something more comfortable. While I was changing, there was a knock on my door.

"Peggy called a few minutes ago," Mom called through the door. "She said that your friends are all meeting up at Daisy's for dinner."

I looked at the clock on my bedside table. It was just after five o'clock. We always used to meet at the diner at 5:30.

"At 5:30?" I asked.

"I think so. She also mentioned you might go dancing afterwards."

Dancing. I sighed. I hadn't done that in a really long time.

"Thanks, Mom."

I quickly changed into something casual but still nice enough to wear to the dance hall if that was indeed the plan. Mom went into Pittsburgh the week before to buy me some clothes that would fit. I ran downstairs, said goodbye to my family, and left for the diner.

I walked, since my old bike now belonged to Jessica. I probably couldn't ride it anyway. My arm was still too weak, and I didn't trust my balance enough to ride one handed like I had seen many of the kids around town do. I arrived at Daisy's early, and stood outside a moment before walking in. I hadn't been here since I left for the war. It felt odd to be standing in front of the building as a grown man and not as a teenage boy. I walked inside and was met with the smell of burgers and fries. It opened a memory, this time a good one, and I stepped back into the past. The diner looked exactly as it had when I left, other than the new jukebox Dottie told me about and some barstools that I could have sworn weren't there before.

I walked right up to the counter where Daisy stood, taking the order of a girl about Jessica's age. Daisy looked up at me and her eyes and smile widened.

"Henry Oakey!"

She quickly finished taking the girl's order and came around the counter to give me a hug. Her once-black curly hair was now graying near her head.

"My, I think you've grown some!" She stepped back from me and put her hands on her hips.

"Really?" I laughed. I didn't think I had, but Miss Daisy had definitely gotten shorter with age.

"Yes sir, I think you have. Now, come sit down and tell me all about your adventures in Europe."

My face fell. I wanted to talk about anything but that.

"Or you can tell me about what you're doing right now, either way." Daisy must have seen my smile fade, and I silently thanked her for understanding as I sat down at the bar and began to tell her about work at the refinery.

CHAPTER 14

June 29, 1945

Dorothy

I received a call from Peggy earlier asking if I wanted to go to Daisy's that night. I never passed up a chance to go to Daisy's, so I wholeheartedly agreed. She told me she was inviting our other friends too, and I suddenly felt nervous, knowing that Henry was going to be there. Why did I feel this way? I told myself it was irrational to be nervous to see my best friends, including Henry.

I ignored the butterflies floating around in my stomach and got ready. Peggy mentioned that it would be fun to go dancing after we ate, so I wanted to look my best just in case. I decided to put on the green dress I was originally going to wear when Bud came home. I even put on a bit of makeup and perfume, things I only wore on special occasions. I considered having all five of us together at Daisy's again something very special. I convinced myself that I wasn't getting all dressed up for Henry, though I felt fluttering in my stomach as I put a bit of rouge on my cheeks.

I biked to Daisy's and got there quickly.

I entered the diner and walked to our spot without even looking around. My friends and I always sat in the same booth, ever since we started looking for a place to spend time together during high school.

There was no one sitting there yet, but I saw Henry at the counter talking to Daisy. He was laughing about something, which I had hardly seen him do since he'd been home.

I sucked in a deep breath before going to sit next to him on a barstool. The butterflies were back at it, but I tried to ignore the sensation.

"Hi, Henry!" I tried to sound natural. I said hello to Daisy as well.

Henry looked directly at me and smiled widely. "Hey, Dottie." The left side of his mouth lifted higher than the other, making his smile look like a smirk.

I loved it when he smiled like that. I caught myself staring at the corner of Henry's mouth and looked away quickly. *You have to stop that*, I told myself.

Daisy looked at the two of us and grinned before walking out from behind the counter to clean tables.

"How was work today?" I tried to act natural.

Henry hesitated a bit before saying, "It was all right, I guess. I'm glad it's the weekend though."

"Me too. I have to work tomorrow, so it's not really the weekend for me until I deliver the last loaf of bread. But it'll be nice to rest afterward."

"That's true; I forgot you work early on Saturdays."

I nodded. "Luckily, I only have a few orders tomorrow, so I won't have to wake up too early."

"That's good."

After a moment of silence, his eyes began to wander, as if he was trying to find something else to talk about. "Hey, I saw the new jukebox you told me about."

I turned toward the machine, which was in the front corner of the diner. "Isn't it amazing? The sound quality is much better than the old one."

"Should we try it out?" Henry's grin became mischievous.

My heart skipped a beat at the sight. I ignored the feeling and nodded. We stood up and walked over to the jukebox to put a coin in.

The new jukebox was made of shiny dark wood and had what seemed like a thousand neon-colored lights running up and down the sides. It was beautiful. I'm sure it cost Daisy a fortune to replace the old one with this newer model.

"You choose," I said. "I've already done it loads of times."

Henry looked at me and smiled shyly, then fished a coin out of his pocket and chose Louis Prima's "Sing Sing Sing". It was one of our favorite songs to dance to before he left. I smiled at the memory, as we sat near the jukebox to listen.

"I'm really glad they kept most of the old records," I said. "When Daisy told us they were getting a new player, we were afraid that the older records would be thrown out."

"I remember dancing to this song all the time." Henry looked at the jukebox with an almost sad expression.

"Going dancing hasn't been the same since you left." As soon as I said that, I regretted it. "I mean, since it's been three girls and only one boy—" I bit my lip so I would stop talking. I was messing things up even more. If Henry still had feelings for me, which I highly doubted, I was just making it worse for the both of us.

"I haven't danced since before the war. I think the last time was about a week before I left." I could feel Henry's eyes on me, as if he was waiting for my reaction to the memory. "The other soldiers tried dragging me along when they went out, but I..." he trailed off for a moment, then breathed in deeply and continued, "I never wanted to."

I thought back to the last week before he left. It had been strange. Henry and I hardly had a chance to talk or say goodbye. Once we knew he had been drafted, things between us became a little strained, like we were trying to keep our distance from each other. I had been scared, and I hadn't known what to do. Now, I couldn't remember most of the details. All that I *did* remember was awkward and embarrassing for the both of us.

"I forgot we went dancing that week," I finally admitted.

"I asked you to dance, and you said yes. That was the best night ever."

I blushed. *Henry, what are you doing to me, making these memories reappear?*

"You were wearing the same dress you are right now, I think," he continued. "And we danced to "Always in My Heart"."

My own heart started to hurt just hearing him talk. When he mentioned that song, I slowly let myself remember what I had tried to forget.

We *had* danced, and everything had been so perfect. It was that night I realized that whatever we had between us had to stop right then and there. He was going to fight in the war, and I didn't know when or even *if* he would come back. I told myself I had no feelings for Henry Oakey and had been thoroughly convinced of that during the time he was away. Only now in the diner, as he reminded me of that dance, I realized I could still open my heart to him if I wanted to. That thought terrified me. I loved being friends with him, and I couldn't bear to ruin that by falling in love with him. What was I even doing, thinking like this?

I suddenly wanted to cry. My heart ached. I didn't say anything, even though I knew Henry was watching me from where he sat.

Finally, the song ended, and I stood up abruptly. I practically ran to our booth without saying a word to Henry. I sat down with my back to him. I heard him call after me, but I ignored him. I knew I was being rude, but I had to get away from the situation or I was going to start feeling something I had no intention of acting on.

I heard the door open behind me and the bell above it ring. From the sounds of back slapping and giddy laughter, I knew it was Jimmy, Peggy, and Marylin greeting Henry as they came in.

They made their way over to where I was sitting.

"Dottie!" Peggy sat across from me.

"Hey, Peggy!" I smiled, trying to forget what I had been feeling moments before.

Henry sat next to me and Marylin sat next to Peggy. Jimmy pulled a chair over from another table. Everything felt almost normal. I let myself breath for a moment and pushed away any feelings I had for Henry. I would not let myself fall for him. It would cause too many problems, and I was not willing to lose him when I had just gotten him back.

My friends and I made small talk for a minute before going over to the counter to order dinner from Carla, Daisy's fifteen-year-old daughter who'd just started working at the diner a few weeks before. Once we had all ordered our food, we sat down again, continuing our conversation.

"So, Henry," Peggy began, turning toward him. "Tell us about Europe."

"I..." Henry began, looking down at his hands.

"I want to hear all about it," Jimmy said happily. "My father always tells me stories from the Great War. Pranks he played on the other soldiers, getting packages from home, recon missions, all of that."

Henry's face went white. He was now staring off into the distance. A part of me could tell he didn't want to talk about that stuff, so I tried changing the subject.

"I'm sure Henry doesn't want to talk about the war. I bet he was stuck in camp the whole time and has nothing interesting to talk about."

Henry looked at me and gave me a small smile, but his jaw was tense. He was at a breaking point, and Jimmy wouldn't let the subject drop.

"Ahh," Jimmy whined. "I'm sure he's got great stories. Henry, did you ever go on recon missions like my father did?"

"Jimmy, I don't want to talk about the war, okay?" Henry's voice came out harsh.

My eyes darted to Jimmy's face, which fell into a disappointed and confused frown. Peggy and Marylin looked surprised. I myself was a bit shocked. I had never heard Henry talk like that, ever.

I instinctively put my hand on Henry's underneath the table. He looked at me and his eyes became sad again. What was going on inside that boy's head?

He looked down at my arm, and I quickly pulled my hand back into my own lap. My fingers prickled where they had touched Henry's hand, and I wiggled them, trying to make the feeling go away. This had to stop.

Trying to relieve the tension, I asked, "I wonder what's taking them so long with the food?"

As soon as I said that, Carla called out our names one after the other with our orders.

I stood and walked to the counter and took my food from Carla. My plate was heavy with a burger and fries, and I had to balance it in one hand since I ordered a cherry coke as well.

As we ate, we talked about our plans for the next few months. Marylin wasn't working now, since school wasn't in session. Peggy wasn't working either. I told everyone about my progress with the Devons' bakery. Jimmy told everyone how school had gone. He was going to the University of Pittsburgh during the week and visited during the weekends. Now that it was summer, he would be here in Ashwood more often.

"I'm thinking of applying there," Henry said out of nowhere.

"Really?" Jimmy said, sounding surprised. "It's great. I love it."

"I have to decide soon, but I know next to nothing about going to college."

"I could talk to you about it sometime. We could even go into the city and I could give you a tour."

Henry nodded and smiled. "That'd be great. Thank you."

I was glad that at least some of the tension had lifted. Once the two boys were talking about school, they forgot all about their earlier conflict.

We all continued talking for a while.

When Peggy had finished eating, she clapped her hands together and said, "I'm just dying to go dancing. We haven't gone together in ages."

We all agreed. After finishing the last few fries and our drinks, we left Daisy's, stopping at the counter to say goodbye to her and Carla before walking out.

"I rode my bike," I said, pointing to the rack where I had left it.

"I'll walk with you," Marylin said.

Peggy and Jimmy had driven their cars, so they left to go park their cars closer to the dance hall.

Henry was left walking with me and Marylin. He had his hands in his pockets and was walking slower than we were at first, but then Marylin asked him a question about work and he looked a little happier.

While we walked, Marylin chattered to Henry about her job at the school. She was catching him up on all of our lives, and I appreciated that, but I also felt a pang of jealousy and wanted to be involved in their conversation. It was yet another irrational feeling, and I ignored it as we walked. It was perfectly normal for two friends to share a conversation about their new jobs, especially when both of them had heard enough about my bakery to be able to quote my plans back verbatim.

We reached the dance hall, and I could hear the music from the sidewalk. Since Peggy and Jimmy were probably already inside, I sped up my walk. I wheeled my bike up to the rack on the side of the building and left it there. When I turned toward the sidewalk, I almost ran into Henry. I jumped, wondering how he had gotten so close without me hearing him. It must have been one of the things he learned how to do in the war, sneaking up like that.

"Henry, you scared me!" I pushed him away playfully.

He smiled and raised one of his eyebrows. "You knew I was behind you, didn't you?"

I shook my head with my eyes wide. "Where'd Marylin go?"

"She went inside already," Henry said. "Let's go."

I nodded and followed him to the door of the dance hall. He opened it for me, and I walked inside, silently cursing the beating of my heart. He was my best friend. Best friends opened doors for each other. It shouldn't make me feel anything.

My thoughts were blissfully drowned out by the combined sound of the music and the hum of the crowd. There were already a lot of people dancing and mingling around the sides of the large dance hall, even though it was just barely after suppertime. Friday nights were always busy, but they were the best nights to go if you wanted a dance partner.

I found Marylin talking to Jimmy on the far side of the dance floor. They were sitting at a table with Peggy's purse and Jimmy's coat on it, claiming it for our group. I sat down next to Marylin, trying not to interrupt their conversation. Henry followed close behind me and sat down. I could feel him staring at me, but I kept my eyes lowered on my hands in my lap, and picked at some leftover polish on one of my nails.

I finally looked up as a new song started playing over the speakers, and saw that Henry was standing up. I watched him walk over to a girl sitting at the table behind us to ask her to dance. I turned away.

I saw Teddy Harrison along the edge of the dance floor, and I waved to him. We sat next to each other in English class in high school, and I hadn't seen him for a while.

He waved back at me and came over to where I sat.

"Dorothy!"

"Hi, Teddy!"

"How have you been? I haven't seen you since—"

"Since graduation," we both said at the same time. I laughed.

"It's been a while." Over Teddy's shoulder, I saw Henry dancing with that girl, and on an impulse I asked Teddy if he wanted to dance. That was it. That was just the thing to take my confused mind off of Henry.

Teddy agreed, looking a bit surprised himself. When the next song started, we headed out to the dance floor. As we danced, he tried to tell me about what he'd been doing since returning home from college, but I had trouble hearing him over the music. I nodded often to show him I was trying to listen. When the dance ended, one of his friends asked me to dance. I recognized him from high school as well, though we didn't really know each other. We danced two dances, and then I danced again with Teddy. I spent some time like this, dancing with guys I vaguely knew, until I wanted a break.

I decided to sit out for a few minutes and made my way to the refreshment table, which had bowls of water and punch. I chose the water, since the punch was occasionally spiked. I shook my head at the memory of a night in high school when Peggy drank too much of the spiked punch, not knowing what had been done to it. Marylin and I had to hold her up all the way to my house. Peggy was muttering nonsense the whole way. We couldn't let her go home by herself in that state, and she lived on the other side of town. I couldn't imagine what her parents would have said if they found her on their doorstep like that. Marylin and I had to sneak her into my bedroom where the three of us spent the night. The next morning Peggy had a terrible headache, but she acted much more like herself. We still laughed about that night sometimes.

I looked out over the dance floor, trying to find Peggy. As I searched, I noticed Jimmy dancing with Marylin toward the middle of the room. He needed to muster up his courage and ask her to go steady already. They had liked each other for years. They only needed to make it official.

I finally spotted Peggy's red dress near the stage. She was dancing with Henry. They were laughing about something, and I found myself feeling a bit jealous. I rejected the feeling. It was illogical to be envious about two of my friends dancing together. Marylin and Jimmy were dancing together, and I wasn't jealous about that, so why should I feel that way about Peggy and Henry?

I pushed away my jealousy about Peggy and Henry with determination and turned my attention to the other couples instead. Maybe it was Peggy's red dress that was so noticeable, but my eyes kept drifting over to her and Henry without my consent.

I decided to turn away completely and walked back to our table as the song ended. I reached it at the same time as the others, and the five of us began talking about how tired we already were, even after only a few songs. We all sat down to take a break.

The music stopped for a few moments, and I looked up to the stage to see that a live band was setting up their instruments. It was a treat when the dance hall got a band to play instead of using records. Most bands didn't want to come all the way out here since we were so far outside of Pittsburgh. After a closer look, I recognized this band as one that had come a few times and always played the best songs.

Once they were set up, the drummer started beating the bass drum. I recognized the first notes of "Sing Sing Sing." I looked up at Henry. I couldn't help but think of him when I heard that song. My eyes met his and he gave me a crooked grin. He gestured to the dance floor with a nod of his head. I smiled in agreement. Henry stood up and held out his hand to me, and I stood and took it. We always danced together to this song, and we weren't going to change that tradition now.

Henry led me out onto the floor, and we began to dance. I hardly had to think about the steps. We had practiced them so many times together that it came naturally to the both of us now. When we were younger, we liked the song so much that we spent an afternoon in Henry's living room inventing choreography for it. From then on, we would do the same dance every time the song came on at the dance hall.

Henry spun me around, and we both started to laugh. I had missed dancing with him so much. Every time this song had come on while he was gone, I couldn't even bear to stay in the building. I would usually make up an excuse that I needed some air, but I knew in my heart it was because of Henry. I couldn't dance to that song with anyone but him. It would be a betrayal of the worst sort.

There was one part in the dance when Henry lifted me as I jumped. When we were twelve, it was hard for him to do since I was taller than he was. As the years went by, he grew much taller than me. Before he left for the war, we were able to do the lift with no problem. Tonight, however, I didn't jump, since I knew Henry wouldn't be able to lift me with his injured arm. I knew it still hurt him. I could see it in his face when he lifted his right arm above his head to spin me around. When I didn't jump, Henry simply nodded and kept going through the steps we had choreographed like nothing had happened. Our friendship was like that. Or at least it used to be. We didn't even have to say much; we just understood each other. Maybe this dance was a sign that our friendship was back to the way it was before he left.

Henry was laughing by the time we finished, and I joined him. He pulled me in and hugged me tightly. I wrapped my arms around him, breathing in his scent. He smelled like he always had —like pine trees and spearmint gum. I relaxed into his embrace, trying not to sigh. I didn't want the moment to end, but I heard the band start playing a new song. It was one of my favorites: "It's Been a Long, Long Time".

Henry didn't pull away from the hug, and neither did I.

"Dance with me?" Henry whispered. I shifted so I was looking at his face. The gleam in his eyes made my heart race. This time, I didn't chide myself for being affected by his smile.

"I already am, silly," I said breathlessly.

Henry laughed under his breath. He was staring straight at me with his blue eyes, and I wasn't shy for some reason. I stared right back and couldn't help but smile.

We started swaying to the music, never breaking eye contact. In the comfortable silence, I started to listen to the words of the song. I had heard it lots of times, but I had never thought about it in the context of me and Henry. It really had been too long since we had been together. Even before he left we were never *truly* together. Not in the way the song said.

We never did talk about what had happened the afternoon before he left. I wished I could go back to that moment and change how I reacted. I don't think I would be surprised by a kiss from Henry now. I might even welcome one.

I blushed at the thought and turned away from looking into his eyes. I couldn't keep having thoughts like that. Henry and I were just fine where we were: as friends. If we tried to become anything more, our friendship would be ruined again. This wasn't a romantic dance; this was a dance between friends. It was no different than a dance between me and Jimmy or between Henry and Peggy or Marylin. It was exactly the same. Henry and I were just friends.

I kept repeating this to myself until the song ended. *We are just friends.* I stepped back from Henry, trying not to betray my internal conflict. I thanked him for the dance and escaped to the refreshment table again to get a drink of water. I tried to calm my heart, which was pounding in my chest.

"That dance was amazing," Peggy said behind me.

I jumped, almost spilling my water on some tall girl in a baby blue dress. I apologized and turned around to see Peggy standing with one hand on her hip.

"Gosh, Peggy. You startled me! And what do you mean 'that dance?' Who were you dancing with?"

"I'm not talking about me, Dorothy Banks. I'm talking about you and Mr. Oakey over there."

"Oh. You saw that?" My voice was practically a whisper.

"Of course I saw it, Dottie. How could I not see it? It's obvious!"

I stared at her with wide eyes. Was it that obvious? I thought I was hiding my feelings well enough that none of my friends would notice. If Peggy figured it out, it wasn't long before Henry himself caught on to how I felt, and I didn't want that. I couldn't have that.

"I haven't seen you look at anyone else like that. Ever. You're falling in love with him." She was whispering excitedly.

"In love? Really, *that's* what you think after seeing one dance?" I took another sip of water, trying to hide my nerves. Were my feelings obvious to everyone but me?

Peggy nodded giddily. "It's not just 'one dance'. I've been watching you two since he came home. Take my word for it, Dot. Henry's smitten. And you're dangerously close to being smitten yourself. You just have to admit it."

"I don't know what you're talking about. I was just dancing with my friend." I tried to make my words show more confidence than I actually felt.

"Uh huh," Peggy said sarcastically. Then she turned and walked away, leaving me alone with my water.

I tossed the last swallow back like it was a shot of something a whole lot stronger and followed her.

I caught up to Peggy right as she approached our table, so I couldn't confront her further about what she said about me and Henry. Could it be true? I knew I could fall for him if I let myself. I swore I wouldn't because I could ruin the friendship I was trying to fix. And, Henry surely didn't have feelings for me after all this time. Or did he? Peggy had only added to the confusion I felt.

"I'm exhausted," Peggy was saying. "And I know Dottie's gotta wake up early tomorrow, so I think we should call it a night."

No one protested. I was ready to go home. I had some things to think over.

"I can take you home, Marylin," Peggy said.

"I'll go with Jimmy, if that's all right," Marylin said meekly, glancing at Jimmy. Peggy and I looked at each other in surprise.

"Dottie, Henry, you both walked, right?" Peggy said.

Henry nodded.

"I rode my bike," I said.

"Perfect. We all have a way home. See you all soon!" And with that, Peggy, Marylin, and Jimmy walked out the door of the dance hall. Henry and I were alone.

"If you want, I can walk with you," Henry said. "It's pretty dark outside already."

"Sure, thanks." I nodded and walked outside, my heart beating erratically. Henry was right on my heels.

I walked around the building and grabbed my bike from where it was sitting on the rack. We started walking toward home.

CHAPTER 15

June 29, 1945

Henry

I had no idea what I had done, but it seemed like Dot was mad at me. She was walking at full speed in front of me, like she was trying to get away. I wouldn't have been surprised if she got on her bike and pedaled off.

"Dottie, wait up," I said, feeling like a little boy.

I suddenly remembered something from when we were younger. During the Depression, Dottie's mom had her sell loaves of bread to the neighbors. Sometimes, I went along with her on her route. We spent the time singing and joking and laughing. There was one day that she was sad about something and refused to talk to me about it. She just pulled her wagon and walked quickly, leaving me to chase after her. Later, I caught up to her and confronted her about it only to find out her Grandma Jane had passed away the day before.

I felt like that little boy now, chasing after her. I wondered if she was sad about something like she had been that day years ago.

"Dot, are you okay?" I caught up to her on the corner by Daisy's, which already had its *Closed* sign up. It must have been later than I thought.

Dot stopped and turned toward me. "Yeah, I'm fine." She smiled, and I believed her.

"That was fun, wasn't it?" I tried making conversation, feeling uncomfortable with the silence between us.

"Yes, it was," Dot said, looking ahead and smiling. When we crossed the road, we walked next to each other with the bike on the other side of Dot.

Seeing her happy made my heart ache, but not in the same way it did when she was sad. I couldn't explain it. She looked beautiful, walking in the dark with her hair all curled like it was. Her big eyes reflected the moonlight, and I wished she would look at me again like she had during our dance earlier.

But then I remembered I was trying to make things right between us by not thinking about her like that. Those feelings were what had messed everything up in the first place, and I couldn't let my heart run away from me like that again. I had to control myself. Dot and I were friends, and that was perfectly fine.

"Henry?" Dot looked over at me.

"Yeah?"

"Are *you* okay?"

"What do you mean?"

"I don't really know, but you seem...different than you were before you left—like when you got sick at the party, and tonight when you got angry with Jimmy—I've never seen you like that before."

"I..." I didn't know what to say. I knew there was something different about me, but it was something I didn't want to talk about, especially right now when I was trying to figure it out myself.

"If you don't want to talk about it, that's okay," Dot continued. "Just know that I'm here, and I'll listen if you need to talk."

"Dot, I honestly don't know how to explain. I have so many things going on in my head right now, but thank you for being willing to listen. You're a good friend."

I smiled at her, and she smiled back.

We reached the corner in front of her red brick house. Dot parked her bike on the lawn.

"Henry, thank you for everything."

What had I done? She was the one who had offered her help, even when neither of us knew exactly what was happening to me.

"No, Dottie, thank you."

She stepped around the bike and walked toward me. She reached out and hugged me, her hands gently placed on my back. After a moment of surprise, I finally wrapped my arms around her. I held her close, and—for the first time—I truly felt like I was home.

We stayed that way for a few moments until Dot stepped back and just stared at me, her face pensive.

"I..." she started.

"Hm?"

"Good night." She turned around and started walking toward her front door.

"Your bike?"

Dot turned around, and with a smile she grabbed the handlebars of her bike and pushed it toward the backyard.

She was gone before I could say goodnight.

Mom greeted me when I came in the door.

"How was it, Henry?" she asked from where she sat on the couch. She always used to stay up until I got home. I guess some things hadn't changed at all. The thought made me smile.

"It was great. We went to Daisy's and then went to the dance hall. It was just like old times."

"Wonderful. Did you dance with Dorothy?"

"Yeah Mom, I did."

"She's a lovely girl, isn't she?"

I nodded and smiled.

"She came here a few times right before you came home. She was always asking about how you were." She almost smirked at me. I wondered if she suspected how I felt about Dot. "She said that she didn't know you had been injured. Didn't you tell her in your letters?"

"I didn't write to her," I confessed.

"Henry Oakey, how could you not write to your best friend?" Her smirk turned into a look of shock.

"It's complicated, Mom. I don't exactly know all of the reasons, but it was just too hard for me." I really didn't want to explain what had happened between Dot and me to my mom.

"Was it hard for you to write to Jimmy?"

This conversation was strangely similar to the one I had had with Bud in London. "No, but Dot is different. Our relationship is different."

Of course our relationship was different. I still had feelings for Dot. It was so hard to move on from what happened two years ago because I never stopped loving her. The last time I confessed my feelings to her, she rejected me. I didn't want that to happen again. But thinking over that night, starting with our conversation at Daisy's and ending with our dance, I almost felt like I could try again. Maybe she wouldn't reject me this time. We were both so different than we were back then. We were older now. Even if she didn't feel the same way about me, we could be mature about it, right? But then I thought about the way she looked at me when we were dancing, and I had some hope that she wouldn't reject me.

"Are you all right?" Mom asked, pulling me out of my thoughts.

I nodded my head. "Yeah, I'm fine. Goodnight. Love you!"

I walked down the hall to my room. I sat at my desk and pulled out a blank sheet of paper. It was time to write Dot a letter, the letter that I had wanted to write the entire time I was in Europe and couldn't.

Dear Dot,

I miss you terribly. That's what I would have said if I had written this letter when I first left, when I should have written it. I still feel guilty for not writing to you while I was gone, and I don't think that feeling will ever go away. Imagine how much closer we could have been if I wrote this and actually sent it.

I tried writing you letters. I really did. I think I must have written a hundred versions of this letter, but they all ended up as fuel for our fires. I gave up on the idea of writing to you after a while. I knew I was too much of a coward to actually send them.

Dottie, I meant what I said to you when I left. I'm falling in love with you. You are the only girl I have ever been interested in, and that fact didn't change during the years I was gone. Most soldiers were mooning over French dames, but all I could think about was you. Memories of you kept me going when I was scared. I hate to admit this, but I was scared a lot. I knew I had to be brave and have hope that I would see you again. I knew that if I was strong and just kept going, eventually I would be where I am right now: Home. Safe. With my family, and with you. You have no idea how many times I wanted to tell you that.

I know the day I left I made a bold move. I am truly sorry for surprising you with a confession of my feelings and for trying to kiss you. I don't regret trying. I only regret that I tried to kiss you without knowing how you felt toward me. I should have waited until I was sure of your feelings, or I should have been less of a coward and told you how I felt sooner. In my mind it was the right time because I was leaving. I didn't know when or even if I'd come home. It was all very selfish of me. I am so sorry I caused you embarrassment.

If I had another chance, I would do things differently. I would go back to that day when I told you goodbye, and I would wait to hear your answer. In all honesty, I would still love you, even if you didn't love me back. But I would respect your feelings and act only as a friend to you. I would write to you once a week, no matter your answer, and I would tell you about even the most mundane things about the war. I would know you wouldn't want to hear about the awful parts, and I wouldn't even mention them. The war would seem like a short trip in our letters, and at the end I would come home and we'd be fine. We would still be best friends, or we would be something more. That's how I wish it had all gone.

Instead, I really messed things up between us. My pride was too hurt for me to send even a single letter to you, and I embarrassed you too much for you to write to me. It was all my fault; don't you dare take any blame for what happened, Dorothy Banks.

Tonight we danced for the first time since I came home. It was amazing. Holding you close like that was something I dreamt about often during the war. Now that I'm home, I can't keep ignoring my feelings for you. Every time I'm with you it gets harder to hold myself back from telling you that I still love you. When I was in your arms, I finally felt like I was somewhere I really belonged after feeling lost and confused for so long.

Dot, I have to know. If you don't feel the same way about me, please tell me. I will still be your friend, no matter what your feelings are toward me. I can't bear to ruin our friendship any more than I already have.

Awaiting your answer,
-Henry

I breathed a sigh as I wrote my name. That was the first time I had been able to write a whole letter with my right hand, which was one accomplishment. But it was also the first letter I had written to Dot where I was completely honest about my feelings for her, which was an even greater accomplishment.

I put the letter in an envelope and sealed it. I would muster up the courage to give it to her tomorrow.

I fell asleep with a smile on my face. It truly had been a wonderful night.

I was burning. I was sure of it. That was the only thing that could cause me this kind of pain. I ran through the trees, hardly noticing as the branches caught on my uniform and scratched my skin. I had to get away. I didn't know why, but terror filled me and I knew I had to keep running.

I heard screaming behind me. I turned and saw soldiers in green uniforms trying to catch up to me, but they all got lost in the trees and the smoke.

I kept running until I saw someone on the ground.

Dot.

I couldn't believe my eyes. What was she doing here?

She was lying on the ground, fast asleep with her hair spread out around her head. She was wearing a beautiful green dress.

I knelt down next to her and gently shook her awake.

"Henry," she said as she opened her eyes. She reached out to cup my cheek in her hand. "You're here."

"Of course I am."

I held her hand in mine and raised it to my lips to kiss it gently.

"Help me up?"

"Of course, darling." I stood and helped her to her feet.

Once we were both standing, she leaned in close to me and whispered, "You can't save me, you know."

"What?" I was confused. What did she mean I couldn't save her?

"You have to save either me or yourself. You can't save us both. You're not strong enough."

"Dot, what are you talking about? Come with me. We're almost to safety."

"No Henry. You have to save yourself. I can't come with you."

"Dottie, please." I felt tears start to fall on my cheeks. "You have to come with me." I grabbed one of her hands to try and pull her along with me, but she wouldn't budge.

"Henry, go. I have to stay here." She pulled her hand away from me and then pushed me into the forest.

I caught my balance after almost falling on my back. I turned and ran a few steps, and then I looked over my shoulder to see Dot.

The last image I saw before I woke up was of her standing in the burning forest with tears running down her face.

I woke up with my heart trying to beat its way out of my chest. I wanted to scream.

What was that horrid dream? Why was Dot there?

I had to get out of here. I tried to sit up in my bed, but I was tangled up in my sheets. I felt trapped in them and struggled to break free of the white fabric, just like I had tried to break free of the trees in my dream.

My vision was blurred by the tears in my eyes. I could hardly see anything. I was reminded of Dot's tears in my dream, which only made me feel worse. What was wrong with me?

I ran to the bathroom and turned on the shower and got in. I left the water running cold, trying to wash off the feelings of burning and guilt left by my nightmare.

I just stood under the running water, trying to calm my breathing. I couldn't catch a breath. It felt like there wasn't enough oxygen. I turned off the water, hoping for more air. I stepped out of the shower and wrapped myself in my towel, finally able to breathe in deeply. I went back to my room to put some clothes on and checked the time. 6:45. It wasn't as early as I thought.

I sat on my bed with my eyes closed, breathing in and out to the sound of the ticking clock. My thoughts were still racing.

Why was Dot in that dream?

What did it all mean?

I felt like my brain was broken. I couldn't control my thoughts. My heart was still beating erratically, even after I tried to calm myself down.

What was wrong with me?

I held my head in my hands. *Breathe in. Breathe out. Breathe in. Breathe out.* I repeated this over and over.

After a few minutes of silence and deep breathing, I finally had a rational thought.

I remembered the man at work, the one who saw me drop to the ground and act like a soldier in danger. He said his father had dreams about the war. Episodes, he called them.

Was that what was happening to me? Were these dreams I kept having some sort of episode? It would make sense. I hardly felt like myself during them. They terrified me and made me feel insane.

I knew I had to talk to that man again. I didn't even know his name, so I would have to track him down next week at work.

But I felt like I needed to talk to someone sooner than that. I wanted to talk to someone right now. Dot had said last night that she was willing to listen, but I didn't want to tell her about this dream. It was too painful, and it involved her. The next person I thought of was Bud. He had fought in the war. Maybe he knew about this sort of thing. Maybe he had episodes too.

That's how I found myself knocking on the Banks' door much too early on a Saturday morning. I knew Dot would be baking and I knew Bud liked to get up early, so I was hoping someone would answer.

And I was hoping that person wouldn't be Dot.

I looked up right as she opened the door. I barely held back a gasp when I remembered the dream version of her, standing in the forest in Belgium and waiting for the flames to take her.

"Henry. What are you doing here?" She was wearing an apron and a smile when she answered the door.

"I need to talk to Buddy. It's urgent."

"Oh." Her face fell. "Well, I'll go see if he's awake yet. Um, you can come in if you want..."

She left to go find Buddy, and I stepped inside and took a seat on their couch. The air smelled like warm bread, and the scent calmed me a little bit.

I was still breathing heavily from my dream and from racing over here. I tried to calm myself down. I touched my forehead and noticed that I was still sweating too. Why couldn't I compose myself?

A few moments later, Dot came downstairs alone.

"Buddy's on his way. But Henry, why are you here so early?" She was folding her arms in front of her, something I had seen both of our mothers do on occasion.

"I just need to talk to Bud."

"So it has nothing to do with our conversation last night?"

Our conversation? Which one?

She raised an eyebrow at me. "I'm here for you, remember? You can tell me."

Oh. That conversation. It had everything to do with that conversation, but I wasn't going to tell her that. Last night, she told me that she noticed a change in me and wanted to know what was wrong. I couldn't even explain it myself, so how could I possibly begin to explain it to her?

"No, Dottie, I'm okay. Really, I'm fine." I knew this was a lie, and I regretted the words as soon as they left my mouth, but I didn't know what else to say.

"I don't believe you one bit, but I'll let it go. If you don't want to tell me anything, I'll just go and check on the bread that's in the oven." Her voice was quiet and serious. She turned on her heels and went back to the kitchen.

I held my head in my hands and tried not to let any tears fall. What was I doing? I was trying to repair our friendship. Lying to Dot was the last thing that was going to help us to be normal again.

Then I remembered the letter. Actually, I remembered both letters. Phrases from the one I wrote late last night burned in my memory.

All I could think about was you. I felt like I was somewhere I really belonged. I still love you.

I realized I couldn't possibly give Dot that letter. This time I knew it wasn't my fear holding me back, but my better judgment. The dream I had just hours ago convinced me that I wasn't in any state to love her or give her anything. My mind was actively trying to destroy me. I hadn't had any nightmares about her before I wrote that stupid letter last night, and if I gave it to her and she loved me back, who's to say I wouldn't have dreams about her dying every night?

I wanted us to be friends. That was all that was realistic right now. Even though that thought made me want to start crying again, I knew that friendship was all I could give her.

Bud came running down the stairs.

"What's up?" he asked with a goofy grin.

"Bud, can we talk outside?" I nodded toward the front door.

"Yeah, I guess." His smile fell.

We walked outside and sat on the front step.

"Bud, I don't know what's wrong with me. I need your help."

"Come on, my friend. After last night, Dot is practically smitten with you! She came home walking on air."

I looked at him in surprise. Was she really?

Then I shook myself out of it. Friends. We were just friends.

"I don't want to talk about that. I have bigger problems."

"Bigger problems than love? I highly doubt that." Bud crossed his legs and knit his fingers together.

"Bud, this is serious. I keep having..." I hesitated, "episodes." The word came out like a question. I was so unsure about all of this.

"What are you talking about?"

"I don't know what to call them. I don't even know what's happening to me. Sometimes I have dreams that I'm back in the war, and I wake up in a cold sweat or feeling sick. Sometimes something reminds me of the war, and I lose control. One time at work, I heard something that sounded like a bomb and I immediately dropped to the ground and reached for my gun. I completely forgot where I was."

Bud sat thinking for a while.

"What's wrong with me?" I put my head in my hands again. "Last night I dreamt I was back in Belgium on the night that I got injured. Dot was there. And a few weeks ago, I dreamt that Jimmy was there too."

"Have you talked to your parents about this?" Bud asked.

I shook my head. The thought hadn't even occurred to me. It didn't make sense to tell them, because they wouldn't know any better than I did what was going on in my head.

"I knew a lady back in England who had some of the same things going on," Bud said. "Every time there was an air raid she would collapse to her knees, no matter where she was, and start crying silently. She would hug her knees to her chest and just sit there rocking back and forth. It took a few of us soldiers to get her to a shelter where she would be safe. She didn't trust us. I can't imagine what she went through to react that way every time. She never talked about it afterward."

We were quiet again. A car drove past and Bud waved at the driver.

"I used to have nightmares when I was little," he said. "One time I heard my Pop and my uncles talking about vampires and Dracula, and I started having dreams about them. I probably had them once every few months for years. They were terrible. Do you think it's something like that?"

"I mean, I had nightmares too when I was younger—but these dreams are different. It's like I'm back in the war. I can smell the smoke, hear the screams, feel the heat of the flames and the pain in my arm. Everything is so real."

"Hm. I've never heard of anything like it. Sorry, Henry."

"There was a man who saw me when I dropped to the ground at work after I heard the crash. He said his father was a war vet and used to have episodes like me, where he thought he was in a battle."

"Maybe he would know."

"Yeah, maybe."

"You'll figure this out, Henry. I know you will."

The door opened behind us. I didn't turn my head to look.

"I made an extra loaf of bread if you want a piece," Dot said quietly. "It's on the kitchen counter."

She left us on the porch and shut the door behind her. Bud and I sat in silence, watching a man across the street try to start a push mower and then become frustrated when it wouldn't work.

A few moments later, Dot walked out of the backyard gate with her red wagon filled with freshly baked bread loaves. She set off down the sidewalk without a word.

"She's mad at you now," Bud said, snorting out a laugh.

"What makes you say that?"

"I know my sister. She is not particularly happy right now."

"Why not?"

"I have no idea. You're the one she's cross with. What have you done since you got here?"

As soon as he said that, I knew. I was talking to Bud about my problems after Dot had offered her help twice. No wonder she was cross with me.

"Well? Go fix it." Bud nudged my arm.

I went running after Dot.

CHAPTER 16

June 30, 1945

Dorothy

How could he? I asked myself. I had just told him he could talk to me about anything, and then he turned around and went to Buddy instead. I knew they were friends too, but Henry and I had always told each other everything. That had to count for something.

But no. Henry didn't trust me with this. I didn't know what was happening to him, and he obviously didn't care to tell me. I wanted to cry, but I was too angry. I didn't like being angry with Henry at all.

I walked up to the first house to drop off a few loaves of bread and tried to smile. Mrs. Anderson thanked me for the bread, handed me a crumpled dollar bill, and told me to keep the change to put toward the bakery. I tried handing back a quarter and a dime but, with a smile on her face, Mrs. Anderson insisted I keep them.

I left the Anderson's porch, thanking God again and again for Mrs. Anderson's generosity. I looked up to see Henry, standing with his hands in his pockets, looking at me sheepishly.

He had followed me.

"What are you doing?" I asked warily.

"I came to apologize." He stepped closer so he was right in front of me. "I know that you offered to listen, but with this situation I really needed Bud's help."

"Why don't you trust me?"

"It's not that I don't trust you, Dottie. I'd trust you with anything." Henry looked right into my eyes, and I knew he was sincere. His eyebrows knit together, and he continued talking. "The thing is, I honestly don't know what's happening with me. Something's wrong. I think it's because of what I saw during the war. I needed another soldier's opinion."

"Oh." I felt relieved that he still trusted me, but I was still very confused. What did he mean something was wrong?

I remembered that we were still in front of the Anderson's house. I grabbed Henry's arm. "Let's keep going. I don't want them to think we're staking their house out."

Henry laughed. "Like Jimmy's games from when we were little?"

"Exactly."

Jimmy used to come up with elaborate games where we had to spy on each other's houses without getting caught. I was always terrible at sneaking around like that. I never had the patience, but Jimmy was always the best. The game was his invention, so it made sense that he would excel at it.

"I'm sorry I was cross," I said once we started walking.

"It's all right. I hope you know that I would come to you about anything else. I know you're a great listener."

I blushed and smiled. "Thanks, Henry." He was always making me blush. Friends weren't supposed to make their friends blush like that.

We were silent as we walked. This silence was comfortable though. It reminded me of other moments Henry and I shared just like this one, when we delivered bread around the neighborhood during the Depression. I wondered if he was remembering those days as well. As we walked, I noticed him glancing over at me occasionally. He looked like he was about to say something, and then stopped himself. I knew how he felt. There was so much I wanted to say to him, but I didn't know if I could do it.

I pointed at a house just up the road, and Henry nodded. He knew what I meant, even without words. We stopped in front of it, and I delivered another loaf of bread while Henry waited on the sidewalk. The Taylors next door had also ordered a loaf, so I took one to them as well.

I walked down their steps back to where Henry was standing. He smiled at me, and I smiled back.

"I have a few more loaves to deliver on the other side of the park. Do you still want to walk with me?"

Henry nodded and we headed toward the park.

After a few more moments, I finally found the courage to ask, "What did you mean earlier? What's happening with you?"

He didn't speak for a while, but then he breathed in deeply. "I don't know how to explain it. My memories of the war aren't exactly happy, and I hate being reminded of it. That's why I lashed out at Jimmy last night. Sometimes my memories seem real. I suddenly feel like I'm back in Europe, and I..." He trailed off, shaking his head.

"Gosh, Henry. That sounds terrible."

"The worst part is that I kind of lose control when it happens. Sometimes I forget where I am, or just get confused. In fact, that's what happened that night at the party. Jimmy looked exactly like a soldier I knew. I thought it was him." His eyes grew wet.

"Knew?"

Henry looked down.

My stomach fell when I realized. "Oh, I'm so sorry. I shouldn't have asked. I guess that's why you don't really want to talk about it."

"It wasn't glamorous. Nothing like what you see in the war bond videos. No Uncle Sam or waving flags. It was horrible. I never knew if the other boys and I would make it home at night." His eyes looked haunted.

I couldn't even imagine what he had been through. I had always pictured the war exactly like what I saw in the war bond commercials before the movies, with soldiers marching in long lines and planes flying in formation overhead. For the first time I realized it was all too glamorous.

"I didn't realize it was like that." We stopped walking when we reached the corner of the park.

"Tragedy is always romanticized, Dot. I thought being a soldier would be like being a hero, like a fulfillment of some childhood fantasy. But it wasn't. It was a nightmare. And now I keep living it. Over and over. I feel trapped in my own mind."

"Henry, I'm so sorry."

"I don't know why I told you all that. I'm the one who should be sorry." He looked straight down at the ground again.

"It's all right. Thank you for telling me." I put my hand on his arm. We were facing each other again. I looked up into Henry's eyes. I could see the tears in them. Before the war, Henry never cried. He was the strong one. The one I always went to for help. Now I had to help him.

I hugged him and it felt very different from the one we shared last night. That hug had held a promise of something—something more than what we were. This hug was one I would give to my brothers if they were upset. I hated seeing Henry like this. He wasn't exactly sad; he looked scared. That made me hug him even tighter. His arms tightened around me too, and we stood there for a while, ignoring the sounds of children playing in the park in the early summer air.

"Thank you, Dottie." Henry stepped back. The uncharacteristic tears still filled his eyes, but he quickly wiped them away. "You're an amazing friend."

I smiled. "Thanks, Henry. You are too."

"Actually, I have something for you. Do you want to follow me back to my house before you head home?"

I agreed, and we set off to finish delivering the other loaves of bread. As we walked, Henry asked me all about my future bakery. He wanted to know everything, from when I'd be ready to buy the building to what I was going to sell.

After I finished describing the menu, he said, "I'm so proud of you, Dottie."

I almost stopped walking out of surprise at his words. "Why?" I looked at him and smiled.

"I can tell you've worked so hard on this, and it's great that you're finally going to have your bakery. You've talked about owning one since we were kids. I just think it's swell."

I laughed. "Thanks, Henry. I'm very excited."

When we finally got to his house, Henry asked, "Do you want to come in?"

I nodded and smiled.

I left my wagon on the porch and followed him through the front door.

I walked into the living room where I had talked with Anna a few short weeks ago.

"I'll be right back, okay?" Henry said as he went down the hall that led to his room. When he was out of sight, I heard him yell, "Feel free to sit down, Dottie!"

"All right!" I sat down on one of the couches. I wondered what Henry was going to give me. My birthday wasn't until August, so it wasn't likely a present. Though after what happened last night, I did wonder. What was going on between us? I didn't know how to feel anymore.

I didn't have to wait long until he was back with an envelope in his hand. He was holding it in the tips of his fingers, like he didn't want to ruin it.

"This is to make up for all of the letters I didn't send you." Henry sat on the couch next to me. "I just couldn't write sometimes. The war seemed too bleak to find anything to write about. I'm so sorry."

"I didn't write to you either. It's not just your fault." His reasons for not writing made perfect sense. The only excuse I had was not knowing how to express my feelings. "I'm truly sorry as well."

Henry smiled at me. All traces of tears in his eyes were gone, and his face lit up.

I smiled back.

"Gosh, Dottie, I missed your smile."

I knew my face was bright red. I felt it get hot, and I looked down at my lap in response. Curse my blushing! I fiddled with my skirt, trying to calm my racing heart.

"I mean it," he continued. "You're always so happy, it makes me feel happy. When I was gone, that was one of the things I missed most about you."

"Thank you, Henry. I missed you too." I looked up at him. He was staring at me with his eyes wide. I felt my heart speed up. What was happening?

"I wrote this when I was in London." He held out the letter to me. I took it from his hand. "I wanted to send it to you, but then it was easier to just bring it with me. And then I forgot to give it to you." He shook his head and laughed. "Also, I wrote it with my left hand since my right arm was still pretty injured, and so the handwriting is pretty sloppy. And I think I rambled a little bit..."

"You're rambling right now," I said through my laughter.

Henry smirked and looked down at the letter in my hand. "I hope it explains some things."

Explains? What did the letter explain?

"Thank you, Henry. This means a lot to me. I'll write you one, if you want." I meant it. I wanted to write him a letter, telling him how I was really feeling. I wanted to tell him that the look in his eyes made my heart beat faster and his smile made me feel warm all over. I wanted to tell him I didn't understand it yet but that I knew I wanted to. I felt too nervous to say it out loud at this point, but I could write it down.

"I'd like that." Henry was staring at me with his eyes squinted, like he was trying to read something in mine.

I knew I was blushing again, and I looked away. Out of the corner of my eye, I saw that he turned away too.

"Thank you again," I said. I really had to get going. I was just going to make a fool of myself if I stayed. "For telling me about how you're feeling and for the letter."

"Of course, Dot. Thank you for listening."

"Anytime." I stood up. "I should probably go." I nodded toward the door.

"Okay." Henry stood up too. We were standing too close together, and I sucked in a breath. My heart was beating quickly, and I knew I had to leave before I did or said something stupid.

"Bye, Henry," I said, as I turned quickly and walked toward the door.

Henry got there first and opened the door for me.

I muttered a 'thank you' and left with the letter in hand and my heart still pounding.

I hurried home, since Peggy, Marylin, and I were going to spend time together as soon as I was done with my deliveries. I wanted to read the letter now, but I had to let myself process my conversation with Henry first. In my head, I rehearsed what had just happened. I had no intention of creating more out of the morning's events than was already there, but my heart was still beating heavily when I walked inside.

I went up the stairs to my room and hid the letter under my pillow for safekeeping until I was free to read it that night.

"How is he?" Buddy's voice came from my doorway.

I made sure the letter was completely hidden underneath my pillow and turned around. "Henry?"

Bud nodded and raised an eyebrow. "Of course."

I sighed. "I don't know, Buddy. I'm worried about him."

"Me too." Bud stood up straight from where he had been leaning on the door frame. "Did he tell you everything?" He walked over and sat on the bed next to me.

I nodded again. "I don't know how to help him."

"I don't either."

We sat in silence for a moment.

Bud cleared his throat. "I think it helped him a bit to talk about it. He seemed calmer when he left our house than he did when he showed up."

"I think so too. I just hate to see him like this." Remembering Henry's tear-filled eyes made me want to shed tears of my own.

Bud put his arm around me and I put my head on his shoulder. "He'll be all right. I'm sure that whatever is happening to him will get better with time. Most things do."

"You don't have nightmares like he does, do you Bud?"

"No. I also didn't see the same things that he did. He was involved in some pretty terrible battles."

"Do you know how he injured his arm?"

Bud shook his head. "He hasn't told me. I don't think he likes talking about it."

"I know. I do wonder, though."

"I do too. The poor guy has too much going on in his head to keep it all inside. He has to let it out or he'll explode."

"Is that why he keeps dreaming that he's back there?"

"Could be. I honestly don't know."

"I want him to be okay. He has to be okay." I looked to my pillow, where Henry's letter lay.

"He will be. Henry's strong. We both know that. He'll pick himself up and be just fine."

I sighed. "Thanks, Buddy. I'm glad you're home."

"Me too." He hugged me tighter. "Hey, weren't you gonna go to Marylin's house?"

I looked over at the clock on my dresser. I was already late. "Gosh, yeah, I was!" I stood up quickly and grabbed my purse off the coat hanger in the corner. "Thanks for the talk, Bud! I gotta go!"

I ran out of my bedroom with Bud following me. "Have fun!" he yelled as I ran down the stairs and out the door.

I rode my bike to Marylin's house, where my two friends were already sitting on the front lawn waiting for me.

"You're late," Marylin said with a smile.

"I know, I got caught up with something." I wasn't going to tell them about Henry. Not yet, anyway.

"We were just discussing last night," Peggy said, adjusting so she was facing both of us with her legs crossed in front of her. She was wearing pants, which she did far more often than I did. I preferred skirts and dresses unless an activity called for pants.

I sat down next to the two of them. "What about it?"

"As you know, Jimmy and Marylin are *in love*." Peggy whispered the *in love* part behind her hand so Marylin wouldn't see.

"You know I can still hear you, right?" Marylin kicked Peggy's leg playfully.

Peggy turned back to Marylin and gave her a big grin. Then she turned back to me and continued. "We were discussing their impending courtship." This time, she spoke like the actresses in the movies.

Marylin rolled her eyes.

"Sounds exciting," I said, laughing. "So, has he asked you yet?"

Marylin shook her head sadly. "Not yet. I'm usually pretty patient, but I feel like we've been dragging this out for forever."

"Has he hinted at asking you to go steady?"

"A little. When we were dancing last night, we were talking about going on another date, just the two of us. He wants to take me into Pittsburgh sometime soon."

How romantic!

"That would be so sweet!" Peggy cooed. "Maybe he'll ask you there."

Marylin smiled. "I hope so."

"We give you our blessing, anyway."

I nodded in agreement. "You two are perfect for each other."

"Speaking of which." Peggy turned toward me. "You. Henry. What's going on?"

I wanted to keep talking about Marylin and Jimmy, or baking, or other safe topics, but from the way Peggy was eyeing me, I wasn't going to get out of answering this question.

"I...I still don't know. We're just getting used to each other's company again."

"You two were adorable last night." Marylin said. "How was your dance?"

I sighed. "It was fine, I guess." But I couldn't hold back my smile.

"Fine?" Peggy asked. "When I talked to you right after, you were all flushed and out of breath. I think it was more than fine."

"I don't know." I didn't really want to talk about this. I was still so confused about what I felt for Henry, and I didn't want my friends to assume I felt more than I did.

"Dottie, do you remember all those dances we went to before Henry got back?"

I nodded. Of course I did. Not specifically, but I did remember.

"You danced with a lot of guys, but never went on a single date. Why?"

I was about to say that no one had asked me, but we all knew that was a lie. There were a few guys who had asked me to go to the movies or to Daisy's with them, but I had turned them all down and given one excuse after another.

"I was never interested in any of them."

"Would you go on a date with Henry if he asked?"

I didn't say anything. I didn't need to. I knew Peggy could read the expression on my face. I smiled just at the thought of going to dinner or to a movie, just me and Henry. I bit my lip and looked down at my hands.

"You would, right?" Peggy asked.

I nodded carefully.

"Now," Peggy eyed me carefully, "would you go out with him just to be nice or because you have feelings for him?"

I knew the answer immediately. I didn't want to be "just friends" with Henry. I wanted to be his. The realization was clearer than anything I had felt since he came home. I was falling in love with Henry Oakey. I couldn't hide my feelings. My smile gave me away.

"Told you so," Peggy said to Marylin. "She was holding out on us."

"Aw, Dottie," Marylin said. "I'm so happy for you!"

Now I knew I had to tell Henry. I had to write him a letter. But I had to read his first.

Later that night, I was sitting on my bed with Henry's letter in hand. I popped open the envelope gently and pulled out the letter inside.

I remembered that Henry said he wrote it when he was in London and that he had written it with his left hand. I smiled when I saw his handwriting. It was crooked, but I could tell each letter was written with care.

I began to read the letter.

Dear Dot,

My, I've missed you. It feels like forever since I left home. When I finally get back, it'll sure be good for me to see you and your smile again. By the time you read this, I'll probably be a few streets away, just like old times.

I smiled as I read. He had told me the same thing earlier today. He had missed my smile. The thought made my heart skip a beat.

I continued reading.

I can't tell you how much I regret not writing to you. The truth is, I didn't want to bore you with details of my everyday life here in Europe. It's pretty dreary here, and I had nothing of value to share with you other than memories of our past, ones you already know and remember.

You'll have to excuse my handwriting. My right arm is still getting better from an injury I got in January, so I have to write with my left hand. I've been practicing. Can you tell?

Dottie, I really have missed you. I don't think I can say that enough. You'll probably get tired of hearing it once I'm home. I'll be shouting it in the streets: "Dorothy Banks, I missed you!"

I laughed.

The world is so dark here, with the war and the horror of it all. It's so different from home. I have needed you more than you can understand.

I paused in the middle of the paragraph and read that sentence again. He needed me. What did that mean? I remembered he mentioned earlier that I helped him feel happy. Was that what he was talking about? I had to find out.

But I imagine your days haven't changed much. I imagine you, Peggy, Marylin, and Jimmy are going to the movies, dancing, and drinking one too many colas at Daisy's, just as if I were with you. I've missed those days so much. I can't wait to spend time with you all again.

He didn't explain what 'needing me' meant. He did miss me though. I laughed and shook my head.

Now, on to the point of my letter. I know I was too forward with you the day I said goodbye to you.

Oh. The day he tried to kiss me. We hadn't mentioned it the entire time he had been home. I thought we would bring it up once we got comfortable with each other again, and here it was. I didn't know if I was ready to talk about it yet.

If you've forgotten what happened, I won't remind you. I'm way too embarrassed.

Embarrassed. He was embarrassed to have tried. That could only mean that he regretted it. My face fell at the thought.

Back then, I was scared I might not ever see you again, and I couldn't bear the thought of never telling you how I felt for all of those years. It took a whole lot of moxie to tell you, but I was young and, frankly, pretty dumb. Dot, I've grown up a lot, and now I realize how you must have felt in that situation. I feel embarrassed to even remember it now. I am sorry I did it. I am sorry for surprising you with such a thing.

And there it was. He *did* regret trying to kiss me. And he gave me this letter to tell me, so he wouldn't have to bring it up to my face.

Henry regretted it. He said he was sorry he did it. He didn't even want to tell me in person, so he wrote this letter instead. My mind was racing through the events of the last week, beginning when I found Henry in the park. I thought of last night's dance and finally today, when I thought that maybe there was something more between us.

But there was nothing. Henry said so himself right here. All of the hope I had felt earlier was now gone. I sat on my bed for a few minutes, trying to process. I could hear Bud and Bobby talking in the next room over. I finally decided to keep reading, bracing myself for more heartbreak.

I hope you can forgive me, and we can be friends, just like we were before. I don't think I could bear it if we weren't friends anymore. So, let's just move on and pretend that day never happened.

I look forward to seeing you again, my friend, and hope you have at least one loaf of bread and a plate full of your chocolate chip cookies waiting for me when I get there.

Love, Henry

I set the letter down on my nightstand, holding back tears. I had wanted to cry more times today than I had in a very long time, and I wasn't going to give in now. Nothing had really changed between us. I just knew his feelings now. That was all. And he regretted trying to kiss me. At that thought, I really did cry a little. Henry was my closest friend, and I wanted to be his closest friend too. It embarrassed him to think about kissing me, and it was obvious that he wanted to forget about that day. He said so himself. *Let's move on and pretend that never happened.*

I resolved myself to do the same. If Henry wanted it this way, that's how it would be. I would hide whatever feelings I was starting to have toward him. I had to forget about them. There was nothing I could do about loving Henry if he said we were just friends. I would forget about any romance between us, which would be easy since it only existed in my hopes and dreams.

CHAPTER 17

July 1, 1945

Henry

I was in a forest. The birds were singing. I could hear a breeze whistle through the leaves above my head. I closed my eyes and breathed deeply. I felt truly and completely at peace.

A crackle of leaves being crushed shook me out of my musings.

I turned toward the sound and breathed out a sigh when I saw her. She was beautiful.

Dot smiled at me from the other side of the clearing. She looked down and her nose crinkled like it often did when she was really happy. She was wearing a long white dress. She looked like an angel.

She quickly walked toward me and took my hands in hers.

I stepped closer to her and felt my heartbeat quicken.

"Henry," she whispered.

"Hmm?" I further closed the gap between us, letting just our foreheads touch. I breathed in. She smelled like vanilla and chocolate.

"I love—" she started.

Without a warning, everything erupted into screams. Fire rained down on us, and I grabbed Dot's hand and ran.

We ran through the forest. Twigs scratched my face and arms as I led Dot through the trees.

I heard the zip of a bullet next to me. Time slowed down. I knew I was going to be hit.

"Henry!" Dot called out. She shoved me out of the way. We both fell to the ground.

Time sped up as I came to my senses seconds later. Dot was lying next to me in the leaves, clutching her arm. My own arm stung with the same pain I knew she was feeling. Red hot blood was already spreading over her arm and staining the sleeve of her white dress.

"Dot, you're hurt."

"But you aren't." She laughed quietly.

"You got shot. That was supposed to hit me."

"I saved you, dummy. Aren't you going to thank me?" She smiled through the tears welling up in her eyes.

I grabbed her uninjured arm and held her hand between my own. I kissed her knuckles.

"Henry?" Her voice was quiet.

"Yes, Dot?"

"I love you." Her eyes wouldn't stay open, like she was too tired to stay awake.

"Dot, no! Stay with me!" I started to cry without tears. They wouldn't come. My breathing got faster and faster. As Dot's breathing grew more and more shallow, mine quickened. I couldn't catch my breath.

"I can't," she whispered, closing her eyes for the last time. I grabbed her body in my arms and held her, willing her to keep on living.

"Dot, please. I love you too. You can't leave!" Even as I said the words, I felt her slip away. I felt her last breath on my neck, and then she was silent.

Someone screamed, and I only realized it was me after I felt my throat burn from the effort. I wanted to run away, to pretend nothing had happened to Dottie, but I knew I couldn't escape this. This was too real, too raw to be fake. I screamed again, but my voice broke and I started crying.

I cried over Dot's body, wishing that somehow she would open her eyes again. That she would come back from whatever place in heaven she was in.

I held her as I sobbed her name, over and over again, until my voice was exhausted and my tears were spent.

⚜

I clung to my pillow, gripping it tightly with both hands, and mouthed Dottie's name like a prayer. Everything was dark.

I lay in my bed for a moment, registering the dark room and the silence.

It wasn't real. She's not dead. I'm here. Dot is at home. She's safe. We're fine. She's alive. I'm here.

I repeated those thoughts over and over in my head, but didn't feel any relief from the affirmations. For the first time after waking up from one of my dreams, I didn't feel sick. I just felt empty.

Absolutely empty.

I wanted to cry, to feel something. I needed some sort of resolution and catharsis to get rid of the emptiness I felt. The tears wouldn't come, and that made me feel even more miserable.

I couldn't even remember what I had been dreaming about now. I knew Dot was there and that she had been hurt. And that she told me she loved me.

I remembered I had said it back. The thought of this should have made me happy, that Dot loved me and I loved her. But I simply sat on my bed, breathing deeply, and stared straight ahead. It wasn't real. I knew that. Dot didn't love me. Only the Dot in my dream did.

I didn't love Dot like that either. I gave her the letter I wrote in England, apologizing for what I did. I just wanted to be friends. That was all. I knew that was what she wanted, and it was foolish of me to wish for anything more than that.

After a few minutes of sitting in silence, I turned to my clock. 4:39. It was still too early to be up. I lay back down in my bed without bothering to put the covers on.

I stayed like that, staring up at the ceiling, until I heard movement from outside my door. It was now 8:00, and I don't think I slept at all.

I got ready for the day quickly, then met my family in the kitchen for breakfast. We always had breakfast together on Sundays. Dad always made potatoes and eggs, and Mom squeezed oranges for juice. With the food rations, we didn't have much.

I sat down at the table across from Jessica, who was wearing a nice dress and had her hair up. "It's Sunday, Henry."

I nodded.

"Aren't you coming to church with us?"

Church. I had completely forgotten. I muttered a yes as I ran back to my room and changed into something more appropriate for the service.

I came back to the table where everyone was already eating.

"Is everything all right?" Mom asked in between bites of toast.

I nodded. "Forgot it was Sunday." I shoveled a bite of eggs into my mouth so I wouldn't have to talk more.

The rest of breakfast was uneventful. I still felt empty. I passively ate and listened to the conversation between my parents and Jessica without wanting to participate. I was completely apathetic.

I finished first and asked to be excused. I sat in the living room and waited for the rest of my family. I closed my eyes and leaned my head back on the couch, only to be tapped on the shoulder by Jessica a few moments later.

"You all right?" she asked.

I nodded a quick 'yes'. "Yeah, just tired."

"Come on sleepyhead, let's go," she said, nodding toward the door.

I followed her outside. I was silent on the walk to the church building. I muttered a 'hello' to the pastor, who greeted everyone at the door, and I slipped inside after my family. I sat next to Jessica and looked in front of me at the other families filing into the pews. The Banks came in just before the pastor walked up the aisle to the pulpit. Dot turned her head to look at me as she sat down. I lowered my head before she realized I had seen her and stayed that way for the rest of the service.

I'm sure my parents thought I was making a show of being pious, but Jessica knew me better than that and suspected I was nodding off. She kept nudging me with her elbow throughout the service and even whispered a few times, asking me if I was paying attention.

I was, though I didn't look like it.

I listened intently to everything the pastor said and prayed that something would shock me out of the apathy I felt. Toward the end of his sermon, he said that if we want peace in this life, we have to make it ourselves. No one else on this earth can give us the peace we need. That phrase did it. I knew I needed peace, and my dreams were keeping me from it. I needed to figure out some solution to what was happening in my head, and I needed to do it soon.

After the service ended, I stood up with my family and left quickly. I knew Dot would want to talk like we used to after Sunday service, but I didn't want to talk to anyone. I just wanted to go home and think about solutions and explanations. With this thought in my mind, I made my way home before anyone had the chance to pull me in to a conversation.

After I got home from the service, I went straight to the backyard where a table and chairs were neatly placed on the patio. Sometimes when the weather was nice, we ate supper back there. I had a lot of happy memories of the four of us around that table, laughing and talking. I wanted to go back to when life felt simple and I didn't have a need to sort out the meaning and purpose of dreams and memories.

Sitting outside in the quiet, I was finally able to think clearly through what was happening. I knew my dreams weren't real, but some felt real enough to remember so vividly afterwards. When I woke up from a dream or got out of an episode, I could still feel the fear. That didn't make any sense to me. I was home and I was safe, so why did my episodes make me feel like I was back in Europe?

The back door opened and Mom walked out. Dad watched her from the back door.

"Are you all right, Henry?" Mom asked. "You left so quickly after church."

I decided to be honest. "I don't know, Mom."

She sat down next to me at the table and looked at me expectantly. I kept talking.

"I keep having dreams that I'm back in the war. But they aren't normal dreams where weird and confusing things happen and then you wake up and you forget. These dreams feel real. I feel like I'm back there. Back in Belgium, where I got injured."

I knew my parents had heard a little about what happened that night, but I also knew that a lot of it was kept secret from them because of the nature of the mission.

"It's like I'm there again, except things are different. People from home keep appearing like they were actually there." Saying all of this out loud made me feel stupid, like it was all in my head.

"Everyone has bad dreams sometimes, Henry," Mom said. Even though her voice was calm, her eyes said otherwise. She motioned to my dad, who still stood in the doorway. He walked out and joined us at the table. He also looked worried.

I continued. "These dreams are different. When I wake up, I feel sick. My heart is racing, and sometimes I'm crying. They are nightmares, but worse." My voice broke. "They don't go away when I wake up."

My parents looked at each other with concerned glances. The more I told them, the easier it was to speak.

"One time, I heard a loud noise at work, and I thought I was in danger. I dropped to the ground and reached for my gun. I panicked when I realized I didn't have one. I felt terrified, like I was going to die. Nothing was wrong, it was just a sound from the refinery. I feel like something is wrong with me, but I don't know what." My throat tightened and I felt tears forming in my eyes. I knew they didn't understand. I wasn't making any sense. I didn't know how to explain how it felt to be trapped in my own head without any way to escape.

I looked up at Mom, who was looking at Dad.

"Mom?"

She looked at me with teary eyes. "I don't know, Henry. I've never heard of anything like this. I know that sometimes soldiers struggle emotionally when they come home, but I don't know in what ways. I don't know how normal this is."

"I feel trapped." I broke. The tears started falling. I felt like all of the weight I had been carrying for the past month slipped off of my back and onto the floor. "I don't know what's wrong with me."

"There's nothing wrong with you." Dad scooted his chair closer and put his arm around me. There was a small ache in my arm where he touched me, but I ignored it.

Mom grabbed my hand and held it in both of hers.

"Henry, it'll be all right. We'll talk to some people, figure this out. You'll be okay."

We sat there for a while and I cried. We didn't talk, we just sat in our embrace.

Finally, I said, "There's a man at work. He saw me when I dropped to the ground that day. He said his father had episodes where he thought he was back in the war. I want to ask him more about it."

"Who is it?" Dad asked.

"I don't know his name. He works in the refinery. I sort of remember what he looks like."

"Hmm. I would have to ask around. We can find him tomorrow."

I nodded and wiped my tears away with my sleeve. "Thank you."

"Of course, Henry. We love you."

"We are so glad you are home with us now. You're safe here."

I gave both my parents a hug and went inside to my room to catch up on some sleep before supper.

I woke up feeling much better. The out-of-body, numb sensation I was feeling earlier was gone. It had been replaced with something akin to how you feel just after drinking hot chocolate, or when you sit in front of a fireplace. I still felt fragile, but I knew I was safe. I knew my parents were on my side and wanted to help me.

I got out of bed and looked at myself in the mirror in the bathroom. As I stood there, I promised myself that I would keep asking for help. I knew I couldn't do this alone. It didn't make sense to do it alone. I thought it was something that I could figure out by myself and then move on from, but, if telling my parents how I was feeling made my mom cry, I obviously needed help. Something was wrong with me. I didn't know what, but I was determined to find out so I could fix it.

※

I enjoyed the rest of the night with my family. We played card games after supper, and I felt happy. I didn't think about the war, or Dot, or anything else. I focused on what was happening right then and there and it helped me feel at peace, just like the pastor said during the service earlier.

I said a silent prayer before going to bed, thanking God for my parents and their help. I also prayed asking for a solution to everything that was happening to me. I needed to figure it out. These dreams and episodes were holding me back. I had to start moving on.

※

That night I slept peacefully. It was the first time in a while I had been able to sleep all night. I had dreams, but they were of the normal sort. I woke up feeling refreshed and ready to go to work. Today was the day when I would hopefully get some answers.

Dad and I got to work early so we could ask around for the man I had talked to. We asked the refinery manager, who had an office right outside the factory. There were whirrings and growlings and bangings of all kinds, and I breathed deeply, hoping I wouldn't lose control. If I was always conscious of where I was, that couldn't happen, right?

The manager told us that the man's name was Alex Hansen, and that he would be in after lunch today.

I breathed a sigh of relief when I left the office with my dad.

"You all right?" he asked as we walked.

I nodded and smiled. "I'm glad we know who he is now."

"I hope he can explain some things."

I did too.

"How did you sleep last night?" he asked.

"I slept really well, actually."

"I'm glad. I've been thinking about you since you told us what's been going on, and I seem to remember reading something in the papers years ago—after the Great War. I remember that some psychologist was researching the effect of war on soldiers, but I can't remember what he found. Just that it happened. That's probably not very helpful." He laughed.

"No actually, it is. If we could find that research, it could help me understand." I knew I needed to figure out what was going on in my brain. Maybe a psychologist would know. They were expensive, and good ones were few and far between, but maybe I could find one who could help me sort out my thoughts and memories.

That afternoon, I went back down to the refinery and found Alex Hansen. He seemed surprised to see me.

"You're that boy, the one who—"

I cut him off. "Yes, that's me. I'm Henry. And you must be Alex."

"Yeah." He looked around, a bit confused.

"I asked your manager who you were. I wanted to talk to you about your father."

He nodded in understanding. "Because of the episodes."

"Yes. They keep happening to me, and I hoped you could tell me more about what happened to your father. Maybe it will help me understand what's going on in my head."

"I'd be happy to help."

"Thank you, sir. Can you meet me after work? We could go to the park and talk."

Alex nodded. "Sounds perfect. I'll see you then, Henry."

Alex was tall and bald, so I could easily pick him out from the other people walking around the park later that afternoon. I waved him down and started walking toward him.

We shook hands and sat on the nearest park bench. I noticed it was really close to the bench where Dot had found me during that lunch break. I smiled at the memory of her trying to cheer me up with her ramblings.

I didn't know how to begin asking about Alex's father, so I was glad when he spoke up.

"My father fought in the Great War," he said. "He was a ground soldier and fought in the trenches. He never really talked about it though. All I remember is that it was very dangerous for him and he came home with a lot of problems."

"Problems?"

"Not physical ones, mind you. More like the emotional sort. He got startled easily. He would wake up sometimes and couldn't breathe. Mother would have to console him and convince him he was at home and not in the trenches. He just couldn't leave it all behind."

"Did he ever talk to a doctor about it?"

"Yeah, the doctor said he was probably crazy. He referred my father to a psychologist. He said that problems of the mind are hard to fix."

Crazy. I didn't feel crazy. When I thought of crazy people I thought of people who couldn't control themselves, who were completely taken over by their infirmity. I wasn't crazy, was I?

"Did he ever talk about what happened in his dreams?"

"He never said anything. He was always really quiet about it. I only saw him break a few times. I heard about some of his other episodes from my mother after he had passed away. Once, I remember my father walking in from work in hysterics. His eyes were red from crying, and he was shaking. He kept repeating over and over 'gotta get out, gotta get out.' I don't know what he was talking about. It was like he really was crazy."

If what Dad said was true and there was research done on veterans and the effects that war had on their minds and emotions, then that must have been what happened with Alex's father. There was no other explanation. I refused to believe he was crazy because, if he was, then what did that make me?

Alex told me a few more stories about his dad—some about his episodes and others about him in general—and then he told me he had to get back to his wife and son at home.

"Thank you for meeting with me, Alex. You've been really helpful."

"Any time, Henry. If you have more questions, I'm just down the hall at work!"

We shook hands and parted ways. I was left with my thoughts.

I had to find a psychologist. I didn't know how, but I just had to. It was also important that I found one that wouldn't assume I was crazy for having these episodes. I needed a solution, not to be told I was unfixable.

CHAPTER 18

July 4, 1945

Dorothy

I spent the morning of the Fourth of July baking cookies. There was going to be an Independence Day celebration in the park, and everyone in Ashwood was going to be there. Now that the war in Europe was over and the war in the Pacific was coming to a close, it would feel like an even bigger celebration. There was going to be a potluck dinner, and that was why I was baking the cookies. Making them took up most of my morning, but I welcomed the distraction from my intrusive thoughts about Henry. I had a restless night after I read his letter. I think I read it at least twice a day since then. That afternoon, I would see Henry for the first time since he gave me the letter. I would see him for the first time since he shattered the tiny hope I had of a deeper relationship between the two of us. I knew now that the only possible relationship was a friendship, since Henry wanted to block out all memories of the day he tried to kiss me. That meant I would have to forget it too.

I decided I had to act like nothing had ever happened between me and Henry. We were friends, nothing more. I had to convince myself I didn't want to be anything more. Henry was just like Jimmy to me, wasn't he? We were friends and that was all. I tried to internalize the thought. It was easier than I thought it would be, since that is what I had been telling myself since before Henry left. I closed my heart to him and swore to keep it that way as I placed his stupid letter in the nightstand drawer, right beside my sketchbooks. I tried to put aside my frustration and sadness and started to get ready for the celebration.

Once I put on my blue dress and red headband, I went downstairs to meet my family in the living room. I almost walked out the door without the large plate of cookies for the potluck, but I remembered it just in time to see Pop carrying the plate behind me.

The five of us walked through our neighborhood with everyone else, all moving in the direction of the park. Bobby and Buddy were on either side of me, talking excitedly about what events would take place today. There would be a potluck, carnival games, and live music. I was as excited as they were, since it would be the first holiday in a long time that we were all together as a family. Holidays had been especially hard without Buddy here, and I knew we were all happy he was back.

"I wish there were fireworks tonight," Bobby said. "I miss watching them."

"Me too," Pop said. "The war will be over soon and we won't have to ration things anymore."

It had been years since I had seen fireworks. We had to ration so many things for the war effort, and holidays like this made it hard to forget that we couldn't have everything we wanted.

"Just imagine," Bobby sighed, "a full breakfast with pancakes, syrup, eggs, and bacon! I miss bacon..."

"Same here." Buddy laughed.

"At least we still get to have a party, even if there aren't any fireworks," I chimed in. "Aren't you excited for that?" I looped my right arm through Bobby's.

"Yeah, I am. I just want the war to be over already."

"We all do, Bobby," Buddy said, holding out his arm for me. "It will be over soon."

We walked the rest of the way in silence, with me between my two brothers, our arms linked. We always used to walk that way when we were little. We used to try running like that, linked together. It never really worked as well as we hoped. I smiled at the memory as we approached the park.

The park was filled with people from all over town. There was Peggy's older sister Julie with her husband and baby boy. There was Daisy, Richard in his wheelchair, and Carla. There were the Devons, who owned the bakery I was going to buy. There were the Oakeys. And there was Henry. His back was turned to us, so he didn't notice me at first. I was glad, because I'm sure my eyes got wide. I wasn't as prepared to see him again as I had hoped. My heart skipped a beat, and that was strictly against the rules I had set. Henry and I were just friends, I reminded myself.

I let my eyes scan the crowd again to find Peggy and Marylin. I saw Marylin by the potluck table, so I took the cookies from Pop and walked over to her.

"Hey," I said when I reached the table.

"Oh hi, Dottie!" Marylin said with a smile. "I've been looking all over for you."

"Sorry, I just barely got here." I motioned to the plate of cookies in my hands. "Where am I supposed to put these?"

Marylin and I looked over the table a few times before we realized the dessert table was behind us. I walked over and set the cookies down. I lifted my eyes to see Henry making his way over to us.

I quickly turned around and grabbed Marylin's arm.

"All right, what do you want to do first?" I asked, already leading her away from the food.

"I was thinking we could go looking for the others and then decide."

"Okay, let's go find Peggy."

I forced myself not to look behind me where I knew Henry was walking aimlessly, trying to find us. I knew I was probably being rude, but I had to explain to Peggy and Marylin what my plan for the night was before I saw him. I couldn't have them trying to push us together the whole night when neither of us wanted that.

We finally found Peggy sitting on a picnic blanket with her family in the middle of the park. As soon as she saw us, she stood up and gave her father a kiss on the top of his head before running over to us.

The three of us hugged and said our hellos.

"Oh look," Peggy said. "There's Henry!" She looked at me, raised her eyebrows, and smiled.

I turned to see Henry walking toward us, waving happily.

I guess I wasn't going to have the chance to convince Peggy and Marylin not to say anything about our conversation from the other day. I could only hope they wouldn't say anything to embarrass me *or* Henry.

"Hello, ladies," Henry said when he got to us. "Happy Fourth of July!"

After greeting him, we noticed Jimmy on the other side of the lawn and walked over to him.

"I was just about to go get food," he said. "Do you all want to come?" We followed him back to the potluck tables and walked around, filling our plates as we made small talk.

"Are these your cookies, Dottie?" Henry shouted from the dessert table.

I laughed and nodded. "Yeah, they are."

"Perfect!" He grabbed two.

I squinted my eyes at him and shook my head. After all, the idea of the potluck was to bring everything we had together so there would be enough for everyone, *not* to take more than one cookie.

Henry saw me glaring at him and brought his finger to his lips in a 'shhh' gesture. I rolled my eyes. We both laughed, and I felt my heart skip a beat.

I quickly stopped myself and went back to choosing my food. *Just friends*, I reminded myself for what felt like the hundredth time.

Once we were done getting our food, we found a spot in the middle of the park and set out the blanket Marylin brought from her house. There were families and other groups of friends sitting on blankets all around us. I saw my parents sitting with the Andersons and Henry's parents over on the other side of the jungle gym. Most of the children were swinging around on the equipment instead of eating. Peggy pointed out her little sister, Abigail, who was showing some other girls her dress with a huge grin on her face.

"She's very proud of her 'new' dress," she told us. "Little does she know it used to be mine, and Julie's before that." We all chuckled. We all knew what it was like to get and give hand-me-downs.

"Hey, Henry," Jimmy said once we were all settled and eating our food. "Do you still want a tour of the university? If you want, I can show you around on Saturday."

Henry looked up at him with a surprised look in his eyes. "Oh yeah, that sounds perfect!"

"Do you still want to go into accounting?" Peggy asked him.

Henry nodded. "Yeah, I'm working at the refinery again, but my boss said I need to be working on a degree in order to get an accountant's job. So I'm thinking about going to school."

"That's so neat. I could never go to college. I don't have the patience for more school." Peggy started laughing. "I barely made it through high school."

"I'm the only reason you survived," I joked. Peggy didn't like school very much and I had to drag her to class most of the time, so the joke held some truth.

"My academic savior, Dorothy Banks everyone!" Peggy held out her hands as if presenting me in front of a crowd.

I laughed and pretended to bow.

"Honestly though," Margaret said. "The only reason any of us made it through math classes was Henry."

"True," said Jimmy.

"You all give me too much credit," Henry said, looking embarrassed. "You just needed the encouragement."

"And a human calculator," Jimmy said under his breath.

We all laughed at that, including Henry. He was shaking his head and smiling. He looked really happy. I was glad to see him smile like that. It wasn't the fake, plastered-on smile that he had been using since he got home. It was the genuine smile he used to wear constantly when we were younger. His green eyes lit up and he showed all of his teeth in a big grin. It was good to see it again.

I caught Peggy's eye. She looked at Henry and then looked back at me with her eyebrows raised. I quickly shook my head, silently begging her not to say or do anything. She must have understood because she narrowed her eyes and pursed her lips, then sat silently.

The five of us chatted about our week and finished eating, then decided to walk around the park together and see what there was to do.

It was finally a little cooler than it had been in the early afternoon, which was a welcome break from the suffocating heat of the last few weeks.

As we walked around the children's games and crowds, I was reminded of a Fourth of July when we were in junior high. Peggy and I were walking around, trying to find a game to play that didn't have a line of children patiently waiting for their turn. Marylin hadn't moved to Ashwood yet, or else she would have been with us too. Peggy and I saw Henry and Jimmy already in line at the fishing pond game, so we joined them. We each had a try at fishing out the best prize. Most prizes were small, metal cars and sweets and things like that, but a few of the prizes were bigger. Henry fished out a small stuffed teddy bear and gave it to me. Peggy tried to steal it from me for the rest of the night, but I wouldn't let go of it. I had misplaced it a few years later and could never manage to find it.

"Do you remember the teddy bear?" I asked.

Jimmy started laughing. "Don't remind me! I was stuck with two whining girls all night. I couldn't tell if you were fighting over the bear or over Henry!"

"It was definitely over the bear," Peggy joked. "Don't get me wrong, Henry, you're great and everything, but that bear was so cute! I wanted it all to myself."

"He gave it to me, fair and square," I said, patting Peggy on the shoulder as if consoling her.

"That's true, Peggy," Henry chimed in. "I did give the bear to Dot."

"I don't even know where it went," I admitted. "I wanted it so badly that night, but now I can't even find it!"

"You lost it?" Peggy cried. "How could you?" She sighed melodramatically.

"Now I guess I'll have to win some more prizes so everyone's happy!" Henry said.

He led us to the fishing pond game, which was right where it had been every Fourth of July since we were little. The game was run by the Devons. We didn't have to wait in line because the kids were all distracted by the new dunk tank a few booths away. I could hear them screaming and laughing as one of their friends was dropped into the water.

"Dorothy!" Mrs. Devon said happily as we approached. "How wonderful to see you!"

"Hello, Mrs. Devon! Happy Independence Day! Where's Mr. Devon?"

"He's not doing so well lately. I wasn't able to open the bakery last week because I had to stay at home with him."

"Oh my goodness. He's getting worse then."

"We're both just getting older and older. He can't move around like he used to, and he's too stubborn to use his cane. He fell last week and hasn't felt like himself since."

"I'm so sorry." I walked over to hug her. She was like a grandmother to me, and I hated seeing her so sad. I also hated to hear that Mr. Devon was feeling so poorly. The two of them had been my Grandma Jane's dearest friends until Grandma passed away. They were like part of the family, even years after Grandma Jane was gone.

"It will be all right. We're patient, and Richard just has to humble himself and start using his cane." Mrs. Devon smiled at all of us. "Are you here to play the game then?"

We all nodded.

"Perfect." Mrs. Devon stood up and made her way behind the curtain so she could give us prizes.

"Who's first?" Jimmy asked.

"You go," Henry said to him, nodding at the fishing poles sitting in a bucket next to the blue curtain.

Jimmy grabbed one and stepped up to the curtain. He swung the line of the makeshift pole over the curtain and we all waited. Finally, there was a tug from Mrs. Devon on the other side.

"I have a bite!" Jimmy cried, making Marylin laugh, then pulled the pole so the prize came up over the curtain. It was a stuffed bunny, with white fur and blue eyes. Jimmy took it off the fishing line and handed it to Marylin. "Now, don't you girls start fighting over this. It's for Marylin."

They smiled at each other. "It's perfect," Marylin said under her breath.

I looked away quickly, feeling as if I had intruded on a private moment. I felt eyes on me, and when I looked up again, I saw Henry looking at me. As soon as he noticed me looking back, he looked down at his shoes.

"My turn!" Peggy said, grabbing a pole from the bucket. She waited for less time than Jimmy had and fished out a princess crown. It was made out of paper and had glitter all over it. "Perfect." Peggy placed the crown on her head and then nodded with satisfaction, which sent glitter falling down her face.

We all laughed.

"Henry, now you have to fish something out for Dot, for old time's sake," Peggy said.

I saw Henry's eyes flick over to me before they settled on Peggy again. "You won't try and steal her prize?"

"No, I already have my crown. That's all I need." She waved and posed like Princess Elizabeth.

"All right then, one prize for Miss Dorothy, coming right up!" Henry grabbed the pole from Peggy and stepped in front of the curtain. "Now, Mrs. Devon, this is for Dottie, so make it good."

I shook my head and held back a laugh. I missed this side of Henry. He used to always joke around like this.

Henry looked at me and smiled, then threw the fishing line over the curtain. A few seconds later, there was a tug on the line and Henry pulled it back, revealing the prize.

It was a teddy bear.

I gasped and brought my hands to my mouth in surprise. Henry started laughing, then Jimmy, Peggy, and Marylin joined in.

Henry brought me the bear and said, "Your prize, m'lady."

"Thank you sir," I said, curtsying. I couldn't stop smiling. This is what I had been missing. Henry was back, and he was acting like himself again. This is what I had been dreaming about during the long years he was away.

I surprised myself with that realization. I had imagined this moment, with Henry in front of me again, the two of us smiling and laughing and joking around like before. I had wanted this for so long. I thought I had just wanted my friend back, but it was more than that. There was a part of me that loved him, and always had. I was terrified to give in to that part of me, because I knew our friendship could be completely ruined if I did. I thought back to the day Henry left: the day I decided that in order to protect the both of us from heartache, I needed to close my heart.

October 21, 1942
The day before Henry left for the war

I sat alone in the living room of my house, listening to the radio and drawing in my sketchbook. I always did that when I felt nervous, or sad, or angry, and I had a mixture of those feelings that day.

My friend was leaving me. My Henry was leaving me. No, not *my* Henry. He wasn't mine. He was going to war, and I didn't know when or even if he'd come home.

I shuddered at the thought. I couldn't bear it if he didn't come home. It was much better to hope for a 'when,' not an 'if.' It surprised me how much it hurt to think that. If I was already mourning his possible death before he had even left for Europe, this was going to be very difficult for me.

I shook those dark thoughts out of my head and continued sketching. I looked out the window to seek inspiration for a new subject to draw when I saw him: Henry Oakey, walking up the sidewalk to my house.

I set my sketchbook under the pillow next to me and stood up to open the door. I threw it open right as Henry reached up to knock. I must have caught him by surprise because he stumbled backward.

"Don't fall!" I said, laughing. I grabbed his hand to steady him. "How are you doing?"

"I—" he started. "I'm nervous, honestly. I keep running around, doing small errands and things because I can't concentrate on just one task."

"Was coming to see me an item on your check-list?"

"Actually, it wasn't. I was planning on saying goodbye to you and your family tonight, but I had to come see you now."

"You had to?" What on earth was he talking about? Henry was so dramatic sometimes, it made me laugh.

"Yeah, Dot. I had to. I can't go to war without you knowing this." Henry took both of my hands in his. Both of our hands shook.

"Knowing what? Henry, what are you talking about?"

"I'm in love with you, Dottie. I have been for a long time."

I stared at him. Henry loved me. Henry loved *me*. Henry *loved* me!

That's when I started to panic. If Henry was in love with me, that made it so much harder for the both of us to be apart. He was my best friend, and I didn't want him to go away. If he loved me, he didn't want to be away from me. What were we going to do? What *could* we do?

"Henry, I..." I started speaking, then I realized what was happening. Henry pulled me closer and gave me a look that pierced me to the center. I swallowed. Was he going to kiss me? It looked like he was. I didn't know if I could do this. I knew I was in danger at that moment, though not in any physical danger. I was safe with him. I was only in danger of losing my heart to Henry Oakey, the soldier who would be leaving for the war in the morning and who I wouldn't see again for who knew how long.

And so I turned my head.

Henry noticed, and quickly stepped away.

"I—" he said.

"I'm sorry, Henry," I said, now feeling sadder than ever. "Let me explain."

"It's all right, Dot. I just wanted you to know. G'bye."

"Henry, wait!"

But he was already gone.

I shut the door behind him sadly and ran to my room. I sat behind my bedroom door, hugging my legs to my chest.

What had I done? My eyes welled with tears as I pictured Henry's face after I had turned aside. He had looked so shocked, so sad, so hurt.

I did that to him. I knew it was all my fault. I turned away not because I didn't love him, but because I didn't know how to deal with the pain of losing him, either for a few years or forever. The more I thought about it, the more I regretted not kissing him. Now I might never know what it felt like to kiss Henry Oakey.

That's when I really started crying.

I fell asleep like that, crying into my pillow and thinking of my best friend—my Henry—going off to a war with an unforeseeable end. I knew I had broken his heart and my own by turning away.

ELIZA STEMMONS

July 4, 1945
The present

Dorothy

I still felt guilty for breaking his heart, for being the cause of that hurt look in his eyes as he stepped away from me for the last time.

That's the real reason I didn't write. I had no idea how to apologize for what I'd done. I wasn't even sure there was an apology appropriate for the situation.

"I'm sorry I turned away, Henry. I wanted to kiss you, but I was too afraid of losing you to let myself admit it."

It felt ridiculous trying to think up an apology.

Part of me was glad to read Henry's letter, to see that he too wanted to forget that day. The other part of me never wanted to forget it. That day, everything could have changed. If I had kissed him back, we would have written each other letters during the war. I would have written to him once a week, like I had written to my brother. I would have helped encourage him when he was feeling sad or lonely. We could have laughed at what happened here at home or there in Europe. I could have done so much. When he finally came home, I would have been waiting for him: searching for him in his uniform, standing out from the crowd. We would have kissed at the train station, not caring who saw us because we were finally together again. Our relationship would be stronger than ever. We could have been going steady by now and planning for our future. If only I had ignored my fears and let him kiss me.

I had to stop myself from thinking about things that might have been. I brought myself back to the present, where Marylin was now fishing for a prize for Jimmy.

"Hey, are you all right?" Henry asked, coming to stand next to me.

I looked at him out of the corner of my eye and nodded. "I'm fine."

"You sure? You look a little sad all of a sudden."

"I'm just getting nostalgic. I'm remembering all of the good times we had when we were kids." I smiled, trying to conceal my true feelings.

I had to be more careful. I couldn't keep remembering things that made my feelings for Henry stronger. I had to respect his decision to forget what could have happened if I had kissed him that day. We weren't meant to be anything more than we were now. *Just friends.*

I hugged the small teddy bear to my chest, then put it in my dress pocket, which was the perfect size to fit the bear.

I looked up to see that Marylin had just fished out a toy car from behind the curtain. She handed it to Jimmy with a huge smile on her face, and I felt a pang of jealousy in my heart. The look Jimmy gave Marylin was very similar to the look Henry had given me on the day he left. I hadn't seen it since.

Marylin held the fishing pole out to me and I stepped up and took it from her.

"Catch something good for me, Dottie," Henry said behind me. I looked back at him and grinned. He was standing there with his arms folded, as confident as ever, and he was smirking at me. He raised one of his eyebrows, and I blushed. As soon as I felt my face heat up, I turned around, praying that he didn't notice.

I stepped up to the curtain with the fishing pole and threw the line over. I waited for a few seconds before I felt the tug on the pole from Mrs. Devon behind the curtain.

I pulled on the line and the prize came tumbling over the curtain. It was a toy soldier.

My eyes went wide. I looked to Henry to see his reaction.

He looked at the toy without expression for a few moments, then looked at me. There was something in his eyes, but I couldn't tell what he was trying to tell me.

"Look Henry!" Peggy said. "He looks just like you! He's in uniform and everything!"

Henry's face fell.

"Oh, how neat! It's a soldier, just like you!" Jimmy said.

I took the soldier off the line and held it in my hands. He was blond with green eyes, just like Henry. He fit in both of my hands perfectly. I held it out to Henry, looking at him carefully. I didn't know if he would want it.

He took it gently from my hand, looked me directly in the eyes, gave me a quick one-sided smile that I suspected he didn't mean, then walked toward where the band was setting up.

"Let's go," he said over his shoulder as he left. He walked quickly and didn't wait for us to follow.

"What was that?" Peggy asked.

"Why'd he leave?" Jimmy wondered.

"Guys, he's going through some hard things right now," I said. "Let him be, okay?"

Then I ran after Henry.

I finally caught up to him in front of where the band was setting up to play.

"Henry!" I called out, hoping he heard me over the crowd.

He looked over his shoulder quickly and, when he saw it was me, he stopped walking.

"Are you all right?" I asked him.

Henry just nodded. His lips were pursed. I knew he was hiding something.

"Here," I said, taking his hand in mine. I had touched his hand since he had been home, but this time something was different. My heart started beating faster and faster, and I was glad the sunlight was dimming so Henry couldn't see my face flush. "Come sit with me."

I led Henry away from the crowd that had gathered. There would be music and dancing soon, so the majority of people were near the stage, leaving the field empty.

I found the same bench where we spent lunch a few weeks ago and sat down. Henry followed my lead and placed himself next to me.

"It surprised me, that's all," Henry said. "I wasn't expecting it." He held up the toy soldier.

"I understand." I realized Henry's hand was still in mine, and my face flushed even more. Even though it felt new and unfamiliar holding his hand, I left it there. I told myself it was so Henry knew I was there for him.

"I'm okay though," he said. "Honestly. I don't feel like I'm going to have an episode. I know that's why you ran after me." He turned away from me to look at the people gathering in front of the makeshift stage.

"I ran after you because you looked disappointed. You looked really sad, and I wanted to make sure you were okay. That's why, not because I thought you were going to start losing control or anything." I hadn't gone after him to make sure he was safe and didn't make a fool of himself for forgetting he wasn't in the war anymore. I went after him because I couldn't bear to have him walk away from me again with that sadness in his eyes. He looked exactly like that Henry who walked away from me years ago with the same hurt look on his face.

Henry opened his mouth and then closed it, like he had wanted to say something and then stopped himself.

"What is it, Henry?" I brought my other hand to where ours were still clasped together and held his hand in both of mine.

"The truth is," Henry started, "what Jimmy said really hurt. I'm not a soldier. I'm not like that. I don't think I ever was."

I thought back to earlier. I remembered Jimmy said something about the toy soldier being exactly like Henry.

"What do you mean?"

"Look at this toy." Henry showed me the toy and gestured to its face. "Look how fearless and heroic he looks. I'm not like that. Not at all..."

I studied his face for a moment before speaking. "Henry, you are one of the bravest people I know. It wasn't part of your plan to be a soldier, but you went anyway because you knew it was the right thing to do. That took so much bravery." I paused for a moment in thought. "Remember how scared we all were when the U.S. entered the war? Remember how terrified I was when Buddy left? You comforted me. You were always brave and hopeful, and I still see that in you. You are just as brave and heroic as any other soldier in the war, maybe even more."

He took a deep breath and frowned instead. "I'm not a hero."

"Of course you are, Henry." How could I help him see what I saw in him? "You fought for your country and you saved people's lives."

Henry was shaking his head back and forth. "I didn't always. I left people behind, Dot. People I could have saved. I left them behind to save myself."

I thought for a minute before I responded. I doubted that Henry saved himself out of selfishness. He was one of the most selfless people I knew.

"Sometimes heroes have to make hard decisions like that. Sometimes we have to save ourselves before we can save other people. Other times we need to let other people save us. We can't always be the hero." I bit my lip, hoping I was saying the right things. "You survived, and we're all extremely grateful that you did. I don't know what I would have done if you hadn't..." I held my tongue after that, afraid of admitting exactly how devastated I would have been.

At my words, Henry relaxed. He lifted his head up a little more and looked at my face again. For the first time that night, I noticed there were tears in his eyes. I had a sudden urge to wipe them away, but I didn't. This time, the expression on his face encouraged me to go on.

"I see you as a man that keeps going no matter what. I see you as my best friend, someone who has always been there for me ever since we were little and who stood up for me when the older kids made fun of my pigtails." He almost smiled at that. "You're still Henry, and you're wonderful. I know you saw horrid things in Europe. I can't even imagine what you went through. I know you keep reliving those things over and over again in your dreams without explanation. I don't understand exactly how you feel, or why. But I want you to know that I'm here to listen, just like I told you the other day. I want to help you, even if the only way I can do that is to listen and be here for you like you are for me."

That's when he hugged me. Even sitting down, he was much taller than I was, and I was drowned in his embrace.

I let my arms wrap around him, and I nestled my head closer to his chest. I breathed in his scent of pine trees and spearmint and let myself relax in his arms. I could feel his heart beating where my head lay on his chest, and I could feel my own heart beating in sync with his.

And I knew. I knew this was where I was supposed to be. I felt like I was home in his arms. What I felt was more than just a physical attraction. It was even more than just an emotional one. It was so much deeper, as if everything that had happened before this moment had led us to this embrace.

I loved him.

The thought shocked me back into reality. The wave of happiness left and in its wake was only sadness. I was living in a fantasy where Henry and I could be together. In this, the real world, Henry had moved on. He stopped thinking about me that way long ago, and I was stuck being in love with my best friend.

I scooted away from Henry on the bench. "Will you be okay?" I tried to bring the conversation back to where it was before that hug, but I knew my voice was shaking.

"Of course. I'll be fine. Thanks a million, Dottie. You're a great friend." He stood up and put the toy soldier in his pocket. "Should we go find the others?"

I nodded and stood up as the knife of reality sunk even deeper into my heart. *A great friend.* That line repeated itself over and over in my head as we walked back to where the music was already playing and the dancing had begun.

I looked around for Peggy, or Marylin, or Jimmy. *A great friend.* Or Buddy, or Bobby, or my parents. *A great friend.* Then I looked back to Henry. *A great friend.*

I heard the intro to the song. "It's Been a Long, Long Time". *A great friend.* I saw Henry hold his hand out to me and heard him ask me to dance. *A great friend.*

I heard myself say that I felt sick all of a sudden and that I was going home. I started on my way, only to bump right into Mrs. Devon, who was taking down the fishing booth.

"Dorothy, dear, why so pale?" she asked, holding me steady then checking my forehead for a temperature with the back of her hand.

"I don't feel very well; I'm on my way home."

"Oh dear, I hope it's not anything bad."

"I'll be fine, Mrs. Devon. I just need some rest, I think."

"Yes, dear. Go home and go to sleep. If you feel better in the morning, come over to the bakery. I want to discuss something with you."

I nodded. "All right." I saw the pile of toys and prizes behind her. "Mrs. Devon?"

"Yes, dear?"

"Could I leave this with the rest of your toys?" I pulled the stuffed bear from my pocket and held it up to her.

"Of course, Dorothy. Did you not like it?"

"I just think someone else will appreciate it more than I will." I gave her a small smile.

"All right, dear." She gestured behind her to the pile of toys.

I set the teddy bear right on the top of the pile, said goodbye to Mrs. Devon, then left the park. I walked home quickly, trying to hold in my tears. I would always be just 'a good friend' to Henry. He had moved on, and I had to as well.

As soon as I got home I went straight to bed. Hopefully the pain in my heart would be gone by morning.

CHAPTER 19

July 4, 1945

Henry

Where in the world had she run off to? Now I was the worried one. Dottie had left me in the middle of the crowd of people with absolutely no explanation, right after I had asked her to dance.

Immediately after she ran away, I started to follow her. She had looked scared. Her eyes had gone wide when she looked at me, and I couldn't figure out why.

I could no longer see her in the crowd of people. I knew she was probably running home, so I started running that way.

That's when I saw it. The pile of toys from Mrs. Devon's fishing game was a few yards in front of me, with a teddy bear right on top. The teddy bear I had won for her less than an hour before. I felt a pang in my heart. What was it doing there? Why did she leave it?

Mrs. Devon wasn't anywhere around the pile of toys, so I had to make a hasty decision. I left my toy soldier on the pile and took the teddy bear off the top. I didn't want the soldier anyway, even after Dot told me that I was like the soldier because I was a hero. I didn't want anything to remind me of what I had done during the war.

I left the toy there and held the teddy bear in one hand as I ran to Dot's house. I had to know why Dot had left it. I also had to know why she left in such a hurry. She had mumbled something about not feeling well before she ran off. I had to make sure she was okay.

I smiled at the memory of her running after me earlier. She said she had to make sure I wasn't sad or angry. I realized that Dot understood that I wasn't crazy or in danger. She understood that what was happening to me was real and that it terrified me. She truly saw me. She saw that I was the same old Henry from high school. I was the same person, just a little older and with more life experience. She saw me as a hero.

I was glad that she knew a piece of what was going on. My other friends had no idea about the episodes. They probably thought I was going crazy. They didn't know what Dot knew. Maybe if I told them they would be able to help me too.

As I finally reached Dot's house, I pushed those thoughts aside for a later time and knocked on the door a few times. No answer. I knocked again. Still nothing.

After a few more tries, I gave up. I just hoped Dot was okay. She looked sad and almost scared when I asked her to dance. It was odd. She looked like she had in my dream, the one where she told me to leave her in the forest while everything was burning around her. That image replayed in my mind, and I felt scared for Dot. I knew it was illogical since she was probably inside her house, safe and sound, but I couldn't push the thought away.

I didn't want to leave her feeling sad, but if she wouldn't answer there was nothing I could do to help until the morning.

She told me earlier that sometimes we can't save other people because we have to save ourselves first. Sometimes we can't be the hero.

I walked home dwelling on that single thought.

I guess I couldn't be her hero tonight.

The next morning I still couldn't get her face out of my mind, so I called her house. Her mom answered.

"Hello?" she said.

"Oh hi, Mrs. Banks. It's Henry."

"Hello Henry!"

"Yes, sorry it's so early. I just wanted to know if Dottie was there?"

"She's not. She went out to talk to Mrs. Devon about the bakery, I believe."

"Oh. Did she seem okay? She wasn't sick or anything?"

"No, she seemed fine. Why do you ask?"

"She went home last night feeling a little sick, I think. She didn't tell me what was wrong, but she looked like she didn't feel very well."

"When she gets home, I'll make sure she's all right, Henry. It was very kind of you to call. I'll let her know that you wanted to make sure she was okay. Thanks for your concern."

"You're welcome, Mrs. Banks. Thank you so much."

"Goodbye, Henry. Have a nice day."

"Goodbye."

I hung up.

I sighed a breath of relief. At least Dottie was okay. For that, I was very thankful.

CHAPTER 20

July 5, 1945

Dorothy

I woke up feeling much better. Henry was out of my mind, and I was prepared to focus on the bakery and my future. It was still early in the morning when I left to talk to Mrs. Devon, but I was used to the early hours of the morning. I actually preferred the peaceful silence just before everyone woke up and just after the birds started chirping. I rode my bike to the bakery and enjoyed the stillness for a moment.

The bakery hadn't changed a bit since I was little. It was a beautiful red brick building with white shutters that had to be painted every few years. I remember painting those shutters lots of times with Buddy and Bobby, the Devons, and my Grandma Jane.

With that memory in mind, I walked through the door. I could smell a fresh batch of cookies and the sour smell of yeast from the bread baking.

I found Mrs. Devon in the back of the bakery, where she was busy kneading bread dough.

"Good morning, Mrs. Devon!" I said.

She looked up, still working the dough with her hands. "Hello, dear! Come, help me knead this bread while we chat."

I washed my hands quickly, then took the other half of the bread dough from the bowl and started kneading it. This was always my favorite part of making bread. My Grandma Jane used to tell me that kneading dough was the best way to get out all of your frustrations and confusions. I understood that more every day.

"I told you that Harold's health has been getting worse," Mrs. Devon started. "He keeps losing his balance and falling, and the doctor in Pittsburgh told him that he needs to take it easy. He can't be on his own anymore." She looked up from her bread dough and turned toward me.

"I'm so sorry, Mrs. Devon." I didn't know how to adequately tell her how bad I felt. Before my Grandma Jane died, it had been the same. She hadn't been able to walk well, so she moved in with us. We helped her all that we could, but it had been a hard time for all of us. She lost her strength and slowly her memory faded away too. She died right before my 10th birthday. I missed her often, but I knew she was watching over me in some way. Every time I made bread, I remembered everything she used to say when we baked together, all of her mannerisms and her quiet sense of humor. I saw Grandma Jane in Mrs. Devon, which is why I felt so sad for her when I heard about her husband.

"I know you're sorry, Dorothy," Mrs. Devon continued. "You have been such a help these past few years, and we are so grateful you want to take over. This bakery means so much to us." She gestured around the room with her floury hands. "I don't know where we would be right now if we didn't know that you'll carry on in our place."

I smiled. "I'm the one who should be grateful, Mrs. Devon. You're making my dream come true."

"Dorothy, would you consider taking over earlier than we had planned so I can take better care of Harold? It would be as soon as possible, maybe at the end of the month."

I was speechless. I thought through my savings quickly, making sure I had enough money to buy the bakery.

"Of course I will!"

"Are you able to buy the building?"

"I'll look through my savings to make sure, but I believe I am. If not already, then I'm very close."

"Thank you so much, Dorothy. It's so hard on us for me to be both here and there. I come here so early in the morning that I can't even make him breakfast, and then I have to close up before the afternoon rush in order to make him supper."

"I would be thrilled and honored to help you, Mrs. Devon. It will help me out too."

She clapped her hands together, sending a poof of flour flying around her face. "Oh good. Harold will be overjoyed! He's been worried I'm spreading myself too thin." She laughed. "He's almost right."

We put the bread dough into separate pans to rise. We talked and laughed, both thrilled at our new arrangement. As we washed up, Mrs. Devon cleared her throat and said, "I saw you and that Oakey boy at the carnival. I haven't seen him in years. He just got back from Europe, if I'm not mistaken?"

I nodded, swallowing my sudden embarrassment at her mentioning Henry. "Yes, he got back the same day that Buddy did."

"You two were always such good friends. I remember the two of you running around town together when you were practically still in diapers." She laughed. "He's grown up into a handsome young man, hasn't he?"

I was glad I was facing away from her when she said that. My eyes were wide and I almost dropped the pan I was drying. "Yes, he has," I admitted, hoping the pain I felt didn't come through in my words.

"You two would make a fine couple."

At that, I almost gasped. I didn't know what to say. "We're not... um..." I stumbled over the words. "We're just friends," I managed to get out, angry with myself for repeating the words that had broken my heart just the night before.

"I see." Mrs. Devon approached the sink where I was drying the dishes. "You'll find someone wonderful, I'm sure of it. You deserve it."

I smiled at her, hoping that her words were true. I needed to believe my own words: *We're just friends.*

"You look so much like Jane when you smile. She would be so proud of you."

Mrs. Devon hugged me, and it was like I was with Grandma Jane again.

Mrs. Devon stepped back and looked around the kitchen with a bittersweet look in her eyes.

"We'll leave all of these things here for you to use. I have no need for them at home." She pointed out the shelves full of cookie sheets, bread pans, mixing bowls, and measuring cups. "You can do whatever you like with the front. It has needed a new look for some time now, and as the new owner you have complete control over the style. I suggest hiring someone to stay in front during store hours to take orders and to make sure no one comes into the kitchen. Harold used to do that before he got too sick, and it has been very difficult for me to do both jobs now that he's at home all the time. You can manage everything else, I'm sure. You've been running your own business from home since you were a young little thing."

We both laughed. I could hardly contain my excitement about how soon the bakery would be mine. Our conversation about Henry was pushed to the back of my mind, and I felt much better.

I helped Mrs. Devon finish up with her work for the morning, then hurried home to work on my plans for the bakery.

When I walked in, Bud and Bobby were sitting on the living room floor, solving a jigsaw puzzle.

"I'm going to take over the bakery at the end of this month!" I exclaimed.

"That's amazing. Congratulations!" Bud stood up to hug me.

I sat down and joined them, putting my planning aside for later.

"That's great, Dottie!" Bobby gave me a pat on the back.

"I just have to figure everything out sooner than I had thought."

"How close are you to putting together a plan?" Buddy asked as he placed a piece down in the middle of the puzzle.

"Not very close, honestly. Mrs. Devon told me that I have free rein over the place since I'll be the owner. There's a lot to plan. I know I want to decorate the storefront differently, but now that the building will be mine soon, I need to decide how. I just need to work faster than I expected. I think I have enough saved up to buy the place, but there will only be a little extra to redecorate, so I need to figure out how I'm going to do it on a budget." Just saying everything I needed to do out loud like that made me realize how much I really did have to do before I'd be ready.

"Well, at least you have a start." Bobby held a puzzle piece up to his face to closely examine it. "Bud and I don't even have jobs."

I turned to Buddy. "Aren't you going to work at the refinery?" He had wanted to work there before he left for the war, and I assumed he still did.

"No." He shook his head. "I don't know. I don't know what I'm doing anymore."

"Hmm." There weren't many other options in town. Most of the men worked at the refinery and had for years. The women worked in the school or in the shops on mainstreet. I couldn't think of anywhere Bud would be inclined to work. No wonder he was confused.

"I don't want to work there either," Bobby practically whispered.

I found a piece of the puzzle and placed it in its spot. "I could use some help with the bakery once it opens. One of you could help me out." It was perfect. I would need to hire someone to run the front of the store like Mrs. Devon said, and both of them needed jobs.

"What would we do?" Bobby eyed me suspiciously.

I laughed at him and reached to ruffle his hair like I always used to, but he ducked his head and I missed.

"I need some brave soul to run the front of the store so no one interrupts me while I'm baking. It's an extremely important job."

"You can count me out on that one, sis," Bud said. "I need to start looking for a more "grown-up" job. No offense."

I stuck my tongue out at him and then laughed.

"It's probably not as exciting as you make it sound." Bobby rolled his eyes and shook his head.

"Oh, it will be very exciting. And whoever gets the job will get free cookies." I had to give Bobby some incentive to take the job, didn't I? He needed work experience, and I needed help. Bud could easily find a different job, since he had the experience of being in the army to boost his resumé.

"I'll do it!" Bobby agreed quickly. I knew the free cookies would make him want the job. I laughed.

"Perfect! You can start as soon as I buy the place. You can work full-time in the summer and part-time come fall. You'll be my official assistant."

"One who gets to taste test new recipes."

"You already get to do that as my brother."

"But now I'll have a title. And you'll pay me, right?"

"I guess." I acted reluctant.

Bobby looked shocked. "I thought it was a job?"

I smiled.

"You tease." He punched me in the shoulder. Hard.

"Ow!"

"Hey, cut it out, you two," Buddy said without even looking up from the puzzle.

Bobby and I punched Bud in both of his shoulders. He looked at us threateningly and the two of us ran out of the room. Bud chased us around the house, trying to punch us back, but he couldn't catch us.

We ended up back in the living room on the couch, laughing and breathing heavily from all the running.

"You two still act like you're in elementary school." Bud could hardly catch his breath long enough to string his words together.

"So?" Bobby asked.

We all broke out into laughter.

"I'm so glad we're all together again," I said. "I missed this." I was sitting in the middle, so I put my arms around both of my brothers.

"I missed it too." Bobby sighed.

"I'm glad to be home." Buddy softly punched each of us in the shoulder.

We laughed, then sat back down on the ground to finish the puzzle.

CHAPTER 21

July 7, 1945

Henry

The next two days went by in a blur. I went to work, came home, and spent time with my family. Everything was almost back to normal, until I started to fall asleep each night. Something stopped me from being able to fall asleep, and I knew I was afraid I would dream about the war. I didn't want to see it again. I couldn't bear to see Dot or Jimmy or anyone else in pain. I felt fine when I was awake because I knew I was in control, but I couldn't control what happened in my dreams. I didn't know how to sleep without dreaming about Belgium. I stayed awake each night until I couldn't keep my eyes open any longer. In the late hours of the night, I would finally drift off into a restless sleep and wake up exhausted in the morning.

Dad had been searching in the local library for every possible piece of information on flashbacks, nightmares, and other similar problems. After hours of research, he discovered the connection to the man who wrote the article that Dad had read years ago. There was a professor at the University of Pittsburgh who helped the psychologist perform the research on veterans. It seemed like fate was working to help us figure this out.

On Saturday, Jimmy and I planned to go into Pittsburgh to tour the university. While I was there, I would be stopping by Professor Adams' office in the medical department.

I planned to tell Jimmy what was going on with me before the day was over. I figured if anyone besides my family and Dot deserved to know, it was him. I was going to tell him everything too, about the soldier that looked like him, about the dream I had where he was yelling at me, and maybe even my dreams about Dot. I needed to tell someone, or these things were going to eat me alive.

Jimmy picked me up early on Saturday morning and we drove to the train station in Riverside. After a few minutes of small talk, I decided now was as good a time as any to tell him what was going on.

"Jimmy, I have to apologize for the way I've been acting lately," I said.

"Apologize?"

"I haven't been the easiest person to be around since I got home, and I have been a horrible friend. Especially to you."

"You're definitely different than you were before." Jimmy chuckled awkwardly.

"I know, and I wanted to explain why." And so I told him. I told him what happened to me in Belgium when I got injured. I told him how hard it was to adjust to being home after seeing so many horrible things. I told him about Jones and Davies and how the first time I saw Jimmy after coming home, it was like I had seen Davies' ghost in front of me.

Jimmy stayed silent throughout my explanation, nodding and listening. I talked the entire drive, filling him in on everything. We got to the train station just a few minutes before our train left to go into Pittsburgh.

Once we were on the train, I told Jimmy about my dreams.

I started with the dream about him, and how horrible it had been to see one of my best friends die in front of me without being able to do anything.

"Golly, that's terrible, Henry. No wonder you haven't been yourself."

"I just hate remembering what happened, and I see it over and over again in my dreams. I don't like talking about the war because it feels like my only break from it is when I'm awake. And even then sometimes I have episodes where I feel like I'm back there."

I told him about what had happened at work, when Alex saw me drop to the ground and reach for my gun.

"I feel like there's no escape from it. Everyone wants to remind me that I did our country a great service. That I fought valiantly and made them proud. But I don't want to remember. I wish I could just forget it all, or at least stop being reminded of it every time I close my eyes."

"Who else knows about this?"

"I told my parents a few days ago. Dot knows too."

"Do you still love her?"

I turned to him in surprise.

"What?"

"Dot. Do you still love her?"

"I..." I didn't know how to respond to that. I had never told Jimmy about my feelings, even before the war. Dot was the only one I had told, and she hadn't taken it all that well.

"Come on, Henry, I've known for years. You were always happier when she was around, and you used to talk about her all the time: 'Dot said this,' or 'Dot thinks that.' It was pretty obvious." Jimmy chuckled and shook his head at me.

I sat there with my mouth open.

"So?" Jimmy sat, waiting for my answer.

When I realized he wasn't going to give up until I gave him one, I told him about the dreams I had about Dot. I finished by telling him about the last dream I had, where Dot took a bullet for me.

"Wow. That was quite a bit worse than the other ones," he said after I finished. "I think it's safe to say that your feelings for her are the same as they were when you left."

"I don't know. I can't love her like that anymore. I see those dreams as a warning. Like they're telling me that if I can't protect her, I can't be with her. I'm terrified of what would happen to our friendship if I let myself love her."

"That's just sad."

"I know. But it feels right. I don't think I can be with her if I'm like this. I feel unpredictable. Dangerous, even. That night at Daisy's, when I yelled at you? She looked at me like she was afraid of me. I can't put her through that."

"You'll get better though, right? My father never has flashbacks or dreams or anything like you do, and he served in a war too. Lots of people who served in the Great War seem fine. Same with Bud."

"I don't know if I'll ever get better. I don't know if there's a name for what's happening. I've heard of other soldiers who have problems like this, but I've never heard of one recovering. I don't even know if it's possible."

"Don't give up hope, Henry. You'll be fine. You'll figure it out."

Jimmy was finally looking at me like we were friends again. I could see the trust we once had returning in the smile on his face.

It felt good to talk about this with people. I never expected that talking about something so horrible would feel so liberating.

"Jimmy, have you heard of Professor Adams from the medical department?"

"The name sounds familiar, but I don't know him."

"My dad said he might have access to some information about my... condition. Could we take a break during our tour to go to his office?"

"You bet! If he has answers, we have to go find him. You need to get better. I know you can."

I smiled again at his encouragement. Jimmy was always so hopeful and idealistic. It was a welcome attitude when my thoughts had been so dark and pessimistic lately.

Once we got to the station by the university, we left the train and started walking.

"This is the University of Pittsburgh!" Jimmy said after a few blocks. He held his hands out in front of him, showing me the entrance.

The gates rose up in front of us, looking both imposing and inviting. I wanted to enter, even though I was nervous to do so. I knew it would be hard if I chose this, but it was what I had wanted to do for a long time. Why should I let a few nerves get in my way?

After taking a deep breath, I followed Jimmy through the gate, and we started our tour.

Jimmy showed me the building where his science classes were held. He had always wanted to become a scientist, and he gave me a tour of the building with pride in his eyes.

He showed me the library, the student center, and a few other buildings. Finally we got to the business building.

"This is where you would be, my friend."

I stared at the building looming over me. It was huge. "Can we go inside?"

"Yeah, let's go."

We walked inside the front door and explored a little bit. Eventually, we found an empty accounting classroom and I snuck a peek inside.

"This is great," I said. The idea of coming here was really growing on me. I wanted to, but some small part of me felt it wouldn't be a good idea. I knew anything could cause me to have an episode like I experienced at work, and I didn't want it to happen here.

"So, do you like it here?" Jimmy asked.

"Yeah, I do. I really do."

"Perfect. Well, that's all I had planned to show you today. Do you want to go find Professor Adams?"

I nodded. "Yes. Let's go find him."

We went back to the science building again. Jimmy took me straight to the medical wing. We quickly found an office with a plaque on the door reading 'Professor Adams' and I knocked quietly.

An old man with scraggly white hair and glasses opened the door.

"Hello, young men. How can I help you?"

"We're, well, *I'm* looking for Professor Adams," I said.

"That would be me," the man said.

"My name is Henry. Do you have a minute to talk? I have a few questions I need to ask you." I silently prayed that he would be a patient man. I also prayed that he didn't find my request odd.

"Of course." Professor Adams gestured to a sandwich and coffee cup on his desk. "As long as you don't mind me eating while we talk. I just started my lunch break."

"Not at all. Thank you."

He motioned for us to come into his office. It was slightly disorganized, with lots of books and papers scattered on the desk and thrown onto the bookshelves haphazardly. After scanning the room, I sat down next to Jimmy in a large red armchair in front of the professor's desk.

"Now, what can I help you with?" The professor sat down in the chair on the other side of the desk and took a small bite of his sandwich. He looked at me through his spectacles while he chewed. The situation would have struck me as funny if I hadn't been so anxious for answers.

I spoke up, my voice shaking slightly. "Professor, my father found your name in the library under the citations for an article about the psychological effects of war on soldiers."

"Ah yes. I helped with some research on shell shock after the Great War. Terrible thing, terrible thing."

"Shell shock?"

"Yes, it's the condition of the mind when unresolved trauma floats around and impairs mental processes. It stops one from moving past the trauma, and it negatively impacts one's health."

I looked at Jimmy. This was it. Shell shock. The name sounded just as horrible as the symptoms.

"Do you know if there's a cure?" I prayed that he knew of one. If he didn't, I wasn't sure what I would do.

"To our current knowledge, the only cure is time. We are still studying the effects of various traumas on the human mind."

"Oh." I tried not to look as devastated as I felt.

"Why do you ask?"

I looked at Jimmy. He nodded toward Professor Adams.

I breathed in deeply and started explaining yet again.

"I served in the war in Europe and just got home a few weeks ago. Since coming home, I keep having moments where I feel like I'm in the war again, and I lose control or I get disoriented. I also have nightmares that are sort of like flashbacks to what I experienced in the war, but some of the details are different. Sometimes people from home are the soldiers or the dialogue is different from what was actually said." I tried to avoid glancing at Jimmy when I remembered the dream I had where he accused me of being selfish and leaving my friends to die. "When I wake up from these dreams, I feel sick or...like I can't breathe. I'm worried that something is wrong with me. I feel like I'm going crazy." I held my hands together in my lap tightly.

"Interesting." Professor Adams held his hands together on the desk and put his hand on his chin thoughtfully. At some point during our conversation, he had forgotten about his sandwich, which sat sadly on the plate in front of him. "All of this started after the war?"

I nodded.

"Many cases of this 'shell shock' occur after the patient—you must excuse my medical terminology—after the *soldier* experiences some sort of disturbing experience. Sometimes this includes an injury to the head. Other times the symptoms of shell shock appear without physical trauma. Whatever the trauma is refuses to leave the brain and appears to affect new memories. The soldiers that experience shell shock often suffer from flashbacks or nightmares like you have."

"So do you think that's what's wrong with me?"

"I believe it could be the cause of your symptoms, yes. Further observation would be needed to fully diagnose you, especially in regards to the physical symptoms you are experiencing. Do these dreams happen regularly?"

"Lately, I've been having dreams a few times a week, and my sleep is really restless even if I'm not dreaming."

"Many soldiers with shell shock suddenly experience intense fear and confusion while going about their day-to-day activities. Have you had any times like that?"

I thought back to the time at work where Alex saw me. I nodded.

Professor Adams was silent for a few moments. Jimmy and I looked at each other. Jimmy gave me a questioning glance, silently asking if I was okay. I nodded once and smiled slightly.

Professor Adams began to search his desk, then finally found a sheet of paper and a pen. He began to write.

"Henry, correct?"

I nodded.

"I want you to call this number. This is the psychologist I worked with to develop the research on veterans. He will know how to help you much better than I will. My area of expertise is the health of the body. He is much more versed in the health of the mind."

I took the paper from him. On it was a phone number, an address in New York City, and the name Doctor Michael Thompson. I held the paper in my hand like it was the most important thing I had ever been given. In a way, it was. Hopefully this psychologist would know how to help me feel like myself again.

"Meanwhile, I can give you some advice to help alleviate any symptoms you've been experiencing. You need to get some sleep. Sometimes victims of shell shock are afraid to sleep because of what they may see in their dreams, but you need energy during the day. If it is too hard to sleep at night, try to sleep for a few hours during the day. That extra sleep would be very good for you. Eat healthy food lots of fruits and vegetables. They will keep your mind awake and alert. Lastly, I think it would be good for you to talk about your experiences from the war. Many of the patients we saw during the time I was working with Dr. Thompson kept too many of their thoughts inside instead of letting them out and letting them go. That is one of the reasons shell shock is so dangerous. Keeping fear and anger inside for too long causes one to lose control, as you have seen on occasion I am sure."

I took that in. More sleep, healthy food, and talking to people. I think I could do that. It was true that I didn't fall asleep quickly anymore like I used to. I knew I could have another nightmare, and that terrified me. I also knew I needed to explain myself to Peggy and Marylin now, since Dot and Jimmy already knew.

Dot. If there was a cure for this shell shock, even if it was extremely gradual, then maybe I had a chance with her. I could feel hope starting to fill my heart.

But then I remembered how she ran away from me when I asked her to dance. If she didn't even want to dance with me, how could it ever work out? I had to respect her feelings, even if they kept us apart.

"I hope you recover from this, Henry," Professor Adams said. "It was a great pleasure to meet you and your friend..."

"Jimmy."

"Your friend Jimmy. Yes. Are you a student here, Henry? I would like to be updated on your progress over time, if I may."

"I'm not a student yet." I made my final decision right then. "But I will be soon."

"Wonderful. I am glad I was able to be of service to you. Hopefully Dr. Thompson can help you even more."

"Thank you so much, Professor Adams."

Jimmy and I stood up to leave.

"And Henry," Professor Adams started.

I turned to look at him again.

"Don't let your fear hold you back. The war is in the past. Have courage, my boy."

That evening after supper, I related to my parents everything Professor Adams had said. I told them about Dr. Thompson and they agreed that it would be very good for me to talk to him so I could sort out this problem.

Later, I lay in my bed thinking about everything that had happened that day. I felt so much better knowing there was a possibility that I wouldn't feel like this forever. I hated living with the weight of the past on my shoulders. I felt like it controlled me. I hadn't felt truly free for so long and I needed to get rid of this weight.

That night, I slept without tossing and turning, without dreaming. For the first time in months, I was starting to hope that freedom from all of this was really possible.

CHAPTER 22

July 11, 1945

Dorothy

I woke up early on Wednesday to get to the bakery before it opened. I had gone through my savings at the bank the day before and had found that I had enough money saved up from years of selling bread to buy the building from the Devons. After the troubles of the Depression were behind us, my parents had encouraged me to save my money instead of helping them with the necessary expenses like I had offered to. Because of them, I had enough money to reach my goal of owning the bakery.

All I needed was a bit more money so I could change a few things in the bakery to really make it mine. I was going in today to start planning what adjustments I wanted to make. I brought along my sketchbook and was ready to figure out how much the new look would cost me.

I reached the bakery right as Mrs. Devon was opening the doors.

"Hello, Dorothy!"

"Hi, Mrs. Devon."

"Are you ready?"

I nodded. "Of course!"

We walked inside, where the scent of bread was permanent. I breathed in deeply and closed my eyes, enjoying every bit of it. Soon, this place would be mine. I let myself relish that thought for a moment and felt content.

Mrs. Devon interrupted my reverie by telling me she was going to get started in the kitchen.

Once she was gone, I pulled out my sketchbook and began to plan.

I drew the entrance as it was, then I wrote notes over the drawing. I wanted to paint the door white. It would be a step up from the faded wood. I would also hang pots of flowers in the windows, so I sketched a few in. Then I moved on to the walls. The entire room needed a fresh coat of paint. The bakery was small, so I wouldn't have to paint a lot. I was still deciding on a color, but I loved the idea of painting the walls either light blue or light green. I imagined photos of people from Ashwood on the walls. I thought it would be fun for people to come in and find a photo of themself or their family on the wall. I would have to find someone with a good camera and a way to print the pictures. It could take a while, but it would be well worth it.

I got a good look at the tables and chairs in the area in front of the counter. They were all made of wood and had been slowly falling apart for years. I pictured metal chairs and tables painted white or black, with cushions that matched the color on the walls. It was perfect! I would put more flowers in a vase in the center of each table. I quickly drew my ideas in my sketchbook.

I made a few more notes about the front of the bakery, but other than a fresh coat of paint and new tables and chairs, it didn't need much. I would only have to focus on the aesthetics of the bakery. Everything else was already taken care of by the Devons.

About an hour after I arrived, I finished taking notes and making sketches in the front of the bakery. I went to the kitchen where Mrs. Devon was busy mixing cookie dough.

"All done?" she asked.

"Yes, thank you so much for letting me change a few things out there."

"It has needed a makeover for many years now. Trust me, you're doing everyone a favor. It's going to look beautiful when you're done with it."

"Thanks." I laughed. "I'm very excited and very grateful."

"Of course, dear. We're grateful to you for taking over. We didn't want this place to change too much when we retired. We couldn't bear to see it changed into offices or be demolished."

"It'll still be the bakery we all know and love."

"Wonderful, Dorothy. If you're all done with your notes, I just took some cookies out of the oven, and you can have one if you want."

"I would never turn down one of your cookies." I smiled at her, then grabbed a warm chocolate chip cookie as I said goodbye.

After arriving home, I spent the rest of the morning writing down estimated costs and creating a budget. That part was much less exciting than planning the changes I wanted to make. In fact, this was part of the reason I had held off on buying or renting a building for so long. Being responsible for and keeping track of expenses was stressful enough without a building to pay for. I had always hated budgeting for ingredients and supplies. The only reason I really made it through math classes during school was Henry.

Of course! Henry! He could help me sort out my budget. That was what he loved doing, so I might as well ask him to help me.

I set my sketchbook down on my bed and ran to the kitchen where I picked up the phone. I gave the operator his number, which I had memorized ages ago, and waited for someone to pick up after being transferred. As the phone rang, I realized I had called on a weekday. Henry was probably at work.

Anna picked up with a perky "Hello?"

"Hi. Anna? This is Dot."

"Hello, Dot. How are you today? I haven't seen you in a while."

"I'm doing well, thank you. How are you?"

"I'm doing fine as well. Are you calling for Henry?"

"Yes, I am, but now I realize that he's probably at work."

"He didn't go in today, actually. He's in his room. I'll go get him."

My heart raced when I realized what I was doing. I had called Henry so I could ask him to come over and help me. I hadn't even spoken to him since I left him in the crowd on Independence Day. He was probably angry with me for running away. What was I doing?

Henry was on the phone before I could think about hanging up.

"Hey, Dottie." He sounded happy. That was a good sign.

"You're not at work." What was he doing at home?

"Not today, no."

"Why not? Are you okay?"

"I had a rough night, but I'm all right now. I slept all morning." Now that he mentioned it, I could tell his voice was a bit rougher than usual, a telltale sign of sleeping late.

"Oh. I'm sorry."

"It's fine. What did you need?"

"I need your help with something for my bakery. I can't figure out how to stretch some of my finances, and I need someone else to help me think through everything. Could you maybe come over and help? You've always been great with numbers and thinking through complicated problems. I could really use your advice." I felt so awkward even asking him for this.

"Of course! I'll be over in a few minutes, is that okay?"

"Yeah, that sounds great." I was both relieved that he was so willing to help me and nervous that he was coming over here. "Thank you so much!"

"Anytime, Dottie! See you in a minute."

"Bye, Henry."

We hung up, and I went to get my sketchbook and notes from my room. I sat in the kitchen to wait for Henry to show up. I tapped my fingers on the counter. I hadn't seen Henry since I realized that I was falling dangerously in love with him. I had to compose myself, or I was going to act like a complete fool.

Sitting with my sketchbook in hand, I realized I might have to show him my sketches of the bakery so he could see my vision. The thought made me extremely nervous. I had never shown my sketchbook to anyone before. It was something I kept private. No one even knew I liked to draw. It was a part of me that I liked to keep to myself, and now I might have to show that part of me to Henry.

As soon as I started thinking about that, Henry knocked on the door. When I opened it, he stood with his hands in his pockets, looking down at the ground. Henry looked at me and grinned. I felt my cheeks get hot and tried to appear calm and collected.

"Hi," Henry said.

"Hi." I studied his face for a moment. He looked really happy. I was glad.

"Can I come in?"

I blushed. "Oh, sorry. Of course."

I opened the door wider and stepped back so he could come inside. He was almost a head taller than me, so I was left looking up at him. He was standing much too close to me. My heart sped up.

"Um, let's go in the kitchen. I left my stuff in there." I stepped away from him and walked into the kitchen. I sat down where I had left my sketchbook and moved it away before he could see what it was. I would only show it to him if I really needed to.

Henry sat down next to me. "Are you feeling better?"

"Huh?" What was he talking about?

"You left the Fourth of July party saying you felt sick."

Oh, that. I thought fast. "Oh, I just had a headache. I went to bed and I woke up feeling much better."

I was satisfied with the partial truth, and it seemed Henry was as well.

"I'm fine though. Don't worry about me."

"Of course not." Henry smiled. "I did come by your house after you left. I wanted to make sure you were okay. You um, you didn't answer."

I lowered my head, embarrassed. I hadn't expected him to follow me. "I didn't hear the door," I apologized.

"I also called the next morning and talked to your mom. She said she would tell you I called, but I guess she forgot."

"She never mentioned anything." I laughed nervously. "Thanks for looking out for me, Henry."

"Of course."

We sat without saying anything for a few moments. Henry gazed at me expectantly, but all I could do was stare back. He glanced down at the papers in front of me which quickly brought me to my senses again.

"Here's what I've been working on." I slid the paper with all of my calculations on it toward him. I had been trying to figure out the cost of the updates to the bakery and trying to decide if everything I wanted to do was possible with the money I had.

"Let's see." Henry began perusing the paper, leaving me to my thoughts.

What must he think of me? He had been asking me to dance when I turned and ran from him. I couldn't believe myself. I felt terrible, and I hated lying to him. But what could I have said? *"Henry, the reason I left so quickly was because I realized I am in love with you, and I couldn't bear that my feelings were unreciprocated, so I ran away."* That would be crazy.

"What do you mean by photos of people?" Henry asked. He pointed to where I had written about the wall of photos.

I turned back to him. "I thought it would be neat if I had someone take pictures of people from the town. They could take a picture of the Devons, for example, or of the Johnsons. I thought it would be fun for people to come into the bakery and see pictures of themselves on the wall."

"Okay, that makes sense. I think that would be swell." He smiled up at me. "And what kind of chairs and tables are you talking about here?" He pointed to my notes where I had written 'white/black metal chairs'.

"The metal ones? You know, like the ones people have in gardens in the movies?"

He looked at me blankly.

I realized the only way for him to understand what I was talking about would be to show him my sketches. I reluctantly grabbed my book from behind me and opened to the page where I drew one of the chairs.

"Like this." I showed him the open page.

"May I?" Henry asked, motioning like he wanted to take the sketchbook from me.

I nodded. If there was anyone I could show my sketches to it was Henry, even though it terrified me.

Henry looked at the sketches of the chairs for a moment, then turned the page.

I almost took the sketchbook back from him when I saw him start to look at my other drawings, but I pulled my hand back when I saw his eyes light up.

"Dottie, these are incredible!" He looked up at me. His green eyes were open wide with amazement, and he was grinning. "Why didn't you ever tell me you were so good at drawing?"

"I haven't told anyone," I said under my breath.

"What? You're a fantastic artist. Just look how realistic this dog is!" He had opened to the page I sketched in the park.

I grabbed his wrist. "You can't tell anyone."

"Why not?"

"It's something I don't like telling people about. Once they know, they'll want to see everything I draw, and my sketches are a part of me. Showing them to people is like opening my heart all at once." I let my hand fall from where it was on his wrist. He had begun to eye it, and I felt awkward sitting with my hand almost on his.

Henry nodded. "I understand. But I still think you're amazing." I wasn't sure he was only talking about my ability to sketch.

I blushed. "Thank you."

"Hey, I have an idea, but I don't know if you would be open to it. Just listen, okay?"

I nodded.

"Since it would cost quite a lot to commission a photographer to take pictures of everyone and then print them all, why not draw them?"

"What?"

"You could sketch people and places from around town—just like you have in your sketchbook—and put them up in your bakery!"

"Henry, I just told you that I don't want people seeing my work."

"What if it was anonymous? What if no one knew it was you who did the sketches?"

I just stared at him, waiting for more explanation.

"You could just draw places. Or people from far away, like this man with the dog in the park. You're so good, Dot. Your work deserves to be seen, even if no one knows that you're the artist."

I nodded. "I'll think about it, okay?" He had a point, but the thought of putting my sketches up for anyone to see was absolutely terrifying.

Henry nodded, then kept looking through the earlier pages of the sketchbook.

"What's this?"

I looked at the sketchbook to see what he was talking about. It was my sketch of a boy standing on a doorstep, about to knock. Henry. It was the same sketch I had looked at a few weeks before, when I had gone back through my book looking for something to improve.

I remembered sitting on my bedroom floor and drawing it a little while after Henry left for Europe. I had been thinking about the day we said goodbye, and the only thing I could do to process my emotions was to draw something. Every line of that sketch felt like it came straight from my heart. I had been so sad that Henry was gone. I had felt ashamed of how I made him feel, and I wanted to pour all of my feelings out onto the paper. This sketch was the product of all of my heartache.

Did Henry realize the sketch was of him? I sincerely hoped not.

"It's a boy knocking on a door, silly." I decided to describe it in the most obvious terms, hoping my tone would make him stop asking about it.

"Oh," Henry said, sounding disappointed. Maybe he did know that it was him in the sketch. I studied his face, trying to read his thoughts, but I couldn't.

When Henry was done flipping through the rest of my sketchbook, occasionally muttering compliments, he set it down and turned back to me.

"Now, Madame Artiste, shall we get back to talking about money?"

I laughed. "We shall."

We continued talking about finances and figuring out a budget for my bakery. I spent most of the time trying to distract myself from the smile Henry gave me whenever we figured out something that would work. Distracting myself was a million times harder than budgeting.

CHAPTER 23

July 11, 1945

Henry

She had drawn me. I almost didn't believe it, but it was me. The boy with worn-out shoes and a patterned sweater, knocking on the door. I couldn't see the boy's face in Dot's sketch, but I knew without a doubt that it was me.

She drew me. I wished I had more time to look at her sketchbook, because then I could figure out when she drew it. Was it recently? Or was it when I was in Europe?

I smiled at the thought. If she had been thinking of me enough to draw me while I was away, that was a good sign.

As I thought about it more, I realized *what* she had drawn. It was the day I said goodbye to her. The day I tried to kiss her and she rejected me. The last time I saw her before I left for the war. I stopped smiling.

Why had she drawn that moment? I had been about to knock on the door when she opened it. I had stumbled backwards from surprise, and she had caught my arm to steady me. Her touch was almost electric, and I remember feeling nervous but ready to tell her how I felt about her. That was the last time I truly had hope for the two of us. That is, until this past week when my hopes had been raised and then dashed repeatedly. Every time we shared a laugh or a glance, I felt like I was where I needed to be. But then I was reminded of the times she has walked away from me, and I knew we weren't meant to be.

My own confusion was driving me insane, and that was part of the reason I hadn't been able to sleep the night before. I knew that if I thought about Dot too much, I could have another horrible dream, and I didn't want that. But trying not to think about her only made me think of her more, and I lay in bed all night trying to quiet my thoughts. I felt surrounded by memories of the past and hopes for the future. I still loved her. Even if she didn't love me, I knew without a doubt how I felt.

And so I resigned myself to living with my feelings for however long they lasted. Now that I had seen her drawing of me at the doorstep, I knew I couldn't tell her how I felt. If she was still remembering that moment, it was embarrassing to her that I had confessed my love to her out of nowhere. She was still hurting, and I was too.

These were the thoughts running through my head as I struggled to focus on the calculations for Dot's budget. Every time she looked at me, I wondered what she was thinking. Was she thinking about what I had done, or what I had become? Neither option was comforting. I had embarrassed the both of us that day, years ago, and it still stung. I had become someone who was dependent on others and who was scared to even fall asleep because of what my dreams held. What could she possibly think of me?

"Henry?" she said, looking at me with her big blue eyes. I saw concern in them, something I was tired of seeing when people looked at me. My parents were treating me like some fragile thing, and now Jimmy constantly asked me if I was all right.

"Yeah, Dot?"

"Are you paying attention?" She laughed. I was glad she didn't ask me if I was okay again.

"Yeah, sorry. I didn't get much sleep, so I'm having a little trouble concentrating."

"Was it because of..." she trailed off.

"Um, yeah. Sort of." I remembered that Professor Adams had told me that talking to someone about my condition would be good for me. "I talked to someone about what's going on with me. A professor from Pittsburgh. My dad did some research and found his name in a study of the effects of the Great War on soldiers."

Dot looked surprised. "What did he tell you?" Her eyebrows knit together.

"I probably have something they call shell shock. It comes from feeling too much stress or experiencing trauma during the war. Whenever I'm reminded of the trauma, I become distressed again. He said that, as of right now, the only cure is time and patience."

"Oh." Dot's smile fell away. "At least you know that you're not sick or crazy, right?" She smiled weakly.

"I still feel like I'm both. I wish I could just stop feeling like this, you know? Being scared of falling asleep is horrible." I shook my head hopelessly. I looked up at her again, and she was staring at me with concern in her eyes.

"Because of the dreams."

I nodded. "I know I might relive what happened to me over and over again in my dreams, and I can't let that happen. I don't want to live through those experiences again."

"But it's not real. They're just your memories. You're safe here." She put her hand on my arm. I was tempted to put my hand over hers, but I held myself back.

"When I'm awake, I'm sure of that. I haven't had any episodes when I'm awake in a while. I think that means I'm recovering, but I don't know. The dreams are getting worse, so maybe I'm not getting better. I can't tell what's real and what isn't in my dreams, even after I wake up. I'm terrified they'll keep getting worse and that eventually I'll just be living in one long nightmare."

I thought back to the times where I felt like I was living in a dream and felt completely numb. I couldn't live like that long term. The feeling of apathy was horrible even for a day. I couldn't imagine what I would do if I felt that way constantly.

Dot moved her hand down my arm and held my hand in hers. I felt the same electricity that I felt the day we said goodbye. It ran up my hand and stopped in my heart, burning and making it beat so fast I was sure Dot could hear it. The feeling grounded me in a way I wasn't used to. I relished the feeling of safety that came from her touch and stared into her eyes, concentrating on them instead of my spiraling thoughts.

"Listen, Henry. I don't know how to help you other than by listening to you. That's what I'm here for. We've always been there for each other and we always will be. You can always trust me."

The burning in my chest spread to my face. If Dot hadn't heard the beating of my heart, surely she could see the redness on my cheeks.

"You can tell me what happened, you know," she said softly. "Maybe it would help you to talk about it."

I knew I wanted to tell her everything. I felt ready to burst with all of the thoughts rolling around in my head, and I knew I was finally ready to get rid of some of the horrors that haunted me. She had shown me her drawings, something she kept close to her heart, and now I could share my memories, however horrible they were.

"We were on a recon mission during the night," I started to say, holding her hand tighter. Once I started speaking, I couldn't stop. All of my memories came spilling out in real words for the first time. My *real* memories, not the distorted ones from my nightmares. I told her everything, how Jones tried to catch up to me, but I let him and the others fall behind in the chaos. How Davies lay dying and I couldn't do anything but watch and leave him there to die. I told her how every time I dreamt about that night, the fire burned through my arm again and again, and I felt like I was there. I could smell the burning wood, feel the cold air interrupted by fire, and hear every scream. My heart ached for the men I left behind to die. I told her about waking up for the first time after that night, and how all I wanted was to see Davies, Jones, and the others in the hospital beds next to me. I told her how I screamed when I found out I would never see them again. I told her how guilty I felt about all of it.

"It's all my fault." I was sobbing. Crying made me feel as weak as the Henry that had begged the doctors for some other news than that his friends were all dead. I felt as weak as the Henry that had dreamt of that night over and over, the Henry that had woken up in a panic and gone straight to the bathroom to vomit like that would somehow purge him of his memories. I felt weaker than ever, crying like that in front of Dot.

"It's not your fault, Henry." She spoke for the first time since I had begun my story. "You keep trying to convince yourself that it is your fault, but how could it be? You didn't leave them to die. You were trying to get away, just the same as they were. It has *never* been your fault, Henry."

Tears ran down my face, and my feelings were still raw. I repeated her words in my mind a few times, knowing that she knew me better than anyone else. If there was anyone I could believe, it was Dottie.

"Henry, remember when I told you that you *are* a hero?"

I nodded, looking off into the distance in front of me.

"This is exactly what I mean. You've been dealing with this for so long on your own. You wanted to be the hero and spare everyone the horrible details of your past, but you don't have to do this alone. You have your family. You have your friends." She put her hand on my shoulder. "You have *me*." Her voice shook on the last word.

I turned to her, looking into her dark eyes. "*You have* me." She had tears in her eyes too. Even though she didn't know exactly how I felt, she still cried because I was crying.

"I know, Dot. I'm here for you too." I reached out timidly to wipe a tear from her face. At my touch she looked at the ground, but then quickly looked up again. One side of her mouth twitched up into a small smile.

I stood up and hugged her. She sat on her stool and wrapped her arms around my waist. I held her for a while, just breathing in the scent of her hair. Dottie smelled like vanilla and chocolate, scents that had always reminded me of her.

I realized two things at the same moment: One, I loved her more than anything. Two, I wanted to kiss her. Badly.

The second thought scared me more than the first. If I tried to kiss her again, it could be a repeat of the last time. She might reject me and we would have to start over again, building up our friendship brick by brick.

I felt Dot move in my arms, and I opened my eyes to look at her. Our faces were almost touching.

She was smiling radiantly, looking up at me. "Henry, I…"

I was going to do it. I pushed my fears aside and tucked a stray curl behind her ear.

Then Bobby slammed open the front door, singing a Sinatra song at the top of his lungs.

Dot and I stepped away from each other, and I started shuffling through some of the papers we had been writing on as if nothing had happened. I wiped the tears off my cheek with my shoulder. I hoped Bobby wouldn't notice the redness in my eyes or on my face from crying.

"Oh, hi Henry," Bobby said, coming into the kitchen. Buddy was close behind him.

"What's up, Bobby?" I tried to seem happy to see him. In reality, I was silently cursing the fact that he walked in when he did.

I could feel Dot staring at me, and I wanted to go back in time to the moments before we had been interrupted.

Bobby opened the refrigerator to look for a snack, so I assumed he would be with us in the kitchen for a while. We wouldn't be getting our moment back. What could have happened was gone.

Now Buddy came into the room as well.

"Henry!" He walked over to me and slapped his hand on my back. "How have you been, my friend?"

"I've been all right," I responded.

In reality, I was disappointed. Something was about to happen between me and Dot, and then it had been ruined.

"Bobby, Mom said that we're eating soon." Buddy turned to Bobby, who was about to slice an apple. "You don't need a snack."

"But I'm hungry." He said it as if it was something obvious.

Buddy put both of his hands in the air. "All right, I warned you. My job here is done."

I looked at Dot again. She was looking down at the table, where her sketchbook was hidden beneath the papers filled with our calculations. I held out my hand to her. She looked up at me, confused. I looked down at the papers and her sketchbook again, then motioned with my hand that she should give them to me. If *I* was carrying around the sketchbook, her family would probably just assume it was something from work, and wouldn't ask about it. Dot must have understood my silent communication, because she handed me the pile and smiled at me gently. I smiled back at her.

I turned my head to look back at the kitchen and Buddy was looking at me, then at Dot, then at me again. He narrowed his eyes and then smiled.

"Hey Henry," he said. "Why don't you stay for supper? I'm sure our parents won't mind it one bit."

My eyes shifted back to Dot who nodded quickly, then I smiled. "Okay, that sounds great."

"Swell." Buddy's smile grew even wider.

An hour later, we all sat at the dining room table together. I sat in between Buddy and Mr. Banks. Dot sat across from me, next to Bobby. Her mom sat at the other end of the table. It felt like a formal supper, complete with small talk and the occasional whispers of 'Please pass the potatoes'.

We were about halfway done when Mr. Banks asked me what my plans were for the school year.

"I'm going to apply to the University of Pittsburgh, sir."

"Wonderful. Are you planning on living here or closer to campus?"

I hadn't thought that far. I had just barely decided to go.

"I'm not exactly sure. I think I'll be staying here, since I'll be working part time at the refinery." I met Dot's eyes across the table. She gave me a pleased grin.

"You worked there during high school, didn't you?"

"Yes. I had an internship in the accounting department. When I got home, my old boss offered me a position there."

"Well done. And you plan on studying accounting at school." He phrased it like a statement, not a question.

"Yes, sir."

"Good work, my boy. Buddy here still hasn't decided what he's going to do." Mr. Banks looked at Buddy with raised eyebrows and a smile.

"I told you Pop, I just need a little more time to decide." It seemed as if they had had this conversation before and were now only joking about it.

I cleared my throat. "I don't know if I would have decided to go to school if my boss hadn't told me that he would help me get in. I probably would have kept working at the refinery in the same position for years."

"I'm sure it's been hard for you to get back to your normal life again since you came home," Mrs. Banks spoke up. "It's been that way for Buddy."

I nodded. "It felt surreal for a couple weeks, but now I feel like I know what I want." I instinctively looked up at Dot. She was holding her spoon over her plate, not moving to bring the potatoes to her mouth. She just stared at me with her mouth slightly agape. I quickly looked down again when I realized what I had said. *I knew what I wanted now.* And then I looked right at Dot without thinking about it. What must she have thought?

"I know now that going on to get a degree in accounting is the best option for me, even though I know it will be difficult." I continued talking, trying to fix the awkward situation.

Dot looked up at me again with a small smile on her face.

I didn't know what to do now. I still felt awkward. I was almost positive Dot could read my thoughts with the look she was giving me.

I couldn't bring myself to look at her, so I focused on my food and didn't say anything else. Luckily, the Banks started another conversation about a film they wanted to see at the theater, so I felt like I was off the hook.

A few moments later, I felt a kick from under the table. I looked up at Buddy.

He was sipping some water and staring straight ahead at Bobby, pretending he hadn't done anything. I nudged his leg with my foot and he turned toward me.

"What?" I asked him under my breath. Luckily, Dot was busy talking to her parents and Bobby was too busy eating to notice.

All Buddy did was nod his head at Dot and then look at me knowingly.

"Huh?" I whispered

"Ah, don't pretend like nothing is going on."

My gaze flicked to Dot and then back at Buddy. I just shook my head at him.

"Come on. Go for it," he urged me quietly.

"I don't even—"

"I saw what was happening when we walked in earlier. Just go for it. Trust me."

He had seen that I was going to kiss Dot? I thought I had stepped away fast enough to disguise the fact that we had been about to kiss. I guess I hadn't been quick enough.

I opened my mouth awkwardly.

"Trust me, Henry." Buddy went back to eating.

I was left thinking about his words for the rest of the night. Buddy thought I should make a move. Did he know something I didn't about Dot's feelings, or was he just guessing?

After supper, I helped Bud and Bobby wash the dishes while Dot cleared the table and put away the leftovers.

Later, I thanked Mr. and Mrs. Banks for the meal and then left before I had the chance to talk to Dot alone again.

I took the pile of papers and Dot's sketchbook with me when I left, since there hadn't been a time to give it to her discreetly. I figured I could bring it back to her sometime soon. This would also give me another chance to look at her sketches. They really were incredible.

I fell asleep that night looking through the book of drawings, noticing all of the little details she had included. Somehow, in her drawings, everything looked more beautiful than it did in real life. The trees were fuller and there were more birds in the sky. The people she drew were always happy. That was how Dot saw the world. She always saw the best in people. She had so much hope and worked hard until she accomplished her dreams. That was what I loved about her. She knew life wasn't perfect, but knew it could be and chose to see it like that instead of dwelling on the negative. Dorothy Banks was just as incredible as her drawings.

After a rare good night's sleep, I went to work the next morning ready to tell Mr. Green that I had finally decided to apply to the University of Pittsburgh. I had thought about it the entire week, and it felt like the right thing to do even though I was terrified. I didn't know how or if I would get better from my shell shock, but I hoped I would be able to learn to control any waking episodes by the time I started school. I was also dreaming less than I had been the week prior. The last time I felt strange was the night before I went to Dot's house to help her with her business plans.

After telling Dot exactly what had happened in Belgium and what kept happening to me in my dreams, I felt a little better about it all. I still felt scared of falling asleep, but I knew that if I had a nightmare or an episode, there was someone who knew a little bit about what I had gone through and believed that I wasn't at fault. I trusted Dot more than I trusted my own memory of the events. I knew that if she saw me as a good guy, a soldier and a hero, then that was what I could be. Even if I didn't feel like it, Dot believed it. When she told me it wasn't my fault, it was as if a wave of sickness and guilt left me. It wasn't my fault. It was the circumstance of war, and I couldn't have prevented any of those things from happening. The war was much bigger than me, a single soldier. I couldn't control those events any more than anyone else could. I just as easily could have been one of the ones to die, but I was lucky. If I was still alive, it must be for a reason. Davies and Jones and the rest of our team died because it was war. They died as heroes, fighting for our country and fighting to protect people. I survived trying to do those same things.

I finally felt real, lasting hope that morning, for the first time since I'd come home. It felt like a fresh start. I was different from the boy that left here years ago, and I was different from the young man that fought in the war. I had a second chance, and I wanted to use that chance to live the best life I could.

I left for work feeling like I could soar through the clouds. Dad even asked me if I was feeling all right. I assume it was because I was acting happier than I had in months.

"I feel great, Dad," I told him, getting out of the car. "I'm going to tell Mr. Green that I'm ready to apply for college.

"That's wonderful, Henry. I'm so happy for you." Dad gave me a huge smile and a quick pat on the back as we walked through the front door of the refinery.

When I reached Mr. Green's office, it was already open. Mr. Green sat at his desk, clicking away on a typewriter. He looked up when he heard me walk in.

"Henry, my boy! How are you doing? I was worried about you yesterday."

Dad had informed him that I wouldn't be coming to work yesterday, since I hadn't gotten much sleep.

"I'm doing much better, sir. And I have some good news."

Mr. Green held out his hand to the chair in front of me and gestured for me to sit. "Well, let's hear it!"

"I've decided that I *am* going to apply to the University of Pittsburgh. I hope it's not too late to ask for your help?"

"That's wonderful! Of course it's not too late. I will inform my colleague that you want to accept the spot in the School of Business."

"Perfect. Thank you so much. And sorry it has taken so long for me to decide. I've been experiencing some health issues."

"Nothing contagious, I hope." Mr. Green laughed and jokingly backed his seat away.

"No, sir. I'm afraid that the issues I've been having relate more to what I went through in Europe. I plan on discussing them with a psychologist as soon as possible."

"I'm sorry to hear that, Henry. Is there anything I can do to help you?"

"At the moment I'm feeling a lot better. But if I need anything, I'll let you know." I smiled. It was easier to explain this problem to people than I thought it would be. Mr. Green was very understanding, even without knowing all of the details. I left his office feeling positive.

I chatted with Jason while we worked, and he told me that his wife was expecting a child. I congratulated him and assured him that he would be a fantastic father. He was always so happy and helped others around him be happy, so I knew he would be a great dad.

Before I left to go home that day, Mr. Green pulled me aside and said that he had contacted his colleague at the university and that I would be officially accepted to the school of business once I filled out some paperwork. I would also need to be interviewed by the dean of the school of business. Mr. Green explained that they were allowing my late admission since I had come home from the war. I was an exception to their usual admissions process, so I would need to do everything I could to be compliant with all of their other deadlines. I wholeheartedly agreed, and I told him I was grateful for the opportunity to even apply.

I was ready to move on with my life. I wanted to leave my memories of the war behind me and feel free again. I could put what happened to me during the war in the past. I needed to for my own sanity. I was going to go to school, become a real accountant, and be who I really wanted to be without the weight of my memories holding me down.

CHAPTER 24

July 13, 1945

Dorothy

I had finally finished planning my budget for the bakery. I knew exactly how I was going to decorate, how many cakes, loaves of bread, and batches of cookies I would bake in a week, and how much my supplies would cost each month. I felt prepared, all thanks to Henry.

Henry was on my mind often. It seemed like every time I closed my eyes, I was met with images of him sitting next to me, holding my hand, and trusting me with his memories of the night he was injured. That afternoon, it seemed like Henry had forgiven and forgotten the night of Independence Day when I had run away from his invitation to dance. The memories of Henry standing in front of me and leaning in closer gave me butterflies in my stomach and warmth in my heart. I couldn't stop smiling every time I imagined what might have happened if Bobby hadn't barged in the front door when he did.

Would Henry really have kissed me? I thought he wanted to stay friends. I thought he didn't love me like that anymore. At least, that's what his letter said. Maybe his feelings had changed? I knew mine had.

I was ready to fall in love with him if he would have me. I was convinced of that when I showed him my sketchbook. It was the first time I had shown it to someone, and it felt like I had opened up a vulnerable part of myself. I trusted him completely.

I even let him see the drawing of him at my doorstep. That sketch was the product of my secret pining for him in the month after he was shipped off to Europe. I had felt too heartbroken and embarrassed to write to him, so I drew that picture and hoped it would be healing. It had worked a little to take the sting of my heartbreak away, and I had eventually bottled up those feelings and hid the pain away in my heart. That drawing represented the guilt I felt because I hadn't accepted Henry right then and there when he came to say goodbye.

I wasn't sure if Henry would know what the drawing was of, or what it represented to me, but if he understood he would know how I felt about him. He would know that I regretted my choice to shut him out that day, and he would know that I still had a place for him in my heart if he wanted it.

At least I hoped he would understand.

As I thought about the relationship between Henry and me, I remembered that when he gave me his letter, I promised him I would write him one in return. And so, that Friday morning, I decided to put my feelings on paper. I was going to be completely honest with him. I wanted him to know how I felt, no matter the consequences.

I wrote the letter in one sitting. I felt good about what I wrote. I only hoped that Henry would understand.

> Dearest Henry,
>
> I told you a few weeks ago that I would write you a letter. I have put it off for too long, and I want to tell you why.
>
> When you came home I couldn't help but remember again and again the day you left. That was a hard day for me, Henry. The night before the day you came to say goodbye, I had finally recognized how I truly felt about you. I was beginning to fall in love with you. I wanted you to stay, and the fact that you were leaving to fight in a war destroyed any hope I had of being with you. I decided the next morning I couldn't let myself fall for you—not because I didn't want to, but because I knew it would hurt both of us. You were leaving, and I didn't know when you would come back. Part of me was terrified that you wouldn't. I wanted to protect myself from heartbreak. It was a selfish decision and one I deeply regret.
>
> You came to my door right after I decided to close my heart to you. If I hadn't made that decision, I would have kissed you. I wanted to, Henry, I really did. My heart still aches when I think of the look on your face when you walked away from me for the last time.
>
> Henry, I am still on the brink of falling in love with you. I think I would if I knew you were falling with me. I want to. When we

danced for the first time after you came home, that's when I knew for sure. Henry, you make me feel like I'm home. In your arms I felt so safe and so loved. I felt it again the other day when you came over to help me. I don't know if it was just me, but I felt like something would have happened if we hadn't been interrupted. Did you think the same?

I need to know, Henry. Are you falling in love with me, or will I fall alone?

-Dorothy

I signed my name at the bottom in relief. It felt good to write my feelings down.

As I put the letter in an envelope, I felt nervous. Was I really brave enough to give him the letter? I wanted to, but maybe I should be a little more sure of his feelings first. I didn't want to pour my heart out to him, only to be rejected. Maybe I deserved it, since that's exactly what I had done to him years ago.

Later that day, I answered the phone. Marylin was on the other line.

"Dottie!" She was out of breath. "He finally asked me! Jimmy and I are going steady!"

"Oh my goodness! That's wonderful, Marylin! How did he ask?"

"Last night we went into Pittsburgh to go to dinner and he gave me a promise ring and everything! Oh Dottie, I cried; I was so happy!" She spoke all in one breath.

"That's so sweet! We need to celebrate!"

"I know! I was thinking we could go to Daisy's and then go dancing?"

I laughed. "Sounds perfect! We'll meet at 5:30?"

"Wonderful!"

"All right! I'll see you there!"

I was happy for Jimmy and Marylin, but I was also a little jealous. Their relationship was uncomplicated. They had been progressing in it since the end of high school. They went on dates periodically, and we all knew they were perfect for each other from the beginning. It was so simple.

I wanted that simplicity. I wanted to know what Henry's feelings were toward me and to be sure of them. I wanted him to know how

I felt as well, but I was so scared. What if he rejected me? What if he laughed and said we were 'just friends'? I couldn't bear to let that happen. Just because he flirted with me a little didn't mean he was in love with me. I would be stupid to think that. I had to know for sure. I refused to be the cause of a ruined friendship again.

Before I left for the diner, I put on my blue dress, curled my hair, and put on makeup. I felt a little overdressed for the diner, but if we were going dancing I wanted to look my very best. I had to dance with Henry and make it up to him for refusing his invitation to dance on Independence Day. My heart beat faster at the very thought.

As I was putting my shoes on, Buddy walked into the living room.

"You should tell him," he said.

"What?"

"You should tell Henry how you feel."

"What...?" I stood up straight and looked at him wordlessly. How did he know?

"I'm your brother, Dottie." He laughed. "I'm not as much of an idiot as you think I am."

I had no idea Buddy even suspected my feelings. I swallowed and shifted my gaze to the floor. If he already suspected how I felt, I couldn't deny it. Buddy knew me better than almost anyone. I met his eyes again. "I want to tell him, but I don't know how he feels."

"If what I saw the other night is any indication, he is very much in love with you."

"You think so?" A burst of happiness filled me. "Wait, just what *did* you see?"

He made a dramatic face and said in a deep voice, "'I know what I want now.'" He looked at me and puckered his lips.

I stood up from where I was lacing my Oxfords. "Excuse me?"

"You know you heard and saw the same thing I did."

"I...I guess I did." I remembered that comment now. Henry had been flustered and gone on talking about school. Had he really been talking about me? Was *I* what he wanted? "Do you really think he has feelings for me?"

"I think you should find that out for yourself. I wouldn't want to meddle." Buddy smiled.

"Thanks for telling me, Bud. You're the best."

"I know." His smile changed to a smirk.

"Hey, why don't you come with us? We're all meeting at Daisy's and then going dancing."

"I guess that would be fun. I'll go brush my hair and try to find something to wear."

"Ah, what you're wearing is fine! And your hair looks great! Come on." I grabbed his arm and pulled him toward the door.

I walked to the diner in high spirits. I was both nervous and excited to see how the night would go. My letter waited in my dresser. I wanted to see what this night would bring before I gave it to Henry. Buddy walked right behind me, trying to keep up. I wanted to get to the diner as soon as possible. My pounding heart demanded it.

When I reached the diner, I walked through the door and the bell above it rang.

I looked toward our table and saw Jimmy and Marylin sitting together on a bench with their backs facing me. Henry was sitting opposite them, and when I walked in, he sat up a little straighter. I felt bold and sat right next to him.

"Hi," I said.

"Hi!" Henry was smiling widely.

I turned toward Jimmy and Marylin. "Congratulations, you two! I'm so excited for you!"

Marylin smiled at Jimmy, then turned back to me. "Look." She held out her right hand to me, which now had a simple gold band with a single diamond in the center.

"It's gorgeous!"

"I know! I love it!" She turned to Jimmy and kissed him on the cheek. Jimmy's face went bright red.

The two of them continued talking, obviously too caught up in each other to focus on anyone else. Noticing this, Henry turned toward me and put his hand on mine. He leaned in close.

"I have your sketchbook at my house." He whispered. "I can bring it by tomorrow if you want."

I turned toward him before I realized that he was still close. Our faces were almost touching. I quickly turned forward again, my face on fire.

"Yeah, that's fine." I tried looking at anything but at him. "I'll be baking in the early morning, and then I'll be back once I've made my deliveries."

Henry gave my hand a squeeze before letting go. Once he had let go of my hand, I glanced over at him quickly, but his attention was on Buddy, who was walking over to us.

Buddy came to the table and dragged an extra chair over.

"Sorry, everyone. I'm crashing your party tonight."

"That's great, Buddy!" Jimmy said. "You even us out. Honestly, you should come more often!"

Peggy strolled in, making the bell on the door ring loudly. She walked right up to our table, smiling at Marylin and Jimmy. As soon as she saw Buddy sitting in her favorite spot at the edge of the table, her eyes got wider.

"Hey, Peggy," Buddy said, smiling softly.

Peggy waved, and her face blushed a soft pink. "Hi."

I looked at the two of them, staring at each other awkwardly. So that was why Buddy was so eager to come with me. *Interesting.* I turned to Henry and raised my eyebrows, hoping to convey my surprise at finding out my brother was sweet on my friend.

Henry chuckled and shook his head.

We all got up to order our food from Daisy, who gushed over Marylin's ring, my dress, and Peggy's hair, which she had recently gotten cut. The three of us stood at the counter talking to her for a while while the guys went back to the table.

When we returned, the boys were immersed in a conversation that promptly stopped before we could hear anything.

"What was that all about?" Peggy asked as she sat down.

"What?" Jimmy asked at the same time Buddy said "Nothing."

"You're acting like high school boys," I said. "All secretive for no reason."

"We're not *that* much older than high school boys, Dottie," Henry teased.

"But I should hope that you were all much more grown up," Marylin chimed in, bumping Jimmy's shoulder with hers. "After all, you're all students or veterans now."

"Or both," Henry said through a laugh.

"Did you apply then?" Jimmy asked, sitting up straighter.

Henry nodded. "Yeah, I'm officially in as soon as I get interviewed by the dean."

"That's great!" Jimmy said, beaming.

"Wait," Buddy said. "Did you ever figure out the...you know..."

Henry looked down at his lap. "I actually wanted to talk to everyone about that."

Just then, Daisy called for us to come get our food at the counter.

While everyone stood up to get their food, I grabbed Henry by the arm and took him aside. "You're going to tell everyone?"

He nodded. "I think Peggy and Marylin deserve to know too. I already told you, Jimmy, and Buddy, so they're the only ones who don't know. I'm sure they think I've gone insane or something with the way I've been acting lately."

I nodded. It made sense that he would want everyone to know why he had been acting a little differently than before. "As long as you're okay to talk about it."

Henry smiled. "I am. Thanks for looking out for me. You're the best, Dottie."

I smiled back. He was wonderful. I stared at him for a few seconds before I realized he was laughing at me. "What?" I asked.

"You're staring at me."

"I was just…thinking."

"About what?" He raised his eyebrows teasingly. My heart skipped a beat.

"Nothing." I said it with the same tone Buddy had used earlier. As soon as I said it, I turned around and went to pick up my burger and fries from Daisy.

Henry stood there for a few more seconds before he followed me to the counter to get his food. I felt his gaze on me the whole time. I couldn't stop smiling, so when I caught his eye, I bit my bottom lip to stop the corners of my mouth from going up any more. This only made Henry raise his eyebrows again, which made me smile more.

Once we were all sitting down again, Henry started to talk. "I've already told the others about this, so Peggy and Marylin, you ought to know too." He paused, looking around to make sure everyone was listening. Then he continued. "Since coming home, I've felt different. I've acted differently too. I have nightmares that are a repeat of the night I got injured in Belgium. I've been on edge with people, and there are times when I can't control my reactions to things." Looking around, our friends had become solemn, listening silently as Henry spoke. Jimmy was nodding supportively, encouraging Henry to keep going. "Anything that reminds me of what happened can trigger an episode. I didn't know what was going on, so Jimmy and I went to see a professor at the University of Pittsburgh who has studied the effects of war on soldiers. He helped me figure some things out about my situation and recommended a psychologist."

Throughout his explanation, I watched Peggy and Marylin to see their reactions. They were the ones that didn't know anything about what Henry had been suffering. At the mention of a psychologist, both of their eyes went wide.

"The professor believes I might have what they call shell shock," Henry continued, slower this time. "They don't know if there is a cure. I might be dealing with problems like this my whole life." His face became sad. He was looking at his lap again, so I reached out for his hand under the table. He gave my hand a squeeze, then looked up again and carried on. "That's why I've been acting so weird. That's why I ran away from the group on the Fourth of July. That's why I don't want to talk about the war. It was traumatic for me, and I'm already reminded of it nearly every time I close my eyes. But the professor did tell me that seeing a psychologist might help me sort through my memories a little bit, and that talking about what happened more often might help me come to terms with it. So, I'll try to be better with talking about the war and being more open. I want to apologize for overreacting in some situations or for lashing out. I'm truly sorry and I'm trying to do better."

I still held Henry's hand under the table. I gave it a squeeze, just like he had done earlier. He turned to me and smiled. I smiled back. What was happening? Henry and I were holding hands. I had reached for his hand to offer him comfort, but now I saw that he didn't really need it. His voice was strong and confident, and he even smiled a little as he told Peggy and Marylin what had been going on.

"It's all right, Henry," Peggy said warmly. "Marylin and I just sort of assumed you weren't feeling well and I guess, in a way, we were right. I can't even imagine what it's been like. Adjusting to coming home is hard enough." Her eyes flicked to Buddy before returning to Henry. "Dealing with nightmares too? That sounds awful."

"We're all here for you, Henry," Marylin said. "I hope you can start feeling better."

"I'm glad you found someone who knows what's going on," Buddy said. "I'm a little familiar with shell shock, but only cases where the soldier reported a head injury. I didn't think it would apply to your situation or else I would have mentioned it when we talked before."

"Thanks everyone," Henry said. "Now, let's talk about something happy." He laughed. "I've had enough of dwelling on the bad stuff."

We talked and laughed together until we finished our food. I still held Henry's hand underneath the table, which made it a little hard to eat, but I didn't care. It felt natural to keep holding on to him, even in such a small way. I started holding his hand to comfort him and give him support, but during the course of the meal, I realized it meant more than just that. I wanted it to mean more.

I didn't know what our hand holding meant to Henry, but I knew I wanted it to be romantic. If it wasn't to him, then I didn't know what I was doing.

With that fear in mind, I slowly let go of his hand to pick up my cola.

I didn't know what to do. I knew I was in love with Henry Oakey. What I didn't know was if he was falling for me or if I was just another one of his friends. The words from his letter kept replaying in my mind, mixed in with what he had said on Independence Day. *I am a good friend.* The confusion circled around my mind for the rest of our time at the diner. I finished eating earlier than the others, and so I sat in front of an empty plate of food and waited, my eyes staring at nothing. In my head, I was going over the encounters Henry and I had had since he returned, and the memories only added to my confusion. If what he told me in the letter was true, he only wanted to be friends. Then how could I explain what had happened on the night of the Fourth of July or the night he stayed for dinner after helping me? It had seemed like he had wanted to be something more. What was I supposed to make of that?

When we left the diner, we all walked to the dance hall. Everyone had walked to the diner since the July night was so pleasant. The sunset gave everything a glow.

Gradually the music got louder and louder, and at last we entered the dance hall. We made our way to an empty table near the refreshments and set our things down on the chairs. Jimmy and Marylin left to go dance together, and we joked that we probably wouldn't see them again until closing time.

When a new song started, Buddy took my hand and led me to the dance floor.

"So?" he asked as he spun me around.

"What?" I answered.

"Are you going to tell him?"

"I don't know. I still haven't decided."

"Just tell him already! You two deserve to be happy. Together!" He eyed me carefully on the last word, almost scolding.

I squinted my eyes at him. "I'll tell him when I'm ready, and I'm not yet." My heart beat fast just thinking about telling Henry how I felt.

"All righty then. But I wanna hear about it when you do tell him.."
I rolled my eyes and ignored him.

By the end of the song, we were out of breath from trying to have a conversation while dancing. We walked back to the group as another song started. I sat out one dance and talked with Marylin and Jimmy, and then I was asked to dance by a boy I knew a little from high school. After that, I looked for Henry but couldn't see him anywhere. Instead, I spotted Teddy Harrison and his friends standing near our table, and I went over to say hello. One of them asked me to dance, and I ended up going from one partner to the next for a few songs.

Once I had danced with Teddy and all of his friends, I told them thank you and escaped to the refreshment table. I grabbed a cup of water and started sipping on it slowly when I heard Henry call my name. I recognized his voice before I turned around to see his face.

"We haven't danced yet," he said, walking up next to me with a cup in his hand.

I took a sip of my drink, feeling nervous. "No, we haven't. I was dancing with Teddy Harrison and his friends. Do you remember him?"

Henry laughed and nodded his head. "Does he still have buck teeth?"

I smiled. "He's grown into them, I think."

"I haven't seen those guys in years, it seems like."

"I think they're all at the University. You'll be there soon."

Henry and I stood there for a few seconds, then Henry spoke up again.

"I was thinking of requesting our song."

It was true—we hadn't heard "Sing, Sing, Sing" yet.

I nodded and smiled. "That sounds wonderful."

"I'll be right back." Henry threw his cup in the trash and walked over to the band. I kept my eye on him the whole time, wondering if there ever would be a right time to tell him that I was falling in love with him. I didn't want to be rejected. I imagined a scenario where I told him tonight while we were dancing, and all I could picture was Henry telling me he didn't want to ruin our friendship with romantic feelings, just like he alluded to in his letter. .My heart started to break at the thought. I didn't want anything to come between us, especially not something this big that could push Henry away from me forever. We didn't talk for almost three years after Henry tried to kiss me, and I couldn't have that happen to us again. I pushed my feelings further down in my heart where I wouldn't be bothered by them. It was exceptionally hard when I could see Henry, as handsome as ever, making his way toward me now, having asked the band to play our song.

He was smiling widely when he reached me. He held out his hand to me, and I lightly placed mine in his, hoping not to feel anything at his touch. I still did, my heart beating a little faster and my face growing a little hotter.

We walked onto the dance floor as the band started a new song.

I knew immediately that it wasn't "Sing, Sing, Sing". The trumpet melody was different. There were no drums. It was slow and soft.

Henry smiled as my eyes went wide. The song playing was "It's Been a Long, Long Time".

"You owe me a dance," he said with a smirk. "I wasn't going to let you forget."

My heart ached at the memory of the Fourth of July. I placed my other hand on Henry's shoulder, trying to ignore the sensation that flitted through my hand and my heart. I took his lead as he guided me through the steps of a much gentler dance than I was expecting. He spun me around and when he brought me back to center, I was much closer to him than before. My mouth went dry.

"What's wrong?" Henry asked.

"Nothing," I lied. "I was only thinking."

"About what?"

"Why did you request this song?"

"I told you. You owed me a dance."

"But you said you were requesting *our* song."

"We danced to this when I came home. We were going to dance to it on the Fourth of July. It's kind of like *our* song now, don't you think?"

"I guess it is now...huh. I was just expecting—"

"'Sing, Sing, Sing'?"

I nodded.

"That's playing next. I couldn't leave tonight without our tradition." He winked.

My breath caught in my throat. I swallowed. Then I smiled, trying to mask my true feelings. I loved him. I had been trying to ignore those feelings for such a long time but now, dancing with Henry, it was impossible to hide them. I felt like they were being broadcast from my heart to his.

His eyes held a challenge. He stared at me and I wondered what he was thinking.

I raised my eyebrow, asking him a question with the simple gesture. He smirked in response and spun me around again in time with the slow swing of the music. When I returned to facing him, he was still smirking at me. The feeling of glee I felt at seeing him smiling like that filled me and I looked up to return his smirk. I was both happy and terrified to be looking at him like that. It all felt too forward, too vulnerable. I looked down again in time with the last few bars of the song that had become ours.

With a few heavy drum beats, the band started playing "Sing, Sing, Sing", and we moved into position to do the choreography that neither of us would ever forget.

We laughed while dancing, and all of the vulnerability I felt slipped away. I pretended everything was normal. I pretended I wasn't completely in love with the man dancing with me. During this song, we were just friends and it felt like familiar territory. I felt safe here, not like I was standing at the edge of a cliff wondering if I'd be caught at the bottom or not. Maybe this was why Henry and I needed to just be friends. Neither of us wanted to step out into uncharted territory or stand on the edge of a cliff. We wanted to feel safe, knowing that everything would stay the same. I loved him, but I couldn't risk ruining our friendship if he didn't love me too.

We finished the dance, and Henry brought me in close for a hug. I stood in his arms and was at war with my feelings. Part of me wanted to keep feeling safe in knowing that we would be friends forever, no matter what happened. The other part of me still stood at the edge of the cliff and wanted to take the leap, hoping beyond all hope that Henry stood at the bottom to catch me.

I thanked him for the dance, my voice barely more than a whisper. Then I left him on the dance floor once again.

I practically ran back to our friends, who were coming back from the dance floor as well. Marylin and Jimmy held hands and their happiness was evident in the looks on their faces. Peggy walked back from a dance with one of the guys I had danced with earlier. Buddy walked back from dancing with a girl about his same age that I didn't recognize

I walked toward Buddy and whispered to him, "I'm exhausted and I have to wake up early tomorrow to bake. What time is it?"

He looked down at his watch. "Almost 10:30. Do you want to go home then?"

I nodded. "Yeah, let's go." I had to get out of there. I knew if I stayed longer, I would be tempted to tell Henry how I truly felt. I couldn't. Our friendship was more important than my stupid feelings for him. Plus, Henry was dealing with too much right now to add this to his plate.

We said goodbye to Peggy, Marylin, and Jimmy, who said they were going to stay for a while longer. Henry still wasn't back yet, so I assumed he was either dancing with someone else or getting a refreshment. I left without saying goodbye to him and felt a familiar stab of guilt in my heart. I was in dangerous territory with him, and I felt like one misstep could lead to ruining our friendship once again.

I followed Buddy back home from the dance hall, feeling so heartbroken that the tears refused to fall.

CHAPTER 25

July 13, 1945

Henry

She left without saying goodbye. Again. She thanked me for our dance and then left, as if *I* made her want to leave. But that couldn't be. She had been enjoying our dances, hadn't she? She smiled and laughed and everything. She had been surprised at the first song I requested, but she had gotten over it quickly and seemed like herself. Had I offended her somehow? I didn't think so, but I ran through the entire night all the same, going over what I remembered of our conversations. I couldn't find any instance when she had seemed offended until she just walked away.

All of this made me more confused. Why had she left so suddenly? I knew I was probably overthinking the whole situation and figured she probably left because she had to bake early in the morning. I settled on that explanation, but a small piece of my brain was left worrying and wondering if I had done something wrong.

When I got to my house, I found a note on the counter that said my parents had gone to visit my grandparents in the city and wouldn't be home until tomorrow afternoon. Jessica was at her friend's house for a sleepover. I was alone in the house.

I sat on my bed after getting ready and noticed the teddy bear from the Fourth of July laying on the floor of my closet. I had forgotten that I threw it there in frustration that night. I went over and picked it up. It was so much like that teddy bear I had given to Dot years ago. Was that why she left it on top of the pile of toys? I was left with even more confusion. What in the world was happening to us? One minute, Dot and I were best friends. The next, she was distant and I felt awkward. The next, she would run away or I would get scared.

I grabbed Dot's sketchbook, which was still in my nightstand drawer, and turned to the page where Dot had drawn me at her doorstep. That was the moment that had changed everything, and it was my fault. If I hadn't tried to kiss her, everything between us would be normal. We wouldn't be in this situation. I felt like it was my fault that Dot had left the dance hall early and that she left the teddy bear I had given her.

I grabbed the teddy bear and the sketchbook and placed them both in the nightstand drawer, hiding them so I could sleep peacefully.

I lay in my bed, trying to relax and fall asleep.

I fell asleep in time.

But I didn't relax.

I ran through the forest, cursing the day I was drafted. The flames grew around me, suffocating me with smoke.

I coughed, trying to catch my breath, but there wasn't enough oxygen. I couldn't taste anything but blood and smoke.

I kept running, though it felt like my lungs would implode from the lack of air. I ignored the branches clawing at me from the trees. I ignored the calls of the other soldiers, knowing somehow that they would suffer the same fate they always did. They weren't who I was trying to save now. I had to find her.

I finally reached a clearing where her house stood. It was engulfed in the same flames that were behind me in the forest. I heard screams from inside and I entered the house, trusting my gut more than my ears to find her.

I finally found her in the kitchen, surrounded by flames. She turned to me and screamed my name, but I hardly heard it above the sound of fire eating wood.

I ran to her and pulled her into an embrace.

"You came," she said.

"Of course I did, Dottie."

A wooden beam fell behind me, startling us both. I pushed her away from it and we ran in the opposite direction, trying to find a way out of her burning house. It was a maze, and it seemed like it would never end. I tried remembering the layout of her house, but it was all different. Everything was blackened and broken. I couldn't find anything recognizable.

We continued our escape, regardless. I saw the front door a few yards in front of me. We ran together, and I kicked away the flaming objects in our path. I held her hand in mine and guided her through the chaos and the terror of the burning house. Right as we approached the front door, I heard a crash and a scream in the same instant. Dot's hand slipped out of mine. I turned my head to see her crushed beneath a wooden beam.

I think I screamed, but I couldn't hear myself. I dropped to the ground and tried pushing the beam away, but it was too heavy. Dot's breathing was already shallow. Her eyes were closed in pain.

"Dot, please. Wake up."

She slowly tried opening her eyes, but they closed again.

"Dot, you can't die. I love you!"

Her eyes fluttered open again and she held my gaze for a few moments before whispering my name slowly.

"Dottie, please. I'm in love with you. You can't leave me. I need you."

I started to cry, repeating myself with every sob. *I'm in love with you. You can't leave me. I need you.*

But I knew she was gone when she let out one last shaky breath.

"Dot!" I screamed.

I shook my head, trying to convince myself it wasn't real. It was all just another dream. I couldn't wake up, which terrified me. I slipped into a panic, which worsened when I finally gained consciousness.

I screamed as I came back to the waking world. Panic overwhelmed me. My thoughts were whirling around my head, and I couldn't remember what was real or what wasn't. I had to get out. The house was on fire. What was I doing in bed?

I stood up, almost tripping over my sheets. I could hardly see. Everything was dark, and the few things I *could* see were blurred by my tears. I needed to get out of here. I had to get out. Nothing was making sense, but I knew that I needed to leave this room immediately. Dot was somewhere out there. I needed to find her before something happened to her. I felt like something had happened to her already. I tried to put my thoughts together. Dot was dead. She had died in my arms as I screamed her name. I felt suffocated by the darkness and my thoughts.

I stumbled across the floor, trying not to run into anything. I finally reached the doorknob and I opened the door. It was dark in the hallway, a stark contrast from the flames I had been expecting. What was going on? In my cloud of confusion, I had a moment of clarity. The house wasn't on fire. I was outside my bedroom, wearing pajamas. It was still dark outside. Nothing was wrong.

It had all been another stupid nightmare.

But I still felt paralyzed with fear. Something had happened to Dot in my dream, and I wasn't entirely convinced it wasn't real.

Part of me knew Dot was safe in her house and that everything had been a dream, but the other part of me worried I had some sort of a premonition of her being in danger. It was so real. She died in my arms. I had to know it wasn't real. I wouldn't believe it until I heard her voice and saw her face in front of me.

I didn't even stop to look at the clock on my bedside table before I ran to the phone in the kitchen. I wasn't thinking clearly enough to care if it was the middle of the night. I prayed the operator would be quick switching the line over, and I dialed the number.

The operator didn't understand me the first time I told her the Banks' number, so I had to repeat myself. I was pacing back and forth in the kitchen, not even bothering to stay calm. I fiddled with the phone cord, wrapping it around my fingers tightly until my knuckles were white. Dot's screams replaying in my mind were all I could focus on while waiting to hear her voice.

Finally, someone answered.

"Hello?" It was Dot.

"Dot, are you okay?" My voice came out weak.

"Henry, what's going on? Of course I'm okay."

"Oh, thank heavens!" I ran my hand through my hair and gave a huge sigh of relief.

"Henry, what's wrong?"

"I thought you were dead." My voice came out in a whisper. I wasn't making sense anymore, I knew it. But the dream had been too real. I could still see Dot laying on the ground in front of me when I closed my eyes. I shook the image out of my head and focused on her voice.

"What are you talking about? I'm just fine. What happened?"

"I had a dream..." I knew my breathing was too fast, but I felt so relieved and yet still panicked. "You were in your house and it was on fire...you were dead."

"Henry, I'm worried about you. Can I come over?"

I managed to get out a muffled 'yes' before I was unable to take in enough air to think straight at all.

I sank to the ground by the phone and leaned against the wall. I was breathing in and out, but I couldn't catch my breath. I felt like I was trying too hard and not trying hard enough at the same time. A pain spread through my entire head, trying to find its way out of my brain. I don't know when I started crying again, but my entire face was wet with tears and sweat.

"Hello, sir?" I heard.

I looked around, confused. Then I noticed I had left the phone off the base, and the operator was still on the line. I grabbed the phone and hung it up.

I waited for Dot to come, still sitting on the kitchen floor with my head buried in my hands.

Finally she knocked on the door. I stood up to answer it, almost falling to the ground again.

She looked like an angel with the sunrise behind her and her hair unruly. She was beautiful. I took in the sight of her for only a moment before I pulled her to me in an embrace.

She was here. She was okay. She was alive.

CHAPTER 26

July 14, 1945

Dorothy

Henry looked like a ghost when he answered the door. I'd hardly had the thought when he wrapped me in his arms and started crying with his head in my hair. I hugged him back, hoping to afford him even a small bit of comfort. His nightshirt was soaked through with tears, and the tears he was crying now soaked through my blouse.

When Henry finally stepped out of the hug, I got a good look at him. His eyes were red and had bags underneath them. His hair was tangled and unkempt. When he saw me looking at his face, he wiped the tears away with his hand. Even after that, his face was still wet with his tears and sweat.

"Henry," I started, almost reaching out to fix his hair or wipe away his tears. I held myself back, feeling embarrassed at the idea of touching him.

He kept staring at me without responding. His breathing was loud and his eyes were wide and scared. He slowly brought his hand up to my face and touched my cheek gently. My skin buzzed where he touched me, and I almost closed my eyes and leaned into his touch but I forced myself to remember what was going on.

"Henry?"

"It's really you, right? I'm not dreaming?"

My eyebrows knit together in a confused frown. I shook my head and practically whispered, "No, you're not dreaming. Henry, what happened?"

His hand left my face and he muttered an apology. He looked down and sighed. "Dottie, I..."

"Wait," I interrupted. "Let's go to the couch." I nodded toward the couch and put my hand on Henry's arm.

He nodded and followed my lead. He sat on the couch in front of the window. I sat down next to him and reached for his hand. He held onto mine so tightly, as if that alone was keeping him from spiraling into another episode.

"It was so real." His voice came out sounding haunted, like he had seen a ghost. "Even after I woke up, I thought it was. You were dead and it was all my fault."

"Start from the beginning." I suggested. I knew it would be hard for him to tell the story, but I knew it would help him process it, just like how telling me the story about the war helped him out a little.

"Sometimes my dreams are exactly like the night I got injured."

I nodded. He squeezed his eyes shut, not wanting to relive the nightmare, and for a moment I thought he would cry again.

"Other times the scene changes so other people are there that shouldn't be, or I'm in another place. Tonight, it was both. I knew I had to find someone and I knew that person was you."

My eyes widened in surprise.

"I ran to your house, which was in a forest, and everything was on fire. I could hardly see anything, and it was hard to breathe. I searched everywhere in your house, and I finally found you in the kitchen. I tried to help you escape, but I couldn't find my way back out. Everything was strange and different inside. It was a completely new place, like a maze."

Henry had a distant look in his eyes. He was staring straight in front of himself without really seeing anything. His hand weakened in mine, like he was using all of his energy to recount his dream.

"We finally found the front door, but as I started to open it, I heard you scream behind me. Something had fallen on you. I couldn't lift it off of you." His voice broke a little. He looked so scared. "I tried to wake you up, but you were already gone. You were dead." His breath caught, and his eyes welled up with tears. "I begged you not to leave me. I wanted to save you Dottie, but I couldn't. You wouldn't listen to me. You wouldn't wake up. Even after I told you I loved you, you were gone."

I didn't hear anything but the words, *I told you I loved you.* My heart was beating in my ears. Chills ran down my arms. Had I heard him right?

"What?"

Henry looked up at me again, pain still evident on his face.

"You were gone, Dottie. I tried to—."

"You told me you loved me?"

His face immediately changed. He looked shocked and embarrassed. His eyes were wide and his mouth was open. "I—" he started.

"Did you mean it?" I asked, hoping beyond all hope that he did.

Henry looked worried, but he finally nodded a few times. His mouth turned up in an apologetic smile.

And so I leaned in and kissed him, barely grazing his lips with mine.

I backed away and smiled widely. Henry stared at me for a few seconds, before surprising me by kissing me back, holding my face in his hands and pulling me in closer.

This kiss was much longer and deeper. I felt like I was finally falling off that cliff, but Henry was holding my hand the whole time. We wouldn't crash at the end because we were together and would keep each other safe. We ended the kiss and just sat staring at each other with grins on our faces. There were tears in Henry's eyes.

"You have no idea how long I've wanted to do that," I said, out of breath.

Henry still held me gently in his arms. "Same here."

"I love you too, you know," I said. I was so happy to finally say it out loud.

"You really do?"

"I kissed you, silly." I laughed. I was ecstatic. I kissed him again, tasting the salt of his tears on our lips. "I'm very much in love with you."

I sat back, looking at Henry. *My Henry.*

Henry grinned. He shook his head and sighed. "Dorothy Banks loves me!" He laughed.

I laughed too, feeling lighter than ever. I was completely content.

"I have something for you," Henry said.

"I actually have something for you too," I answered, remembering the letter. "But first, are you really going to be okay?"

"Yeah, I'll be fine. I just needed to talk to someone—to *you*, really—and know you were safe. I feel a little better now. Exhausted, but okay." Henry sighed and smiled again, bumping me in the arm with his elbow teasingly.

I smiled back and wiped a tear off Henry's face. "I'm here. That dream wasn't real. None of them are."

"I thought I was doing so much better," Henry said, now looking a little sad. "Yesterday, I felt so happy. I was peaceful and felt great all day. Then I fell asleep and my mind attacked me..."

"Have you talked to that psychologist yet? He'll be able to help more than I can."

"You've helped me more than you know, Dottie, so don't say that. But I haven't called him yet." Henry stood up. "In fact, I'll call him right now. It's a decent time, right?"

"It's still early. It was 5:00 when you called."

"Oh gosh, I'm sorry. Did I wake you up?"

He had, but I didn't care. "It doesn't matter. Helping you is much more important to me than sleep."

"Wow, you really do love me!" Henry grinned, giving me his hand to help me stand up.

I took it and stood. To my surprise, Henry spun me around and then pulled me in close. Our faces were almost touching. He placed his other hand on my back and began leading me in a slow dance.

"Dancing with you last night was torturous," he said, now sheepish.

I looked at him in shock. "What?"

"You looked absolutely gorgeous, and I wanted to tell you that I love you. I could hardly stand not telling you."

"Why didn't you?"

He let go of my hand and tucked one of my loose curls behind my ear.

"I was so scared to lose you, Dottie. I kept having dreams like the one I had last night, and I knew that if I loved you I could lose you. It doesn't really make sense, looking back."

"I understand." I really did. I had been scared to lose him too. "I was terrified to ruin our friendship," I admitted. "I couldn't bear losing you after I knew I loved you."

"What idiots we were," Henry said, laughing and kissing my forehead.

I laughed in agreement. "I'm not scared anymore." My eyes found his, and I let go of a breath I felt like I had been holding in for a long time.

We danced in silence for a while, occasionally letting our lips find each other's.

We were finally interrupted by the clock chiming the hour.

"I have bread I need to bake and then deliver," I admitted sadly. I didn't want to leave, but I had to get that bread delivered today or else my reputation as a baker would be ruined before I even had a bakery.

Henry stopped leading us around in our slow circle. "Meet me back here later? I want to give you something." He dropped his arms, letting me go.

I nodded and stepped towards the door. "Aren't you going to give me a goodbye kiss?" I asked.

"Of course, Dottie," he said, sounding hesitant.

I knew why. I shook my head apologetically. "I wish I could change that day more than anything." I kissed him, trying to convey all that I felt. I would explain everything when I gave him my letter. When the kiss ended, I looked into his green eyes. He was smirking now, looking at my lips.

"You're really good at that, you know."

My eyes grew wide, and I just knew my face was an unattractive shade of red.

Henry touched my cheek. His fingers were cold on my face, which further confirmed that I was blushing.

"You're good at blushing too, you gorgeous girl." He practically whispered. He leaned in and placed a kiss on my other cheek. "You'll come back, right?" He spoke right next to my ear.

I nodded slowly. My heart was pounding in my chest. "See you later?" Henry smiled.

I walked toward the door again, looking back at him quickly. He grinned at me and chuckled.

I didn't want to leave, but I did have work to do and Henry had to get ready.

I left and ran home quickly, wanting to finish my baking and deliveries as fast as possible so I could go back to Henry and give him my letter.

❧

A few hours later, I knocked on the Oakeys' door with a loaf of bread in a basket and the letter in my pocket. The bread was still warm, and the smell was comforting.

Henry opened the door, looking serious.

"What's wrong?" I asked.

"I called Dr. Thompson."

"Oh?"

Henry let me in and I went to sit on the couch.

Henry shut the door and followed me.

"So? What'd he say?" I asked..

"He's in England." Henry shook his head. "His secretary said that he wouldn't be back in the States until at least April."

"April? That's so far away! Why?"

"He's helping other veterans with shell shock." He paused, sighing. "Just not me."

I closed my eyes. This Dr. Thompson was his last hope, and he wouldn't be back until April!

"The only thing I can do is keep living my life until then. I'm getting better at handling this on my own and with help when I need it, like this morning." Henry started nodding resolutely. "I'll be all right." He looked at me and smiled. "I will. You'll see."

"Of course you will. And you know that I'm always here for you. When you need to talk, you can always call me like you did this morning. I want to help you in any way I can."

"It's not a burden?" The redness in his eyes was gone now, but they still held a hint of sadness and fear. "I don't want to be a burden to you, Dottie. I really don't."

"You will never be a burden to me, Henry. I'm here to help you. That's what friends do." I thought about that phrase and changed it. "That's what people who love each other do."

Henry wrapped me in another hug.

"I'm here for you too, Dot. I'll always be here for you. Thank you for everything."

"Of course, Henry. We'll get through this together." I hugged him even tighter.

"Do you really want that? To be together?" Henry asked.

"Yes. I really do."

Henry kissed the top of my head then released me from his embrace.

"I don't have a promise ring or anything, but I do have something for you." Henry's cheeks got a little pink when he said 'promise ring'. I liked it when he blushed too.

I laughed. "Me too." I took the letter from my pocket and held it out in front of me. "I wrote this yesterday morning."

"A letter?" Henry asked, laughing.

I nodded. "Yeah, it's a letter." I said it like it was the most obvious thing in the world.

Henry then pulled an envelope out from behind him. "I have one for you too!"

I laughed. Of course he did.

"Will you read yours to me?" Henry asked. He looked almost giddy.

I hesitated, then nodded. Henry put his arm around me and I scooted closer. He held me there protectively.

I opened the envelope carefully, then pulled the paper out. I cleared my throat dramatically, making Henry laugh, and then began to read:

"Dearest Henry,

I told you a few weeks ago that I would write you a letter. I have put it off for too long, and I want to tell you why.

When you came home I couldn't help but remember again and again the day you left. That was a hard day for me, Henry. The night before the day you came to say goodbye, I had finally recognized how I truly felt about you. I was beginning to fall in love with you. I wanted you to stay, and the fact that you were leaving to fight in a war destroyed any hope I had of being with you. I decided the next morning I couldn't let myself fall for you—not because I didn't want to, but because I knew it would hurt both of us. You were leaving, and I didn't know when you would come back. Part of me was terrified that you wouldn't. I wanted to protect myself from heartbreak. It was a selfish decision and one I deeply regret."

I felt a tear in my eye and wiped it away, praying Henry wouldn't see. He did see it, and he gently wiped away the next tear that fell.

I continued reading the letter, taking comfort in the fact that Henry seemed to have forgiven me for my stupidity. "*You came to my door right after I decided to close my heart to you. If I hadn't made that decision, I would have kissed you. I wanted to, Henry, I really did. My heart still aches when I think of the look on your face when you walked away from me for the last time.*" I looked up at him, and his face showed exactly what I felt when I remembered that day.

I practically had the next part of my letter memorized, so I read it and glanced up at Henry often. "*Henry, I am still on the brink of falling in love with you. I think I would if I knew you were falling with me. I want to. When we danced for the first time after you came home, that's when I knew for sure.*" I stopped again to look at Henry. His eyes were wide and he was smiling. I blushed, remembering the night before, as I was sure Henry was remembering as well.

"*Henry, you make me feel like I'm home. In your arms I felt so safe and so loved. I felt it again the other day when you came over to help me. I don't know if it was just me, but I felt like something would have happened if we hadn't been interrupted. Did you think the same?*

I need to know, Henry. Are you falling in love with me, or will I fall alone?
-Dorothy."

"Of course I'm falling in love with you," Henry said. "I never stopped." He reached out to grab hold of my hand. He brought it gently to his lips and kissed my knuckles.

My heart skipped a beat. "I knew I loved you when we were dancing last night. You requested that stupid song that makes me want to cry happy tears, and I knew." I laughed again. "It scared me. I thought you just wanted to stay friends and not have anything romantic come between us. I thought that's what I wanted. But last night I didn't think I could go another minute without telling you the truth, and I didn't want to ruin anything. So I ran. I guess that's what I always do when I'm scared. I run away. That's what happened when you told me how you felt the first time, and it's what happened on the Fourth of July, and what happened last night."

"You should stop running," Henry said, leaning in to kiss me gently.

"I know," I said against his lips.

"Also, I think I really like you calling me 'dearest Henry'. You should use that more." He winked.

"All right, dearest Henry," I said in the most dramatic Hollywood starlet voice that I could muster. "Why don't you read me your letter now?"

Henry raised his eyebrows. "Of course, darling Dottie."

I couldn't take it. I broke my serious gaze and started giggling like a little girl. I even snorted, which only made me laugh harder.

Henry stared at me in confusion. "What? You don't like being called 'darling'?"

"Not when it's with my name like that! It sounds like what an old woman would call her cat. 'Darling Dottie, come eat your supper!'" I mimicked an old British woman's voice, which made Henry laugh with me.

"You're right. It does sound kind of like that. I'll have to come up with something else."

I nodded matter-of-factly. "Yes, you must." I was still using the British accent.

Henry rolled his eyes at me. "Stop it now; I'm going to read you this letter." He smiled and started opening the envelope. He dropped my hand to do so, and I felt sad at the lack of contact between us. With a wink, he began reading the paper that was inside.

"*Dear Dot,*

I miss you terribly. That's what I would have said if I had written this letter when I first left, when I should have written it. I still feel guilty for not writing to you while I was gone, and I don't think that feeling will ever go away. Imagine how much closer we could have been if I wrote this and actually sent it.

I tried writing you letters. I really did. I think I must have written a hundred versions of this letter, but they all ended up as fuel for our fires. I gave up on the idea of writing to you after a while. I knew I was too much of a coward to actually send them.

Dottie, I meant what I said to you when I left. I'm falling in love with you. You are the only girl I have ever been interested in, and that fact didn't change during the years I was gone. Most soldiers were mooning over French dames, but all I could think about was you." Henry looked at me and sighed. "It's true, you know." He interrupted the letter-reading. "You're the only one I've ever loved like this."

I leaned in closer to him again and pressed a kiss to his cheek. I didn't think I would ever get tired of kissing him.

After a moment, Henry kept reading the letter. "Memories of you kept me going when I was scared. I hate to admit this, but I was scared a lot. I knew I had to be brave and have hope that I would see you again. I knew that if I was strong and just kept going, eventually I would be where I am right now: Home. Safe. With my family, and with you. You have no idea how many times I wanted to tell you that.

I know the day I left I made a bold move. I am truly sorry for surprising you with a confession of my feelings and for trying to kiss you. I don't regret trying. I only regret that I tried to kiss you without knowing how you felt toward me. I should have waited until I was sure of your feelings, or I should have been less of a coward and told you how I felt sooner. In my mind it was the right time because I was leaving. I didn't know when or even if I'd come home. It was all very selfish of me. I am so sorry I caused you embarrassment.

If I had another chance, I would do things differently. I would go back to that day when I told you goodbye, and I would wait to hear your answer. In all honesty, I would still love you, even if you didn't love me back. But I would respect your feelings and act only as a friend to you. I would write to you once a week, no matter your answer, and I would tell you about even the most mundane things about the war. I would know you wouldn't want to hear about the awful parts, and I wouldn't even mention them. The war would seem like a short trip in our letters, and at the end I would come home and we'd be fine. We would still be best friends, or we would be something more. That's how I wish it had all gone.

Instead, I really messed things up between us. My pride was too hurt for me to send even a single letter to you, and I embarrassed you too much for you *to write to me. It was all my fault; don't you dare take any blame for what happened, Dorothy Banks."*

"But it *was* partly my fault." I was the one to interrupt now. "I never even put a pen to paper to write to you or even tried to tell you how I felt."

"You heard the letter Dot," Henry said, faking a strict glare. "Don't you dare try to take any blame for my own cowardice."

I gave him a mischievous grin. "It still seems like it was a little bit my fault."

"Then let's blame fear. I'm not at fault, and you *definitely* aren't at fault. Fear is. We just gave in to our fear a little too much."

I nodded once, officially accepting the accusation against 'fear'. This was the Henry I remembered from our past. His old, joking self was coming back more and more every day, and I loved it.

"Well then, now that that's settled, shall I continue?"

I nodded.

Henry continued reading: *"Tonight we danced for the first time since I came home. It was amazing. Holding you close like that was something I dreamt about often during the war. Now that I'm home, I can't keep ignoring my feelings for you. Every time I'm with you it gets harder to hold myself back from telling you that I still love you. When I was in your arms, I finally felt like I was somewhere I really belonged after feeling lost and confused for so long.*

Dot, I have to know. If you don't feel the same way about me, please tell me. I will still be your friend, no matter what your feelings are toward me. I can't bear to ruin our friendship any more than I already have.

Awaiting your answer,

-Henry."

I was left breathless. He hadn't regretted our almost-kiss. He had never stopped loving me. He had tried to write me letters.

Part of me wanted to cry for all the time Henry spent taking the blame for our confusion.

"I like this. Writing letters, that is." I smiled.

"Me too."

I nodded. "We shouldn't stop. We owe each other lots of love letters."

Henry smiled and pulled me in closer. I rested my head on his shoulder.

"I wholeheartedly agree, my love," he said.

"That's it."

"What?"

"My love."

Henry turned his head and tried to look at me.

"My love," I repeated. "That's what you should call me."

"Ahh. Perfect. My love." He kissed the top of my head.

I bit my lip and then smiled.

"I have something else for you too," Henry said, sitting up a little straighter. I lifted my head. "Actually two things." He reached next to him. I couldn't see what he was grabbing, since he blocked my view.

Henry pulled out my sketchbook and the pile of papers we had worked on together. He handed them to me.

"I really think you're an amazing artist. That's not just my biased opinion. It's the complete truth."

"Thank you." I took my things out of his hands.

"And I think you should display your artwork at your bakery."

That made me pause. I was terrified to show anyone my drawings. But I had also been terrified to kiss Henry, and yet I did it. And look what was happening because of that!

"I think I will." I heard myself say it before I had actually internalized what it meant. "I've been running away for too long. I need to do something daring."

Henry smiled. "And the second thing." He pulled out the teddy bear from Mrs. Devon's fishing game.

I gasped. "How?"

"I followed you. I saw the pile and wanted to leave the toy soldier there for a kid that would actually appreciate it, and I saw the bear sitting right on the top."

"I regretted leaving it there the next morning, but I thought that there was nothing I could do! I didn't even mention it to Mrs. Devon. I was so embarrassed."

"Well, my love, here it is. Safe and sound."

"Just like old times."

"That's when I realized I liked you, you know."

"Way back then? We were just kids."

"I know. But I knew that you were something special. I knew I couldn't let you go."

I smiled. "I love you."

"I love you too," Henry said, wrapping his other arm around me and pulling me in for another kiss. It was true. I would never get tired of this.

EPILOGUE

June 14, 1946

Dorothy

It was Friday, one of the busiest days at the bakery. I had been working since the early morning, and my lunch break was finally approaching. I cleaned the flour off of the counter, put away various ingredients, and threw the dirty mixing bowls in the sink to soak. I always did this before my break, since I hated coming back to a dirty kitchen. I was almost finished organizing the kitchen area when I heard a low voice in the dining area behind me. Through the door, I could hear someone talking, but I couldn't make out what they said or who it was. I heard Bobby's voice respond "She's in the back." Thank goodness he was willing to work here during the summers. I needed to consider getting a full-time assistant to man the counter since Bobby would be going back to school again in a few months.

The stranger came right through the swinging door into the kitchen, something I specifically told Bobby not to let anyone do. I turned around, intending to ask him to leave, but instead I was met with a familiar face.

Henry stood before me, as handsome as ever. He had been gone for a few months now, meeting with a psychologist in New York weekly. We sent letters as often as we wanted, which was usually multiple times a week. I had only talked to him over the phone twice, since the phone line was poorly connected to the apartment he was renting in the city.

But now he was here, in person.

"Henry! You're back early! How?"

He answered with only a smile, then he drew me into his arms. I sighed in his embrace. I had missed him so much. I hated it when he was away. We stayed there for what felt like forever, but even then it was too short. He pulled back and just stared at me.

"You're even prettier than I remember."

"Oh stop, you haven't been gone for *that* long." I laughed.

He interrupted my laugh with a long kiss.

He broke the kiss and stared at me, dreamy eyed. "I feel like I have. I missed you so much, Dottie."

"I know. I missed you too. How have you been?" We had talked in our letters, but Henry was always very quiet about what he discussed with Dr. Thompson.

"I've been so much better, Dottie. I can sleep through most nights without dreaming now. And I can tell the whole story of that night without problems too!"

"Henry, that's wonderful!"

"I know!" He smiled like a little boy. "But we can talk about that later. Bobby said you have a break soon?"

"I was just getting ready to leave."

"Perfect. Come with me?"

I nodded.

We left the kitchen and said goodbye to Bobby. Henry and I passed the pictures on the wall, all sketches I had done myself. I had drawn everything: the bakery, people in the town, even the cakes and cookies I sold.

"I told you," Henry said, nudging my side with his elbow. He looked at me and smiled. "You did it."

"Thanks to you." I looked back at him and couldn't contain a grin. I sighed happily and looked back at my drawings. I never thought I'd be brave enough to display my drawings so the whole town could see, but Henry's encouragement and example of bravery convinced me I could do it. He made me feel brave.

We walked out of the bakery arm in arm. I let Henry take the lead, since he seemed to have a destination in mind. He was strangely silent the whole time, but it was a comfortable silence.

Henry led me to the park. We walked along one of the paths through the grass and the trees to a bench. As Henry sat down and motioned for me to do likewise, I realized it was our bench. It was the same place I had talked his ears off that day he was feeling down. It was the same bench where we sat together on that Fourth of July night. I smiled at the memories.

"I missed you so much, my love." Henry gazed at me softly. "I wanted you by my side the whole time I was in New York. I knew that you being with me would do me more good than anything else, so I told Dr. Thompson I needed to go home. He told me he believed I was ready to live a normal life again, especially if I kept my family and friends close."

"It worked then."

Henry nodded. "I'm not exactly cured, but I know how to manage now. But that's not the reason I brought you here."

I looked at him with confusion.

"Dottie, I've been thinking a lot these past few weeks. Mostly I thought about you. I couldn't stop myself from missing you, and I hated that feeling more than anything. Every time I thought of you, it hurt to know you weren't with me. I've been so stupid in the past, thinking that loving you like this would ruin our friendship, but now I see that it has only grown stronger. You have always been a part of my life, and I want you to be with me forever."

I threw my arms around him. "I missed you too, Henry. Letters weren't enough."

"No, they really weren't, were they?" Henry leaned back and looked at me intently. "Next time I go away, I want you there with me. I never want to leave you again."

Then, the love of my life got down on one knee in front of me. I felt a tear roll down my cheek, and I laughed at the thought of crying in a situation like this. I could hardly believe this was happening, and yet I had always prayed it would. Somewhere deep inside, I had always wanted to hear the words Henry spoke next from him and only him:

"Marry me, my love?"

Even before he could finish the question, I was already nodding my head in agreement. "Of course. Of course I'll marry you!" I started crying even more, which made me laugh. I reached out and practically fell into Henry's arms. He caught me and held me close for just a moment before he shifted and his lips met mine.

"I love you, Dottie." Henry spoke between kisses, his breath grazing my lips. I kissed him again and then repeated "I love you too." He pulled my head closer to his and I was met with his lips again and again and again. I would never grow tired of Henry's kisses, and I never had to. As long as he was next to me, I was exactly where I needed to be.

We were home.

The End

AUTHOR'S NOTE

This book deals with the effects of war on a soldier's mind. Henry suffers from post-traumatic stress disorder and survivor's guilt. The diagnosis for PTSD did not exist in 1945, when this book is set. PTSD was greatly misunderstood for years, even after it was finally put in the Diagnostic and Statistical Manual of Mental Disorders in 1980 (see Matthew J. Friedman's article "PTSD History and Overview" on ptsd.va.gov).

With Henry's symptoms, I have tried to accurately represent what I understand about PTSD and what I have personally experienced with my own anxiety and depression. Trauma response is not the same in everyone, and Henry's is just one experience out of many and is fictionalized.

If you are suffering from PTSD or any other mental health disorder, know that you are not alone. The best thing that you can do is find someone you trust and talk openly and honestly about the things you feel. You are a hero, just like Dot helps Henry realize. If you know someone who suffers from a mental health disorder, be present in their lives and be patient. Recovery may not always look like recovery from the outside. Don't give up on them and don't give up on yourself.

-Eliza

ACKNOWLEDGEMENTS

There are so many people who helped me write this book, even if they didn't realize they were helping me. I'd love to thank every single one of them, but I think I'd run out of pages to do that pretty quickly. Instead, I'll stick with thanking the people who helped me directly.

First, my family: (Hi, Mom! Hi, Dad!) My parents have always been so incredibly supportive of my dream to be an author and are just amazing people. I owe so much of who I am to them. My siblings are the inspiration behind a lot of the friendships in this book, and I want to thank them for being my forever best friends. Love you guys!

Next, my roommates and friends: Thank you for not thinking I was insane when I would randomly shout things like, "What's a word that is like 'awesome', but isn't 'awesome'?" or "How do you describe this sound?" or "Is this a normal thing that someone would do?" You were so patient with my crazy outbursts, late nights, and rants about the history of mental health diagnoses. You are all the best.

To my beta readers, who read through and helped me organize my own thoughts: Jen, John, Nannette, Diana, Kendra, and Gerberta, you were all so helpful in the earlier editing stages. This book would have been an absolute mess without you.

To my amazing editor and friend: Tori, you're a rockstar. Thank you so so so much for helping me be a better writer and a better person. You helped me so much throughout this process, and I can't thank you enough. Love ya, girl!

To Naomi, Maddie, and Jake for helping me out with the cover: Naomi, your photography is pure art. Maddie and Jake, I'm so happy for you guys and I'm glad you got to pretend to be Dot and Henry for a morning.

To my junior high, high school, and college teachers and professors: Thank you for inspiring me and your other students to keep reaching for the stars. You are doing something so incredibly important.

To my Great Grandma, Marylin Jane Oakey Neubert. I put your full name in here because I want people to know how much you inspired this story. Reading your life story was very influential for this book and also for my life. I remember the first time I told you I was writing a novel set in 1945 and you lit up and wanted to know all about it. Well, Grandma, you don't have to wait anymore to find out what happens to Henry and Dot! I love you so much and I'm so glad that you are my grandma and my friend.

And to my readers: I might not know you, but I am still so incredibly grateful that you decided to read this book. It was a labor of love. Writing this book helped me heal from a very hard experience, and I hope the story of Henry and Dot helps you too. I love you all. Thanks for believing in me. Happy reading!

Photo by Naomi Linnell

Eliza Stemmons began writing books when she was ten years old and knew she wanted to be an author by the time she was thirteen. Since then, she has written many beginnings, middles, and endings of books, but As Long As You're Next to Me is the first where they all appear together.

Eliza grew up in Provo, Utah, and still lives there near her family. She attends Brigham Young University and is pursuing a degree in English and editing. She spends her days reading, doing homework, making jewelry, and teaching piano.

You can find her on social media @elizastemmonsauthor or on her website elizastemmonsauthor.com.

Made in the USA
Monee, IL
18 May 2023